CANDLELIGHT
Ecstasy Supreme

"IN OTHER WORDS YOU'RE VOLUNTEERING TO BE MY BODYGUARD?"

"I can't think of a body I'd want to protect more than yours," Marc drawled.

Juliet had to grin. "And who will protect me from you?"

"No one. That's the most important part of my devious plan," he whispered, but he was grinning, too, as they walked together up the steps.

Now she was alone with him and, dangerous as that could prove to be, she was unable to deprive herself of the pleasure of his company. With him she felt warmer, more alive, and happy. She was only human. She didn't want to try to escape such good feelings, and so she made her reckless decision. . . .

CANDLELIGHT ECSTASY SUPREMES

WARMED BY THE FIRE

Donna Kimel Vitek

A CANDLELIGHT ECSTASY SUPREME

Published by
Dell Publishing Co., Inc.
1 Dag Hammarskjold Plaza
New York, New York 10017

Dell ® TM 681510, Dell Publishing Co., Inc.

Candlelight Ecstasy Supreme is a trademark of
Dell Publishing Co., Inc., New York, New York.

ISBN: 0–440–19379–6

Printed in the United States of America
First printing—August 1983

To Our Readers:

Candlelight Ecstasy is delighted to announce the start of a brand-new series—Ecstasy Supremes! Now you can enjoy a romance series unlike all the others—longer and more exciting, filled with more passion, adventure, and intrigue—the stories you've been waiting for.

In months to come we look forward to presenting books by many of your favorite authors and the very finest work from new authors of romantic fiction as well. As always, we are striving to present the unique, absorbing love stories that you enjoy most—the very best love has to offer.

Breathtaking and unforgettable, Ecstasy Supremes will follow in the great romantic tradition you've come to expect *only* from Candlelight Ecstasy.

Your suggestions and comments are always welcome. Please let us hear from you.

Sincerely,

The Editors
Candlelight Romances
1 Dag Hammarskjold Plaza
New York, New York 10017

CHAPTER ONE

After putting on her herringbone suit jacket, Juliet York automatically smoothed her loosely upswept hair. As usual, one wayward strand had escaped confinement to fall in a wispy blond tendril that grazed her right temple and cheek. She tucked it back and deftly secured the end with a pin, defying the fact that the pesky strand would be brushing her cheek again within five minutes. When she stepped around her desk to take several folders from her secretary, Susan, she noticed for the first time the other woman's irrepressible smile.

In response to that smile and the secretary's genuinely warm expression, Juliet's emerald-green eyes sparkled with amusement and a natural hint of curiosity. "You look just like the proverbial cat that ate the canary," she told Susan with a grin while shifting the stack of file folders from one arm to the other. "Care to tell me why? Or am I supposed to guess?"

"Oh, no secret. It's just that you're on your way to meet Marc Tyner for the first time, and you'd better believe you're in for a real treat. He's really something else." Susan sighed dreamily. "Did I ever tell you that I was alone with him on an elevator one day and he actually talked to me! I couldn't believe it. I mean, some of these news media 'stars' are so conceited, they'd never stoop to speaking to a peasant like me. But Marc Tyner was as friendly as could be."

"Hmmm, that's nice," Juliet responded absently, glancing through the folders to be certain she had all the information for the meeting. Satisfied she had everything she needed, she glanced at her wristwatch. It was nearly five to three, and she immediately started toward her office door. "I can't wait for Tom any longer or I'll be late getting upstairs. When he gets back from the studio, send him up to Tyner's office, please. He may as well start getting accustomed to meetings up in the inner sanctum with the top brass."

"Sure you don't want me to grab my steno pad and come along with you?" Susan called after her. "I could take notes for you, and I certainly wouldn't mind being around Marc Tyner again. That man makes me positively swoon."

Glancing back at her secretary, Juliet chuckled. "Better not let your husband hear you saying things like that. I doubt he could understand why Tyner makes you 'swoon,' and truthfully I can't either. Needless to say, he is a top-notch television journalist and I respect his talent and professionalism. But other than that, as far as I'm concerned, he's just another man."

"That's easy for you to say right now. You haven't met him face-to-face yet," Susan retorted good-naturedly. "By the time today's meeting with him is over, though, I bet you'll be singing an entirely different tune. I'm telling you, Juliet, the man's a real charmer."

"So I've heard, from nearly every woman I know who's ever met him." With a brisk movement of her left arm, Juliet shot her cuff back and checked her wristwatch again. Her small straight nose wrinkled. "Unfortunately I've also heard Tyner can be a real tyrant, too, so I'd rather not be late for my appointment with him. He might

10

yell at me, and I'd really hate to have to yell back. Not the best way to start a working relationship." She stepped out of her office, paused, and looked back. "Oh, and while I'm in this meeting, please phone the hotel in Boone to confirm the reservations for the crew, and tell the clerk we'll be arriving early tomorrow evening as planned. And remember to send Tom up to join me when he gets back."

Leaving Susan to her tasks, Juliet moved across the diminutive outer office and out into the corridor, turning toward the center of the towering steel-and-glass building where the banks of elevators were located. Her pace was brisk but unhurried as she walked along the long hall, and the natural elegance of her graceful gait elicited a frankly admiring look from a young man walking toward her. She responded with a sincerely pleasant smile, one that was friendly but that in no way encouraged him to continue thinking what he was thinking. Juliet York wasn't a flirt and never had been, although she could have been a very successful coquette with a minimum of effort. The rare but natural shade of her golden auburn hair, her wide green eyes, plus her porcelain-smooth complexion and delicate features were enhanced by a slender shapely body that could not be completely camouflaged even by the tailored lines of a suit such as the one she was now wearing. And her long shapely legs had caught many a male eye. Although Juliet never flaunted her appearance, she was no more coy than she was flirtatious and would readily admit to herself that it was actually rather gratifying to know men found her attractive.

Yet it was hardly Juliet's physical attributes that drew attention to her a few moments later, and she knew that only too well. The instant she moved into the open reception area across from the elevators, all eyes turned to her. Staff members who had been idling away their afternoon breaks by the row of vending machines now turned away

11

from each other toward Juliet, watching her with avid interest. Lighthearted chatter that had already diminished considerably became a nearly deafening silence, and although an unpleasant sinking sensation dragged at Juliet's stomach, she valiantly produced for her spectators her best devil-may-care smile. Her small chin lifted slightly higher and her shoulders were perfectly straight as she turned toward the elevators and reached out to press the upper button. Even as she was hoping a car would stop on that floor quickly, she heard the muted whispering begin behind her.

The edge of her teeth sank down into the soft, full curve of her lower lip as tears of sheer frustration pricked at her eyes. She had prayed that she would leave all the vicious, unfounded rumors about herself behind when she resigned from Lancaster Broadcasting six weeks ago. As time had passed, however, it had become patently obvious that the gossip had made the transition to Union Broadcasting with her and, judging by the whispers still buzzing behind her, Julie was afraid she might have to endure her fellow employees' speculations for some time to come. It still amazed her to realize such stories were circulating about *her*—stories without a grain of truth to them—but at the moment she wouldn't allow herself to dwell on the unfairness of the gossip. Instead, she concentrated on holding her head high, then stepped with dignified slowness onto the next elevator going up, careful not to show any sign of relief as she turned to press the thirtieth-floor button and the doors glided shut, closing her away from all the staring faces.

It was only as the car she occupied alone was wooshing upward that she relaxed once more. Taking her first deep breath since she had entered the reception area below, she stared at the scrolled pattern of the carpet beneath her feet and shook her head bewilderedly, wondering for about the millionth time how the situation at Lancaster had grown out of proportion so swiftly. She imagined it had begun with some catty remark made by a jealous colleague, a remark that had raced along the company grapevine, embellished here and exaggerated there, until in the end it had become, crazily, a full-fledged scandal that even some newspapers had mentioned. Much ado about nothing, Juliet thought, but the unfavorable publicity had at last resulted in her resignation from Lancaster. And it remained almost too incredible for her to believe that the entire scandal had arisen simply because of her meteoric rise—from her rather lowly position of assistant to the assistant news director—up the ladder to associate producer. Granted, it was rare for a woman just turned twenty-eight to be promoted to associate producer, but it had been a promotion Juliet had deserved. Intelligent and with natural talents for organization and diplomacy, she had earned the respect of the executive producer of Lancaster's news magazine program, Henry Alexander. In a sense she had become his protégée and given practically free rein, she had produced two well-done innovative news exposés for the program. Unfortunately people preferred to believe she had gained her promotion by sleeping with Henry Alexander, ignoring the facts that she was talented and that he was a married man over thirty years her senior.

If those people only knew, Juliet thought. She smiled ruefully as the elevator glided to a smooth stop. Because her career was predominant in her life, she had never been seriously involved with any man, and when and if she did become involved, it wouldn't be with anyone like Henry. She was quite fond of him; she respected him, and she knew that the fact that Henry was, in his late fifties, a distinguished-looking man and a powerful executive, would cause many women to be attracted to him. But not her. Her regard for him simply did not extend beyond that for a professional mentor and good friend—no matter what other people thought.

No one at Lancaster, however, had known how Juliet felt. Perhaps even if they had known, it wouldn't have mattered. The gossip about her fictional affair with Henry proliferated; the scandal mushroomed, becoming so pervasive that even Henry's career began to suffer. And on the day he had reluctantly confided that his wife of twenty-seven years was beginning to act worried about his relationship with Juliet, she had written a letter of resignation, unwilling to let the man who had exhibited such faith in her talent suffer anymore simply because she was young and a fairly attractive female. It often occurred to her that it might have been different if she were a young man. Then she would have probably been considered a boy wonder whose meteoric rise would have been accepted as his due. But Juliet was a woman and . . .

Ah, well, she was being given a second chance here at Union Broadcasting now. As Juliet stepped from the elevator and turned down the wide plushly carpeted corridor toward Marc Tyner's suite of offices, she was extremely grateful the president of Union had offered her a position as an associate producer. She suspected his old friend, Henry Alexander, had something to do with the offer, but right now, the reason she had been hired didn't really matter. All that mattered was this second chance, and she wasn't going to jeopardize it in any way whatsoever.

Thrusting the memory of her ordeal at Lancaster far back in her mind, Juliet stopped at the third door to the right, smoothed her skirt, then entered the reception cubicle of the suite with a friendly smile to the young woman behind the desk. After the receptionist found her name in an appointment book, Juliet entered another, larger office

14

that was occupied by Tyner's private secretary, Mary Bedford, an attractive and stylishly dressed woman in her early fifties.

Looking up from her typewriter, Mrs. Bedford nodded expressionlessly as she said, "You're Miss York."

"Yes, to see Mr. Tyner, please," Juliet responded, unable to determine whether the secretary's words had been a statement or an accusation since her voice had been totally devoid of inflection. Deciding the woman had only been confirming her identity, Juliet smiled. "I have a three o'clock appointment."

With a glance at the clock on the wall, Mrs. Bedford returned Juliet's smile. "And it's three on the dot right now. That's good. Mr. Tyner's time is far too valuable to be wasted on those who won't bother to be punctual. He's such a busy man."

"I'm sure he is." Juliet's smile deepened slightly as she recognized the older woman's fondly protective tone. And she was oddly reassured by it. A man who engendered such loyalty and affection from his staff must be a fairly personable individual. After waiting until Mrs. Bedford had buzzed Tyner to announce her arrival, Juliet approached the double mahogany doors beyond and to one side of the secretary's desk. She knocked once softly, and the deep, resonant voice that bade her enter was instantly recognizable from the many times she had heard it on television. There was a sudden dryness in her throat as Juliet realized what a novice she was in this business compared to this man. But she was a talented, highly competent producer and this assignment with him was her chance to prove that. By chanting that reminder mentally, she was able to produce a convincingly self-assured smile when she opened the doors and entered Marc Tyner's spacious office. The office was simply but expensively furnished, she noticed. The cream-colored walls were accent-

15

ed by several excellent original paintings but that detail had barely a second to register in Juliet's mind before her complete attention was claimed by the man who slowly rose to his feet behind a mammoth teakwood desk.

"Mr. Tyner, how do you do?" Juliet began, her easy smile still gracing her lips. "I've seen you from a distance since you returned from your last assignment last week but we've never been introduced." As Tyner strode forward to meet her in the center of the room, she extended her right hand which was immediately enfolded in a firm warm clasp. "It's a pleasure to finally meet you."

"The pleasure's mine, Miss York," was his gracious low-timbred response. While he gestured toward a comfortable leather chair then she took a seat in it, his gaze roamed over her, expressing a man's appreciation of attractive femininity and absolutely no sign of disrespect or a sexist attitude.

And Juliet could hardly resent his intent appraisal since she was examining him quite closely too. His appearance came as something of a surprise. He was taller than she had imagined and the subtle muscularity of his lean body was not nearly as apparent on the television screen as it was now. Also, the camera obviously darkened his hair and eyes, because he was actually sandy-blond with eyes the clearest and yet the most unusual shade of blue Juliet had ever seen. And most surprising of all, he was only in his mid-thirties.

"You're younger than I thought you'd be," they said to each other simultaneously, then laughed together as Marc Tyner sat down on the edge of his desk, extending his long legs out before him.

"Why does my age surprise you?" he asked Juliet, amusement in his deep melodious voice, a smile still crinkling the corners of his eyes and fanning out to his lean

16

sun-bronzed cheeks. "Are you trying to tell me I look old on television?"

"Oh, no, I didn't mean it like that," she answered, laughing and relaxing back in the chair as she spread her hands out in a somewhat apologetic gesture. After shaking her head, she automatically tucked back the troublesome wisp of hair that had once again escaped to graze her temple. Then she confessed. "To tell the truth you look as young on television as you do in person but I . . . well, I had just always assumed that you had a great makeup artist . . . I mean, I thought you must be older than you looked because it usually takes longer to make career advances in the national news business than it's obviously taken you."

Marc Tyner raised dark brown eyebrows questioningly. "If that's true, then how do you account for the fact that you're already an associate producer though you can't be more than twenty-one?"

"Oh, I know I look younger than I am but not that much younger, I'm sure," Juliet told him, casually dismissing his deliberate exaggeration. "I'm twenty-eight."

"That's still young to become an associate producer. But I do know exactly why you were promoted so rapidly," he declared, crossing his arms across his broad chest, his eyes narrowing as he observantly noticed her suddenly stiffen. But he continued. "I happened to catch those two segments you produced for Lancaster—I try to keep an eye on the competition—and your work is good, Miss York. I was impressed."

Juliet murmured sincere gratitude for the compliment, then breathed again at last. For one despairing moment she had thought Tyner was going to throw that sordid scandal right in her face and tell her quite frankly that he believed the stories he had undoubtedly heard about her were true. Thank God he hadn't done that. Her patience

17

had worn extremely thin in the past several weeks. She had little tolerance left for those who presumed her guilty on the basis of vicious rumor. Defensive pride now prevented her from even attempting to plead innocence so any snide remark he might have made would have aroused great antagonism; no way to begin a relationship, especially when they had to work closely together for some weeks to come. Thinking of that work, Juliet dismissed her irrelevant personal problem from her mind but as she started to open one of the folders she had with her, Marc Tyner's next words stilled her hand.

"With your career flourishing at Lancaster, I'm surprised you left them. What was your reason for resigning?"

Juliet's eyes darkened with renewed suspicion as they darted up to meet the striking sapphire-blue of his. Just what kind of question had that been? Was he trying to bait her, to provoke her into admitting that scandal had finally left her with little alternative except to resign her former position? She honestly couldn't tell if he was baiting her or not. The expression laying over his finely carved features was inscrutable, and all she could really detect in the clear depths of his azure eyes was the unmistakable glimmer of intelligence. Uncertain what his question had truly meant, she tossed it right back to him.

"Why do you think I resigned?"

A puzzled frown nicked his brow. "I have no idea why. That's the reason I asked you."

Juliet's tension dissolved immediately. Something deeply instinctive assured her she could believe him. *He actually had not heard the rumors about her.* After all, he was often away on assignment and even when he was in New York City, it was unlikely he was a member of any of the cliques that gathered at vending machines to exchange

18

gossipy tidbits. Feeling greatly relieved, Juliet smiled up at him.

"Resigning from Lancaster was the best thing I could have done since it gave me the opportunity to come over to Union Broadcasting. After all, your program *Perspective* earns consistently higher ratings than *News Probe,* and I'm like most people—I want to be a member of the most successful team," Juliet said simply, her gaze never wavering as she looked up at him. What she had said wasn't the whole truth, but it wasn't a lie either. "Besides, Union offered me a considerable raise in salary. And more importantly I couldn't pass up the chance to work with such experienced and respected correspondents as Terry Kendall, Jeff Blakemore, and of course, you."

Her final comment was made in earnest and was in no way an attempt to gain points with him, and with a brief inclination of his head he accepted the roundabout compliment with as much ease as he obviously accepted her explanation. Then for a long moment he was silent, looking down at her before he abruptly said, "Beverly Joyce was the correspondent on one of the *News Probe* segments you produced. What do you think of her?"

"She impressed me very much and we worked well together."

"Do you like her personally?"

"Yes, I do."

"Although she has quite a reputation for being a bitch?"

Juliet laughed. "That reputation preceded her, I must admit. But after we met I realized that if she seems demanding to some people, it's probably because she's a perfectionist. She's committed to doing a first-rate job, but so am I. So we got on fine. Why do you ask?"

Marc Tyner gave her a slight smile. "I think you will also. But I was just curious. I like Beverly too."

"Then we already have something in common," Juliet

drawled, amusement lighting her delicate features as she once more tucked back that wayward strand of hair. "Now, if you've finished sizing me up and have decided we can work together compatiably, perhaps we should start discussing our assignment. Agreed, Mr. Tyner?"

"Marc," he corrected firmly, though there was an answering glint of amusement in his eyes. "Agreed, Juliet? It's only logical for us to be on a first-name basis since we are going to be practically inseparable during our assignment."

Looking up at his tanned finely carved face, Juliet felt as if her heart skipped a couple successive beats. Foolish reaction! Marc hadn't meant anything personal by that comment, yet something in his low tone . . . Oh, what nonsense, she told herself. Simply because this was her first real assignment for Union, she was a bit on edge but couldn't allow herself to succumb to an overactive imagination. Refusing to be flustered because a highly attractive man made a remark that could be misinterpreted, she withdrew a thin sheaf of papers from the folder in her lap.

"I'm more comfortable with first names too, Marc," she answered calmly. Crossing her shapely legs, she leaned slightly toward him, extending the sheaf of papers so he too could see them. "Now, I have several details to discuss with you. First, the travel and accommodation plans. Our departure time is four forty-five tomorrow evening, and that's from Kennedy. Our E.T.A. in Greensboro is approximately six o'clock, and there will be a charter plane ready for our flight to Boone. My secretary's booked rooms for the entire crew at a rustic but very comfortable inn there. It's actually a ski lodge in winter—very lovely, I'm told." Vaguely sensing disapproval, Juliet glanced up and saw a barely perceptible tightening of Marc's strong jaw. "Something wrong?"

"Why the accommodations in Boone? When I go out on

20

assignment, I think it's best for the entire crew to stay where the story is. I refuse to be accused of conducting a sneaky investigation. This time, I especially want every public official in Talbot County to know *Perspective* is investigating all the charges of corruption against some of them."

"Oh, I'm sure they will. In fact, some of the higher officials probably knew we'd been given this assignment almost as soon as we did."

"Fine. I prefer quarry who are prepared to give me a challenge so there's no point in staying in Boone. I'm sure it's not too late for your secretary to make reservations for us in a motel near Trenton, the county seat. Have her do that today please."

Juliet smiled faintly. "I don't think you realize how rural Talbot County is," she demured. "My secretary discovered there are only two motels. Unfortunately one was recently condemned and the other . . . well, suffice it to say the rooms aren't what you might call reasonably comfortable."

A sudden steeliness came into Marc's eyes, graying over the blue. "I'm sure I could survive a less than luxurious motel room for a few weeks since I managed to endure far more primitive conditions in Vietnam jungles when I accompanied recon patrols for days at a time."

"Yes, I realize that," Juliet said softly, sensing that memories of those reconnaissance missions were bitter and probably still horrifying. She caught his introspective gaze and smiled at him. "I know you even survived several White House press conferences too." When her attempt to lighten his mood brought a fleeting smile to his firmly shaped lips, she added, "I still think we should stay in Boone during this assignment, however."

He stared steadily at her. "If we stay there, how close to Trenton will we be?"

"It shouldn't take more than a twenty-minute drive across the county line to get there. And since Boone is a university town, the crew will be more content there. We certainly don't want a bored, disgruntled crew. Bored people rarely put their best effort into their work, and it would be a shame to do this assignment sloppily, wouldn't it?"

Marc threw up his hands in mock surrender, muted laughter coming from down deep in his throat. "Enough! You've convinced me. There's nothing worse than a mutinous crew."

"We'll certainly need all the team spirit going in we can muster," Juliet stated flatly though her expression sobered. "The arrival of our entourage isn't likely to be welcomed with a marching band. I'm sure you've been told our executive producer has received a couple of anonymous letters advising *Perspective* to stay out of Talbot County business."

"Yes, Pete told me about them, but letters like that aren't at all unusual when you do an exposé news program," Marc said without much concern as he regarded her speculatively. "But maybe you see them as threats. Does this assignment frighten you, Juliet?"

"No, it doesn't frighten me," she answered honestly. "But I do know how potentially controversial this story could be. I mean, we have a case of proved corruption in a small rural county; three local officials convicted of corruption, yet given suspended sentences; and most disturbing of all, several implied indications a United States senator might have bribed or coerced a district judge to hand out those light sentences."

"There's no concrete proof of that. That's the main reason to do this story." Marc tapped a forefinger against his jaw thoughtfully. "People may suspect the senator's

22

guilty simply because he is very influential in that 'good ole boy' group of his friends."

"Yes, he is," Juliet agreed, then politely took exception to Marc's choice of words, unaware that her chin was now slightly jutted out. "*However,* we should avoid using the terminology 'good ole boy' in this story. It gives the impression that every rural area in the South is rife with corruption, which of course isn't true. I personally know some very nice 'good ole boys' who are scrupulously honest."

"You're absolutely right. It's a terminology we will avoid," said Marc as he regarded her intently. "I know some very nice 'good ole boys' too; consider them good friends. But none of them have the same sort of drawl you do, Juliet. I would guess you're from western Tennessee."

Juliet's emerald eyes widened in surprise. "How did you know that?"

"Regional accents have always interested me." He smiled down at her rather teasingly. "You know, you're the first fiery little Rebel I've ever had as a producer."

"Well, don't let it worry you. You're not the first damn Yankee I've ever worked with, so I'm sure we'll manage just fine," she retorted perkily, returning his smile, pleased that thus far their working relationship was beginning smoothly. Millions of viewers might consider Marc Tyner a superstar in television journalism, but he didn't act as if he thought he was God's gift to the airwaves, and for that she was truly thankful.

During the following fifteen minutes as Juliet and Marc discussed various aspects of their assignment, she became increasingly more comfortable with him. He was an attentive listener, enthusiastic about some of her ideas and willing to share his own. Together they mapped out a flexible strategy for their pursuit of a factual story and

23

with that accomplished, Juliet began to gather up the material she had brought to the meeting.

"Well, we certainly have a lot to go on here. The research team has supplied us with many good leads," she commented. "And I agree with you that your first interview should be with Trenton's mayor. Hopefully he won't try to avoid us and will talk freely in front of the cameras."

"I wouldn't count on that. I have a very strong feeling this will be one of those assignments in which very few people will be eager to talk to us," Marc told her, rising up from the edge of his desk as she stood. He smiled. "But I'm sure we'll manage to persuade most of them to consent to an interview."

"I'm sure *you'll* be able to persuade them," Juliet countered, smiling back. "You have the reputation of being quite an aggressive hunter."

He raised one dark brown eyebrow. "Now, Juliet, do I really seem like the aggressive type to you?"

Although there was, at that moment, a glimmer of amusement in his incredibly blue eyes, she imagined that in some situations, he would be awesomely aggressive. "Perhaps *assertive* is a better description of you," she replied tactfully.

A smile tugged upward at the corners of his mouth. "How diplomatic you are."

"I try my best," Juliet murmured, and turned her attention to a note she had scribbled on one folder to serve as a reminder. "Oh, one last detail. I realize many correspondents have certain writers they prefer to work with. We have Jenkins and Merriam going on this assignment—if you have no objections."

Marc lifted his broad shoulders in a casual shrug. "I hear they're both talented. But I write my own material."

"Oh. I see." Juliet observed him thoughtfully for only

24

a few seconds before making her decision. "Even so, I want at least Jenkins along on this one."

"Whatever you say," Marc replied offhandedly, though there might have been a veiled note of challenge in his low tone. "You're the field producer; staff selection is your prerogative."

"Yes. It is," she said but with a warm smile. Once again, she extended her right hand toward him. "Well, Marc, I'm happy to be working with you."

"I'm looking forward to the next several weeks myself" was his soft reply.

And as he continued to hold her hand in his longer than was necessary, long hard fingers pleasantly rough-textured against her soft palm, Juliet experienced a sudden forceful surge of excitement that very nearly made her catch her breath. It was as if he were too close to her, and for a moment she could concentrate only on the strong column of his neck rising above his open shirt collar and loosened knot of his tie. His skin was darkly tanned and very smooth; and with his shirtsleeves rolled up above his elbows, exposing subtly muscled forearms, he seemed much more approachable than the rather imposing hard-hitting journalist she was accustomed to seeing on her television screen. That was the problem. She was suddenly far too aware of him as a virile, attractive man, and that awareness made her uneasy. When she saw his gaze discreetly wander over her, she gently withdrew her hand from his and took a small backward step away from him. She managed a seemingly casual smile.

"Remember our flight time tomorrow evening. Four forty-five," she reminded him, turning to leave. "See you on board."

"If not before," he said softly as she moved away from him.

Something disturbing yet undefinable in his deep voice

seemed to make Juliet's heart skip several beats again, and it wouldn't have surprised her much if she had started blushing like an adolescent simply because she could feel his eyes on her as she walked across his office. But she didn't blush; the moment she closed his door behind her, she began justifying her reaction to him. After all, he was one of those rare men endowed with a very dangerous combination of qualities—sex appeal and a fascinating intelligence. And she was a woman. It was natural for her to find him attractive. Contrary to Susan's dire predictions, she hadn't felt like she was going to swoon in his presence.

Smiling wryly at that thought, Juliet exited the suite and was nearly run down in the corridor by Tom, her assistant.

"Oh, damn, you're not leaving?" he exclaimed, running his fingers through his hair. "You mean, your meeting with Tyner's over already?"

"Afraid you missed it."

"Hell. I wanted to meet him, but I was held up at the studio. I got up here as soon as I could."

"Don't worry about it. You can meet Marc tomorrow on the plane," Juliet said comfortingly.

"Well, what's he like in person?" Tom inquired eagerly, obviously suffering from a rather severe case of hero worship. "What did you think of him?"

"Very intelligent. Strong-willed but very pleasant," Juliet answered but didn't add what she now knew only too well. Marc Tyner was also a powerful man, one who probably wouldn't hesitate to use that power to his advantage. She could only hope that while they worked together no major disagreements arose between them, because technically—as field producer—she might be in charge of this assignment, but in the boardroom of Union Broadcasting it was Marc Tyner who had the clout. He was the

26

superstar. She was merely another associate producer, as expendable here as she had been at Lancaster. If Marc became her ally, she would finally be fairly secure in her career, but she didn't like to think what might happen to her if, for some dreadful reason, he became an enemy.

CHAPTER TWO

The next evening as the sun was setting, Juliet left her room in the rustic little inn. She stepped directly out onto the balcony that circumvented the entire building and breathed deeply of the clean mountain air as she moved to the wooden railing. Propping her elbows on the top-most slat, cupping her chin in her hands, she gazed westward where the enormous fiery orange sun was drifting down behind the mountain. In its wake, blue sky was bathed in a reddish-gold glow, and eastern slopes lay in dusky shadow. Rolling hills and steep inclines that would become winter's ski runs were now lush dark green, reminiscent of Alpine meadows. There was serene silence in the cooling air that accompanied the deepening twilight. Caught up in the peaceful beauty of the countryside, Juliet began to unwind from what had been a hectic day filled with last-minute assignments and preparations followed by the flight from New York then the transfer in Greensboro to the charter plane.

The *Perspective* team had only arrived at the inn a scant two hours ago, and most of the time since their arrival had been spent over a long shop-talk dinner—enlivened by the enthusiasm that usually accompanies the beginning of a new project. Listening to the crew's chatter, Juliet had wondered if everyone would still be this enthusiastic when they were wrapping up this assignment. She suspected they all would be, simply because Marc Tyner was the correspondent. He possessed a rare ability to slice swiftly down to the core of every story he went after, yet he did so with such finesse that it was a fascinating experience to watch him go about it.

That was the distinct impression Juliet had received from everyone who had ever talked to her about him; as she stood on the balcony while dusk cloaked the countryside in darkening shadow, renewed excitement surged through her. She was looking forward to watching Marc in action and could hardly wait for the next morning, when their assignment together would officially begin. Practical though Juliet was, she was not immune to occasional daydreaming. In the twilight she stood very still, staring at the purple-shrouded mountains while she imagined putting together such a brilliant story that it would earn accolades for Marc as the correspondent and for herself as producer.

Pleasant as her somewhat feasible fantasy was, she was rather reluctant to let go of it even when a large hand descended unexpectedly onto her left shoulder. Turning her head, she found Marc towering above her, his face visible in the light that spilled from her room onto the balcony.

He looked down at her. "You didn't even hear me coming. Did you fall asleep on your feet? Or were you as lost in a world of your own as you seemed?"

"Trying to run through a checklist in my mind," she admitted easily, smiling back at him. "Tomorrow will be pretty hectic."

"Maybe you should get to bed early then."

"I doubt that would help. Even if I were dropping from sheer exhaustion, I wouldn't be able to fall asleep. Too excited about tomorrow, I guess." Tilting her head slightly to one side, she looked into his eyes, her expression

29

questioning. "Do you ever have that problem, or are you such an old pro at this that you don't really get very excited about a new assignment?"

"When I stop feeling excited about each story I do, I'll retire," Marc stated seriously, but then grinned. "And if you must call me an 'old pro,' try not to make it sould like you think I've been in this business since the television was invented. You said yourself that I'm not quite as ancient as you'd imagined I'd be."

"I wasn't insinuating you were ancient, and you know that," Juliet replied, responding to his almost teasing tone by returning his grin. "I called you an old pro because compared to me, that's what you are. You've done countless stories like this, but I . . . well, suffice it to say, I'm not nearly as experienced."

"Experienced enough obviously, or Pete Martin wouldn't have given you this assignment. I personally know what fine work you did for *News Probe* before you left Lancaster. And I doubt the quality of your work has changed since you came over to Union."

Juliet grimaced rather comically, wrinkling her small nose. "Well, to tell the truth, I've only been at Union about six weeks. I guess you didn't realize that. And I've been spending my time studying Pete's style by viewing videotapes of *Perspective* stories or visiting some of the other associate producers in the field. Actually this is my first real assignment for *Perspective.*"

"In other words you're saying I'm something of a guinea pig?" Flicking back the sides of the casual tan jacket he planted lean hands on lean hips and stared down at her, his face devoid of any readable expression. "Pete tossed my story to you as a test of your ability?"

Gazing up at him, unable to decide whether or not he was actually serious, Juliet said rather tersely, "I beg your pardon, Mr. Tyner. This isn't exclusively *your* story. It's mine, too, because I'm the associate producer. And I'm not an amateur whose ability has to be tested. I assure you, I know what I'm doing."

"Exactly. And it's reassuring to know you realize that," Marc said with a sudden unabashed smile. "You were beginning to sound apologetic because you didn't have twenty years of experience behind you."

"I wasn't apologizing. I was merely telling the truth," she said with some degree of frustration at his abrupt turnaround. "You seemed to think I'd already done stories for *Perspective* and I thought you should know this was my first assignment."

"That fact doesn't bother me in the least . . . now that I'm sure you don't have doubts about yourself. You obviously have confidence in your abilities, Juliet, which is an absolute necessity for anyone who hopes to succeed in this business."

Juliet raised her eyes heavenward in mock exasperation but at last had to laugh at herself. "Taken in by that old reverse-psychology trick. You attack me to make me defend myself. And it worked. No wonder some of the people you interview call you a manipulator."

"Believe me, I've been called much worse than that, and on more occasions than I'd care to count."

"I guess that's the price you pay for being able to make people tell you more than they really want to but you think it's worth it, don't you? How does it feel to have so much power?"

"Ah, yes, I have power—but not enough . . . yet," he said theatrically, the fanatically fervent note in his deep voice almost convincing. He lowered his head until his face was close to Juliet's but his megalomaniacal expression was too exaggerated to be at all sinister. "Today I have power over the people I interview, but tomorrow . . ."

"Yes, I know. Tomorrow the world," she said wryly, leaning back against the railing on her elbows, entertained by his impromptu performance. "But until you're able to accomplish that little feat, I'm just glad I won't ever have to be the target of one of your interviews."

"Why? Do you have secrets you wouldn't want revealed? Some scandal in your shady past?"

Juliet's answering laugh was cold and cynical-sounding. The crazy scandal she had been involved in hardly qualified as a secret since everyone in the broadcasting industry had heard about it. Yesterday she had assumed Marc hadn't heard the gossip about her but perhaps he had and perhaps this was his way of trying to bring up the matter discreetly. If that was his objective, he had failed in it, because she had no intention of discussing the rumor that she had been having an affair with Henry Alexander ever again. She was thoroughly disgusted with the entire ridiculous business.

Taking her cue from Marc, she leaned a bit closer to him to whisper "Sorry to disappoint you, but my life is a very predictable book."

"I don't believe you," he whispered back, looking deeply into her eyes. "Everyone has some secrets. And besides, if your life's such an open book, why should you be glad I won't ever interview you?"

"Because I've seen how you operate, and as I said, you're very adept at getting people to say more than they want to," Juliet murmured. Marc was so close to her now that his warm breath caressed her cheek and she eased closer back against the railing to put more distance between them as she continued. "I certainly wouldn't want you to cajole me into blurting out some of my most personal thoughts before millions of viewers. They might be shocked."

"Oh? For example?"

Juliet fought a smile. "Well, for example, I've always had this wicked desire to go skinny-dipping in the ocean in the moonlight, but I've never had a chance to do it."

"That *is* shocking."

"I know it is."

"Yes, indeed," Marc said as soberly as she had spoken despite the amusement lighting his eyes. "That may be the most shocking confession I've ever heard, because I truly believe everyone should have at least one chance to go skinny-dipping in the ocean in the moonlight. Now I can understand why you wouldn't want to risk publicly admitting how deprived you've been."

"And speaking of interviews, the mayor of Trenton cannot possibly talk to us tomorrow, according to his secretary," Juliet said hastily, heeding an inner need to steer the conversation to a more serious but impersonal topic. As Marc moved from directly in front of her to stand beside her at the railing and gaze out into deepening darkness, she turned around too. "And when I asked very politely for an appointment with him on Thursday instead, she claimed he would be out of town. Since you can't interview him first, as we'd planned, I'll try early in the morning to get an appointment with the county sheriff."

"No, we should bypass the sheriff for the time being," said Marc, rubbing his jaw, deep in thought. "Two of his top deputies and a town councilman were the ones convicted of corruption, but our sources tell us it should be fairly easy to prove the mayor and sheriff himself were equally guilty, especially in the bid-rigging on county public-works projects. And if the mayor refuses to talk to us now, we won't talk to the sheriff either. Instead, we'll interview some of their harshest critics first, starting with the county district attorney. Then it shouldn't be long before the Mayor will start thinking he'd better say something in his own defense."

"But by interviewing their critics first, we'll be giving them the perfect opportunity to accuse us of deliberately slanting this story against them," Juliet reminded him. "I'd rather not give them a chance to do that."

"I'd rather not either, but my instincts tell me we're going to have to go that way on this one. Besides, the moment they accuse us of slanting the story, we'll request interviews again—and they'll be more inclined to grant them."

"And if they don't, we'll take a camera crew into their offices to film them actually refusing to be interviewed."

"Only as a last resort, Juliet. I never like to do that." Marc turned his head to look at her, and a grim smile moved his firm lips. "Their refusal to be interviewed caught on film will seem proof of their guilt to most viewers. But in an interview we have a better chance of getting down to the real truth. Throw a few unexpected questions at guilty people, and most of them will begin to unravel. Their answers aren't consistent. Their own lies confuse them, and it usually shows in their faces and the way they start shifting restlessly in their chairs. They condemn themselves, and the audience *sees* the truth."

"Always the relentless pursuer, aren't you?" Juliet asked softly, her soft gaze exploring his firmly carved features. "Never give up until you get to the truth."

"And what about you? Why did you choose your particular career?" he asked her. "Because you think it's always important to look for the truth? Or did you just want all the glamor and excitement that come with being a producer?"

"Oh, it's definitely the glamor and excitement I'm after," she answered, returning his knowing smile. "There's nothing more thrilling than all the background work we do on these stories—the tedious research, the dry holes that we were sure had been hot leads, the battle to keep everything organized and on schedule. But it's worth it, isn't it? It *is* exciting to expose the truth—for me, especially when we can do stories that actually get help for people who really need it."

"A fiery little Rebel with a social conscience. Intriguing," Marc said softly, his narrowed eyes wandering over her delicately contoured face. "But does your career and your need to help people occupy all your time? Or do you occasionally allow yourself to relax?"

"Of course, I do."

"How?"

"I read as much as I can. I enjoy the theater and ballet. And, as I mentioned, I do love to swim," she added with a mischievous grin. Juliet tilted her head to one side questioningly. "Why do you ask?"

"Just curious. I wondered why you didn't go into town with the crew to check out the nightlife."

"Why didn't *you* go with them?"

"I had some notes to go over." Marc turned toward her, one arm resting on the railing, his long legs crossed at the ankles. "Okay, I've told you my reason for staying here this evening. Now tell me yours."

Juliet gave him a wry smile. "All right, I didn't go check out the nightlife because it's fairly obvious what the crew will find. Most college towns are pretty much alike: three pizza parlors, one movie theater, two ice cream shops, three bars, several fast-food places, maybe a disco, and the inevitable little stores that stock overpriced preppie sportswear. Some will probably enjoy reliving their college days in those places, but luckily for everyone else, the university's offered us the use of all its recreational facilities while we're here. And the drama department has two plays scheduled for this last month of the summer session.

Since I knew all that already, there was no need for me to go into town tonight, and like you I had some notes to go over anyhow. Besides, as I told you, I am tired."

"But still too excited about tomorrow to feel sleepy. There's something you'll have to learn, Juliet. No matter how involved you become in getting a story, you need to forget it completely sometimes and relax," Marc said softly, raising his hands to curve them around her arms, his grip light. Long fingers began a gentle stroking message, and when Juliet's eyes widened, he smiled indulgently. "Your muscles feel very tight, but I could easily remedy that if you'd like me to give you a real massage in your room."

Juliet stiffened as her eyes flashed defiance. "What I want is for you to take your hands off me. Immediately."

Ignoring her command, he shook his head. "Hmmm, you really are weary, aren't you? And obviously too tense to realize I was only teasing you."

"Your helpful suggestion sounded like a genuine proposition to me." she retorted skeptically.

"Maybe it did, but it wasn't. We only met yesterday, and it would be ridiculous for me to try to get you into bed with me tonight," Marc said succinctly. "Maybe if you weren't so tired, you would give me credit for having more finesse than that."

With the realization that she had obviously overreacted, Juliet sighed and conceded, "I guess I am even more tired than I thought. But I still don't think you sounded like you were teasing."

"Only because you don't know much about me—yet. But by the time this story's wrapped up, you will. And I'll know all about you. We'll be working together so closely that we'll learn much more about each other than people usually can in only a few weeks."

"Yes, I expect we will," Juliet murmured agreeably,

trying to appear calm and collected although the stroking fingers that had slowly slipped up beneath the cap sleeves of her pristine white blouse were causing powerful tingling sensations that seemed to dance over her skin. Instead of relaxing her with a soothing impersonal massage as Marc was apparently trying to do, he was arousing in her an altogether different kind of tension. It wasn't weariness that was bothering her now—it was Marc himself. The same uneasiness she had felt in his office yesterday stole over her again; that uneasiness borne of her overpowering awareness of him as a man. The palms cupping her arms were evocatively warm and hard, and to escape their disturbing touch she looked out over the darkened sloping meadows while half turning away from him. Her move was executed with such natural unhurried grace that Marc automatically released her. Yet Juliet felt as if the imprint of his fingers still lingered caressingly on her skin. A slight tremor ran over her that he mistook as a shiver, and he removed his jacket to drape it around her shoulders.

"Thanks," she murmured, smiling back at him. "Now I can never say chivalry is dead, can I?" When he silently turned her to face him, crushing the jacket's lapels in his hands to gently draw her nearer, her smile faded, and she only barely suppressed an audible catching of her breath. Unnerved by his continued silence and narrowed intent gaze, she moistened suddenly dry lips and was dismayed at the frantic pace of her heartbeat.

It was as if, in an instant, the stillness of the night had enveloped them. The faint scent of pine perfumed the air; the sliver of an ivory moon glowed luminously in a black sky festooned with sparkling stars. A light breeze, refreshingly cool for early August, stirred in the surrounding trees, whispered over the leaves, and drifted over Marc and Juliet. Habit caused her to reach up toward the strand of hair that swept forward to brush her temple and cheek, but before she could tuck it back in place or even touch it, Marc caught her hand in one of his.

"Leave it," he commanded softly as his own strong fingers moved up to run lightly as a feather through the silken tendril. Moonlight reflected warningly in his eyes as they caught and held hers. "I like your hair better this way, with this little wisp free to graze against your cheek. In fact, I'd probably like it even better if it was all free. What does it look like that way, Juliet?"

Before she could even think of some sensible response, his palms were brushing the sides of her neck and his fingers slipped into the loose chignon on her nape. With spellbinding slowness Marc removed pin after pin until the swathe of soft auburn-gold hair unwound to cascade down over his hands. He ran thick vibrant strands between his fingers as if he found the texture fascinating. And when one fingertip moved in slow circles against her scalp, keen tingling sensations scampered over every inch of her skin. She trembled, unable to divert her bemused gaze from his.

Marc's slow lazy smile warmed his eyes. "Such lovely hair shouldn't be confined when it can be down like this, shimmering in the moonlight," he said almost in a whisper. "It looks beautiful, Juliet."

Managing to conceal her sudden breathlessness long enough to murmur an appropriate response, she stood very still; she knew that if she was sensible, she would put a stop to this little scene at once. Yet her characteristically good common sense seemed a thing apart from her present feelings. Some persistently nagging part of her brain wanted her to simply walk away from Marc, while another part wanted her to stay with him. And, caught up in a quandary of those conflicting emotions, she could do nothing at all except continue to gaze up at him.

Marc moved closer. Intently surveying her upturned

38

face, which was framed by gently waved hair, he cradled the back of her head in one large hand while the other was drawn slowly around to lie lightly against her collarbone. The ball of his thumb feathered across the pulse beating in her throat, lingered there a moment, then trailed up to brush slowly back and forth along the fragile line of her jaw and chin.

"Did you know you have an incredibly beautiful mouth?" he murmured, his deep voice appealingly husky. "It looks so soft, so—"

If he finished that sentence, Juliet didn't hear his words because her heart thudded wildly against her breast, pounding loudly in her ears the instant he started tracing the outline of her lips with one fingertip. Then he brushed the edge of that finger across them. She could have stopped him then, but she didn't. She had heard lines before, but Marc's was spectacularly effective . . . and arousing. Warmth was rushing in waves over her. Some powerful force was drawing her inexorably to him, making her want to touch him. Perhaps it was the expertise of his caresses and his aura of potent virility combined with the respect she already felt for his intelligence and his character that suddenly made her want very badly to be much closer to him. But whatever it was that made her feel as she did didn't really matter at that moment, because when Marc tilted her head back slightly and lowered his, her eyes fluttered shut as anticipation caught at her swiftly drawn breath.

Firm warm lips barely grazed her temples—skimming the natural arch of her eyebrows and even touching the tips of her thick lashes—before seeking her contoured porcelain-smooth cheeks. A shiver of delight trickled along Juliet's spine as the kisses that followed the curve of her neck increased in pressure from a teasing touch light as a butterfly's wing to a thrilling caress exerting still gentle but undeniable demand. She lifted her hands, laid them against his chest, and felt the warmth of his flesh emanating through his shirtfront and seeming to permeate deep into her skin. Then an inner warmth was kindled in her when Marc raised his head to seek her mouth again, touching first one corner then the other.

As Juliet clenched the fabric of his shirt Marc's lips took possession of hers, parting them but with an exquisite tenderness that savored their sweet taste. His warm minty breath mingled with hers as his sensuously formed lips playfully explored the fullness of her own, and when the breathtaking contact of flesh against flesh was suddenly broken, disappointment gnawed at Juliet. Her eyes opened and darkened to lambent pools of emerald impaled by the piercing light that glinted hotter and hotter in the blue depths of his. His sun-browned face filled her vision and she felt an odd vulnerability, as if her very soul were exposed to his view as he studied her every feature closely. The way he was looking at her caused her heartbeat to quicken to a rapid tempo that unraveled the last remnants of her composure.

"Marc, I—"

"Your lips are soft, Julie," he interrupted gently, his alteration of her name spoken like an endearment. "Soft and sweet. So sweet." His thumb brushing her chin pressed down lightly in a persuasive hint of a tug and he commanded unevenly, "Open your mouth a little."

She did, and waves of sensual pleasure rushed deep down within her when his lips descended with only an instant of initial gentleness before hardening to part and plunder the enticing tenderness of hers. With a low nearly inaudible moan, she uncurled her fingers against his chest, swayed toward him, and kissed him back. Their lips touched and parted, touched and parted, their tongues entwining in erotic dance of desire until at last a groan sounded in Marc's throat; his large hands spanned her waist to pull her forcefully to him. Muscles rippled in the arms that gathered her up onto her toes and fast against the hard lithe length of his body. The enchanting pliancy of her softly curved form, pressed so closely to him, aroused unmistakable passion, and his hard mouth claimed hers with fervent demand.

Lost in the moment, aroused by his subtly aggressive masculinity, Juliet slid her arms up around his neck; as the kiss they exchanged deepened, her lips clung to his. Her fingers feathered through the vibrant thickness of the sandy blond hair grazing his nape. She allowed the supportive arms that tightened around her to mold her amply curved body against the firm muscular contours of his. Powerfully taut thighs pressed against her own; the hard plane of his broad chest warmed the yielding flesh of her breasts; the arms holding her conveyed an insistence tempered by tenderness.

Fascinated by the very feel and clean male scent of him, she ardently gave him back kiss for kiss until his mouth left hers. Arching her back slightly in his embrace, he reached up and discovered the first button of her white blouse already undone; with swift, deft fingers he unfastened the second and third. Juliet's heart began hammering when Marc pushed his jacket and her blouse aside, lowered his head and trailed a strand of nibbling kisses over the creamy curve of her shoulder. His breath tantalized yet seemed to scorch her skin, and as weakness dragged at her lower limbs she began to recognize the danger of the rapidly growing desire he was arousing in her. Partial sanity restored, she took a long deep breath and was able to resist her own need to be kissed when he started to seek her lips with his again. Bending her head to rest it in the hollow of his shoulder, her unconfined hair fell forward like a luxuriant silken curtain over her cheeks.

41

"Don't," she whispered. Despite the revealing breathless tremor in her voice, her hands were almost completely steady as she reached behind her to take hold of Marc's wrists and withdraw his arms from around her. Yet something akin to shyness warmed her cheeks when she at last looked up at him. An obviously indulgent smile touched his lips. Glad there wasn't sufficient light for him to see her deepening blush, she managed a weak smile in return. "We're both tired—too tired to think straight, so it seems. I guess I'd better go in now."

Before she could turn to step away from him, his hands came out and caught hers. "You don't really believe being tired had anything to do with what just happened?" he asked softly. "Do you?"

"I'm sure that contributed to—"

"*Julie.*"

Once again his caressing tone as he abbreviated her name disconcerted her. But she tried her best to conceal that fact from him. Instead, she maintained at least an outward semblance of composure by directly meeting his watchful gaze. "Really, Marc, let's be honest about this. It's a beautiful night, and we're alone out here. And . . ."

"I kissed you because I wanted to, because as I said, you have an incredibly lovely mouth," he interrupted gently, his resonant voice deepening. Releasing one small hand, he cupped her chin in curved fingers and, without warning, brushed his thumb across her lips. The instant they parted beneath his grazing touch, his eyes impaled hers. "And I enjoyed kissing you, especially since you gave me every indication you were enjoying it too. Weren't you?"

"All right, yes," she confessed with a resigned gesture and wry smile. "I did enjoy it."

"Then why the pretense?"

"I didn't want you to get the wrong impression."

42

"Wrong impression?"

"You know. I didn't want you to think I expect what happened to lead to something more. I certainly don't expect anything of the sort. We're here to work not to— What I'm saying is, I don't get involved."

Marc smiled provocatively. "But it can get very lonely on assignment, Julie."

"Oh, come now, Marc. That's a line a married man would hand out." Juliet grinned at him, relieved she had been able to seize a chance to make light of a conversation that had been rapidly becoming too serious—at least in her opinion. As he smiled back at her she extracted her hand from his and shook her head. "Besides, I doubt very much that you ever get lonely on assignment—there are women in every town who would be happy to help you occupy your time."

"Why should I bother with other women when you're right here?" he countered. "And we are attracted to each other."

"Yes, I guess we are, but as I said, I don't get involved," she reiterated. "So what happened tonight won't happen again."

"Julie," he murmured, stroking a hand over her evocatively tousled hair, then leaned down to touch his lips to hers in a light yet astoundingly electrifying kiss. When he moved away from her after a moment, a little smile was tugging at the corners of his mouth. He inclined his head toward her room. "I think you're right. You should go to bed. We'll have a busy day tomorrow."

"Yes. Good night, Marc" was all Juliet said as she slipped off his jacket and returned it to him. Leaving him leaning against the railing, she crossed the balcony, stepped inside her room, and closed the French doors behind her.

"The last thing in the world you need is to get involved

43

with Marc Tyner," she muttered aloud while walking to the mirrored dresser. "With all the influence he has at Union Broadcasting, everyone would assume the worst." She certainly didn't want to do anything that would start more gossip about her. Besides, she had her career to concentrate on; she really didn't want to get involved with any man, even one as magnetically personable and attractive as Marc.

And Marc Tyner was dangerous. Juliet knew that now without a doubt. Surveying her reflection in the mirror, she touched her fingertips to her lips. A tiny frown knitted her brow. Only seconds after assuring Marc that what had happened between them tonight wouldn't be repeated, he had kissed her again. And she had responded! Not with uncontrollable passion, but she *had* responded. And even now, her breath caught a little with the memory of how his kisses had made her feel. Oh, Marc had finesse with women all right; far too much finesse for Juliet's peace of mind.

CHAPTER THREE

The next afternoon Juliet, Marc, and Paul Phillips, the director of their *Perspective* segment, left the office of Talbot County's district attorney. Camera and sound crews, carrying out their equipment, straggled along some distance behind the three of them as they exited the old gray stone courthouse building on Trenton's Main Street. As they stepped outside into bright sunlight Juliet breathed a silent sigh as local residents who had been strolling along the sidewalks stopped to stare at the *Perspective* team.

"They're eyeing us like we're visitors from another planet. Unwelcome visitors at that," Paul remarked laconically. "I get the impression they're not really glad to have us here."

"Perfectly understandable. According to the D.A., most of the people in the county are disgusted by the corruption that's already been uncovered," said Marc. "They're probably afraid we'll air a story that makes everyone in the county seem corrupt and will badly tarnish the image of Trenton as a nice little town."

"Then we'd better prove that's not the type of story we've come to do," Juliet declared, halting in the blessed shade provided by an ancient sprawling oak tree. Adjusting the collar of her ivory suit jacket, she watched the camera and sound teams descend the courthouse steps, then she turned to Marc and Paul decisively, nodding her head. "We're going to do some man-on-the-street interviews. And since we have the crews in town, we'll do them right now. We'll ask them questions that give them every opportunity to air their own opinions—then assure them that at least some of them will appear in the segment *Perspective* airs. That way they'll know we're not here to do a hatchet job on the whole county, and word will get around that we're playing fair. All right?" she asked rhetorically while opening her briefcase. She removed a large brown envelope containing waivers and handed it to Paul with a grin. "Be sure—"

"I know, I know. Be sure everyone we talk to signs a release so we can't be sued for airing an interview without permission." Paul recited Union Broadcasting's litany in a bored tone. "Waste of time if you ask me."

"It's just a little extra precaution that can't hurt," Juliet said. "And since it *is* company policy . . ."

"Well, I guess it isn't really that much trouble," Paul conceded, tucking the envelope under one arm and rocking back on his heels. "Might as well get started then. Do you want me to shoot them with Ben off-camera so we can mit him out later and Marc can voice-over the questions he asks?"

"No," Marc responded flatly. "That's a technique I've never cared for. I'd rather do my own interviews."

"I think you should, especially in a situation like this," Juliet said, agreeing readily. "Some of these people might be reluctant to talk to Ben, but because they see you practically every week on national television, they feel like they know you in a way. They'll be more open in answering questions, I think." As she watched Marc remove the jacket of his charcoal-gray suit, she handed her briefcase to Tom, who was listening nearby, gleaning production ideas for future reference. When Marc tossed his jacket to Tom also, she nodded approval. "Yes, you look more approachable without the jacket. People will feel more comfortable talking to you, and I think you should remove your tie too."

"Take it off for me, will you, while I undo these cuffs and roll up my sleeves," Marc requested, one long stride bringing him close up in front of Juliet. When she hesitated for a split second, his gaze imprisoned hers; there was an odd flicker of light in the depths of his blue eyes that seemed to express amusement while issuing a challenge. "Come on. The crew's beginning to look surly, standing out in the sun."

Choosing to ignore the teasing note in his voice, Juliet maintained a neutral expression while she swiftly undid his tie and pulled it around and down from beneath his crisp collar—though her assistance seemed to her like a strangely intimate gesture. And when Marc reached around her to roll up one sleeve and then the other, she realized she was actually in the circle of his arms, and she had never felt more self-concious in her life. It was ridiculous really. He wasn't touching her nor was she touching him. There was at least a foot between them, yet it was almost as if she could feel the eyes of the crew members boring into her. She wondered bleakly how many of them were assuming she was playing around with Marc now simply because they believed she had had an affair with Henry Alexander at Lancaster. Maybe all of them assumed that, and with the mere thought, defiance erupted in Juliet. She wanted badly to prove to the crew that her relationship to Marc was strictly professional. Also she wanted to prove to Marc himself that she intended to relate to him only as an associate, but more importantly she *needed* to prove to her own satisfaction that she could touch him without her foolish heart starting to pound.

When Marc finished rolling up his sleeves and lowered his arms again, Juliet stepped back, a hand on her hip, and examined him with cool businesslike detachment. After several long moments she approached him again, reached up, and casually undid his collar button, taking no great care in keeping her fingers from grazing the strong brown column of his neck. "There. That's better," she stated with a prim little smile. "Suits are for interviews with district attorneys, but open collars and shirtsleeves go over better with the man-on-the-street."

Marc's answering smile was practically tongue-in-cheek. "Would you like to rumple my hair a little too? I'd like to rumple yours," he said low enough so only Juliet heard him. And amazingly when she reacted to his provocative words by compulsively smoothing back that notorious tendril of hair, he promptly brushed it forward again with a flick of a finger. "I told you I like it better like this."

That *had* seemed like an intimate gesture; one that left Juliet speechless. Her eyes, however—now a stormy gray-green—spoke volumes as she glowered up at him. Suspecting he realized he had caused her embarrassment, she started to turn away on one heel but was brought to an abrupt halt midcircle when Marc caught her by the arm.

"Don't rush off yet. I want to give these back to you." From a trouser pocket he withdrew the hairpins he had so slowly removed from her hair last night. He allowed them to rain down into the cupped palm of her extended hand, giving nearly every member of the crew a clear view of what it was he was returning to her. No doubt they immediately began speculating about how her hairpins had come into his possession. As if speculation were needed!

Juliet groaned inwardly. He had just undone whatever she had managed to achieve a few minutes ago. Now the gossip would surely fly simply because he had had her hairpins. God, she was so tired of having to worry about such silly little things! But as long as that insane scandal

48

that had mushroomed at Lancaster continued to hang over her like a pall, she knew she was going to have to watch her every step. But of course, Marc didn't know the predicament she was in. Fair-minded though she was, she could be angry with him for returning the pins to her in front of the crew, but she knew that he hardly understood the ramifications of his gesture. Dropping the pins into her jacket pocket, she murmured her thanks.

"I thought you might need them, but I see you had others," he replied softly, his voice once again so low, only she could hear. His gaze roamed slowly over her loosely upswept tresses. "Pity you did. You should get rid of all your pins and clasps and always wear your hair down, Julie."

"You're an incorrigible flirt," she murmured accusingly but smiled wryly despite herself. Marc had caused her feeling of frustration, then had somehow managed to ease it, but she had no time to wonder how he had accomplished that feat. Now there was the business at hand to attend to. "All right," she said, addressing both Marc and Paul. "Since you don't need me here while you do this, I'm going back to the inn to do some rearranging of tomorrow's schedule. Then we'll all get together to go over our plans when you both get back there." She turned to her assistant. "Tom, you come with me."

Walking toward her rental car parked in front of the courthouse, Juliet smiled at several crew members in passing. Everyone smiled back, but a few did so with a smugness that irritated Juliet immensely. Those damn hairpins! Why couldn't Marc have just tossed them in the trash instead of giving them back to her in front of these people? Frustration began mounting in her once more; the final straw came when she turned her head to say something to Tom and found him watching her curiously. Tired of the

49

nonsense, she felt an abrupt and overwhelming need to be alone for a while, away from prying, suggestive stares.

"Now that I think of it, I want you to stay here," she informed Tom as she opened the door on the driver's side of car. "You've never seen Marc in action in interviews like these, and he's considered one of the best in the business at persuading the public to talk freely to him. Watch how he operates. It'll be a good learning experience."

Tom was unable to conceal his eagerness to observe his hero at work, and after retrieving her briefcase from him, Juliet watched as he rushed away after the crew that was following Marc along the sun-washed sidewalk. She smiled to herself, tossed the briefcase across the front seat, and slipped into the car beneath the steering wheel to drive back to the inn.

Juliet's blessed solitude lasted only ninety minutes, but even that brief a quiet time relaxed and refreshed her. She had a tentative schedule for the next day completed when Marc and Paul walked into the room adjoining hers, which they were using as a temporary office.

"We got some great footage over there," Paul announced with a flashing smile before Juliet even had a chance to ask how the interviewing went. Plopping down in a chair across the table she was using as a desk, he unfastened the second button of his rather limp sport shirt. "Hotter than hell on that street, though, but we sure can't complain about the response we got from nearly everybody. These local people are really friendly, and they got even friendlier when they realized we weren't here to smear them. Plenty of them volunteered to talk to us, and we got some pretty eloquent statements of outrage. Marc's questions didn't give them much chance to pull their punches. They're mad about this situation and let him know it."

"Sounds great," said Juliet, and her tone made the

words an expression of appreciation of a job well done. She looked at Marc, who was sitting in the chair next to Paul's, his long legs outstretched, his sleeves still rolled up to just below his elbows. She smiled at him. "I guess we won't be thought of as the enemy now, since you've won over the local populus. But you do have a talent for winning people over, don't you?"

"I hope so," Marc answered, his voice low. It seemed as if his eyes were darkening to a deep indigo, and they never left her face as he added, "Some people are more difficult to win over than others. But I never give up easily, Julie."

Was that a warning or a promise? Juliet thought. But she didn't know. She knew only that there had been an unspoken message in his words, a personal message for her. He wasn't making her life any simpler by implying he considered her a potential romantic conquest. She didn't want to spend the next several weeks fighting the attraction she felt toward him; that was a complication she didn't need. This assignment demanded her full attention, and that was what she must give it. Lowering her gaze to the yellow legal pad that was lying atop the table she used as a desk, she coughed and picked up her pen.

"Okay. Here's what we have tomorrow. We have an appointment with Trenton's police chief at two in the afternoon, and he's agreed to an on-camera interview. Our sources tell us that in private Chief Michaels acknowledges that the mayor was deeply involved in the recent bid-rigging scandal, but he can't provide enough concrete evidence for the D.A. to press charges. Without that proof he obviously won't make accusations against the mayor when he talks to us. But, Marc, I'm sure you can lead him up to a point where he'll at least admit he's still investigating the mayor."

"According to our researchers, there are rumors that

51

the mayor paid some people to keep quiet about his involvement," Marc said, the expression on his lean face contemplative. "But I'm more interested in the other rumor about the sheriff intimidating people to keep them from talking."

Paul spoke up, removing his glasses to wipe the lenses. "I have this sinking sensation we're going to have some trouble getting this story. I realized that when District Attorney Martin told Marc he had received a number of threats he took seriously enough to send his family out of the state to stay with relatives for the summer."

"That wasn't exactly reassuring, was it? In fact, I was thinking about what Martin said while I was driving back here from Trenton, and my imagination began working overtime. I actually started wondering if I was being followed by this nondescript dark sedan behind me on the road. I felt pretty uneasy for a few minutes until I realized I was just jumpy because of what the D.A. had said." Juliet smiled rather sheepishly at Paul, but her smile faded when she looked at Marc. There was a grim set to his hard mouth and a look in his eyes that was both disturbed and disturbing. It seemed as if her story troubled him, and that rearoused her own uneasiness. She chewed at her lower lip and gestured uncertainly. "I really don't think the . . . sedan was following me."

"Probably not," Paul agreed. "But it wouldn't hurt to mention the incident to the police chief tomorrow. Who knows? He might tell you that some elderly little lady around here owns a dark sedan and her hobby is taking leisurely drives." When his lighthearted comment caused Juliet to smile, Paul changed the subject. "Now, since we aren't taping the police chief until two tomorrow, maybe the morning would be a good time to take the camera crew over to Trenton to get our place-setting shots."

"That's what I have scheduled as a matter of fact,"

Juliet told him. "And I especially want you to get Main Street and that lovely old courthouse with those huge oaks in front of it. You know, let the viewers see a vivid picture of Trenton as a quiet peaceful small town. We'll want to use those shots in the segment right after Marc's opening stand-upper then go directly to D.A. Martin talking about the corruption investigation and the threats he receives. The contrast between a peaceful-looking town and a man who's been made to fear for his family's safety will be striking."

Paul grinned. "That should certainly get their attention fast."

"Justifiably because that's what this story's really about —a small town that *should* be as quiet and peaceful as it looks but isn't anymore because of a few corrupt individuals. We won't be misrepresenting the situation in Trenton with that beginning," Juliet said evenly, then turned to Marc. "I think you should do your stand-upper opening from that bluff that overlooks Trenton. We'll have a great panoramic view of the town as your background. How do you feel about taping that tomorrow morning?"

Marc shook his head. "I nearly always wait and tape openings after we've gotten the entire story. Makes for more effective lead-ins, in my opinion."

"We'll wait then." Juliet paused to glance over the papers on her desk. When she found the ones she sought, she handed them to Marc. "Here's the opening Todd wrote for you if you want to read it over. We won't be taping it until later, however."

After a cursory glance at the neatly typed pages, Marc sat back and, linking his fingers across his flat midriff, smiled blandly at Juliet. "Sure, I'll read it. Todd's a fine writer. I'm always interested in his approach to a given story. Sometimes he even influences my own efforts—to a certain extent."

That subtle reminder that he always wrote his own material was not lost on Juliet. Her elbows resting on the tabletop, her chin nestled in cupped hands, she studied him closely, intrigued by the strong sense of responsibility she sensed in him. Her voice was low when she finally spoke. "Some correspondents rely heavily on writers for their material."

"That's their style. It isn't mine."

"I've heard you even keep an eye on the videotape editors, so you obviously get very involved in the entire production process, don't you?"

Marc's eyes narrowed. "Does it bother you that I do?"

Before Juliet could answer, Paul cleared his throat and rose to his feet. "Unless there's anything else you wanted to talk to me about, I'd like to go give my wife a call before I get ready for dinner."

"Oh, sure, go ahead. There's nothing else to discuss right now anyway," Juliet told him, bewilderment darkening her eyes as she watched him rush out of the room. When he had closed the door behind him, she turned back to Marc with a questioning frown. "Wonder why he seemed in such a hurry to leave?"

"He probably just didn't want to get caught in the middle."

Juliet's frown deepened. "Caught in the middle of what?"

"You never answered my question," Marc said, ignoring hers. "*Does* it bother you that I get involved in the entire production of a story?"

"No," was Juliet's emphatically honest answer as she continued to stare at him questioningly, not knowing where this conversation was leading. But correctly interpreting his expectant expression, she elaborated her reply. "In fact, I'm glad you want to be involved in everything.

Your interest can only improve the quality of the final product."

"Some producers don't feel the way you do," Marc said, then smiled wryly. "That's why Paul was so eager to get out of here. We've both worked with people who refuse to listen to anyone else's ideas. In other words Paul's a director and nothing more, and I'm only the correspondent; the producer makes all decisions and we take orders. I imagine Paul thought the questions you were asking me were swiftly leading up to a haughty declaration of absolute authority over this story, and I guess he just wasn't in the mood to deal with that. As he quite often says, and I quote: 'Producers like that are real little dictators, and working with them is a pain in—' "

"Well, Paul doesn't have to worry about me. I'm no fool," Juliet assured Marc, laughing at the quotation he hadn't needed to finish. She spread her hands in an expressive gesture. "Considering the experience you and Paul have, I'd be stupid if I refused to listen to any of your ideas or advice. And besides the fact that I know both of you can teach me a great deal, I happen to believe that this story is as much yours and his as mine." She shuffled some papers on the tabletop as they spoke. "Even though producers do have final authority, technically anyway, I hope that if you, Paul, and I have disagreements, we'll be able to compromise somehow. I'd rather have partners than enemies."

Marc's slow smile gentled his features as his warm gaze wandered over her. "Producers with that attitude don't come along every day," he said very softly. "I think I'll try to arrange to keep you with me, Julie."

"Be careful what you say. You might change your mind by the time this assignment's wrapped up," she quipped, then swiftly diverted her eyes from his face to the desktop. A list of telephone numbers provided her a valid reason

55

to change the subject. "I tried to get an appointment with the mayor for tomorrow morning, but the answer was no again. Of course, after we see the police chief tomorrow, your strategy has a better chance of working. By then Mayor Haynes should be getting very edgy, don't you think?"

"It probably all depends on how far above the law he thinks he is," Marc responded rather absently as he got up from his chair. Hands in his pockets, he strode across the room to the balcony doors to stand gazing out for several seconds. Then he half turned to look back at Juliet. "Why don't we go for a walk while we talk? It looks like it would be so much cooler out under those trees up there. We could change to more comfortable clothes, and—"

"You just talked me into it," Juliet said with a quick smile. "I've been wanting to get out of this suit since noon. I'll straighten these papers, lock up in here, and meet you on the balcony in fifteen minutes."

After Marc nodded agreeably and left the room, Juliet locked the door after him. She wrinkled her nose at the material strewn atop the makeshift desk, but didn't bother to put it in order. In a very few minutes she was in her room, locking the connecting door to the "office" from her side. Humming softly, she tossed her suit jacket on the bed.

Juliet sighed with pleasure as she slipped out of her shoes, skirt, and blouse. Her full-length white slip dropped silently down around her feet. Already she felt ten degrees cooler but ecstasy came when she removed her summer-weight panty hose. The simple act of undressing after a long hard day made her feel so free-spirited that for a moment she was tempted to leave her clothes where they lay. But an inherent propensity toward neatness won out at last. Padding about, clad only in bra and panties, she carefully put her suit away on a hanger in the closet,

56

placed her blouse and slip in a laundry bag, then even dropped her panty hose into a basinful of soapy water in the adjoining bathroom.

Despite the time she took to tidy her room, Juliet was dressed in creased khaki shorts, a blue sleeveless cotton blouse, and sandals—with three minutes to spare. In front of the vanity she unnecessarily smoothed her hair but didn't even bother to try to confine her most rebellious tendril of hair. After smoothing a tiny amount of gloss containing sunscreen onto her lips, she went out on the balcony, apparently only a couple of seconds after Marc had stepped from his room. He was locking the French doors, and Juliet locked hers too. She pocketed the key and turned to wait as he strode over to her.

She smiled. "Promptness is a virtue."

"Good timing *is* important," he said, his tone expressionless. Yet his striking blue eyes expressed unmistakable approval as they swept up over long shapely legs, lingered a moment on an insweeping waist cinched by a narrow khaki belt, then lifted to Juliet's face. He smiled too. "You look much cooler now."

She nodded. "You too." And he looked not only cool; he was so casually attractive in chino slacks and tobacco-brown polo shirt that a flutter of excitement raced along Juliet's spine as they walked together down the outside balcony stairs to the gently inclining ground. In a silence she found unexpectedly companionable and comfortable, they started to ascend a grassy slope less steep than others around it. Seeking shade, they followed a line of lofty pines and more than once Juliet watched with near fascination as dappled sunlight glinted gold in Marc's sandy hair as it shone down on occasion between the needled boughs above them. At last she managed to fix her gaze on the not-too-distant crest of the hill, and soon the natural beauty surrounding her brought relaxation.

"About that dark sedan on the road behind you this afternoon," Marc said abruptly, turning his head to look at her as she walked beside him. "Tell me everything you remember about it."

With some reluctance Juliet lifted her eyes to meet his gaze. The feeling of tranquillity she had experienced was fast receding. She gestured uncertainly. "There really isn't anything to tell."

"You can remember more than you realize, if you try," Marc persisted. "Now, think. Do you have any idea what kind of car it might have been?"

"Not really. Like I said, it was nondescript."

"Late model?"

"I think so . . . yes. At least I know it wasn't a really old car."

"You said it was dark. Dark what? Brown? Blue? Green?"

"Actually I think it was black. If not, then dark blue. But what—"

"How many people were in it? Only the driver? Or were there passengers too?"

Juliet's grimace was involuntarily apologetic as she admitted, "I don't know how many. I guess I didn't pay that much attention to it."

"Obviously you didn't," muttered Marc, his voice sharp-edged. Impatience tightened his strong jaw and hardened his features. Staring at her, he shook his head. "For God's sake, Julie, it crossed your mind that maybe you were being followed, so why didn't you pay attention to the car?"

"Because that thought only crossed my mind for a second, then I dismissed it since it seemed too damn silly," she retorted, her own patience beginning to wear thin. "And I still think it's silly."

"Silly or not, tell me when you first noticed the car behind you."

"Somewhere in the outskirts of Trenton." She heaved a heavy sigh. "Really, Marc, I don't remember precisely."

"Did the car stay behind you all the way back here?"

"Well, yes, but it went on when I turned onto the drive up to the inn."

"You can still see the road from the drive. Did you notice if the car slowed down at all as it went past?"

"No. I didn't notice." Juliet stopped suddenly, hands on her hips as she met his piercing eyes. "Why are you grilling me like this? You're acting as if you know that car was following me, but you can't be sure it was."

"No, and you can't be sure it wasn't. I just want you to realize it's a possibility that you were followed, because in our business we can't afford to rule out any possibilities," Marc warned. "Journalists are sometimes followed; sometimes they're harassed and now that you've become an associate producer, you'd better learn to be more observant than you were this afternoon. Always keep your eyes open and stay alert."

Juliet gave a dismissive wave of one hand. "Oh, surely we don't need to be continually looking back over our shoulders. After all, we're not international spies."

"Dammit, we might seem just as dangerous as spies to people who have something to hide," Marc almost growled, one long stride bringing him very near her as he grasped her shoulders. "Julie, listen. You said earlier that there are things I can teach you about this business, and here's lesson number one—keep up your guard. Be aware of what's going on around you." When Juliet's emerald eyes dilated and darkened with concern, he relented a little. Some of the hardness went out of his face, and he turned her around to lead her a short distance into the stand of pines to where a weather-worn outcropping of rock rose from the ground.

He leaned with one shoulder against the pitted surface of rock; that casual stance was somewhat reassuring, especially when a faint smile moved his firmly shaped lips as he looked down at Juliet. "I'm not an alarmist, Julie, and I'm certainly not trying to frighten you. If you face reality and keep up your guard, you're less likely to be scared if someone does harass you. And that could happen. Media intimidation in this country is usually subtle, but it exists —and it's unpleasant, no matter how subtle it is. You can deal with equipment sabotage and nasty threats much better if you've prepared yourself in advance for possible harassment. I'm trying to tell you that you can't assume it will never happen to you or you'll be very vulnerable when it does."

"In other words: Beware of people in dark sedans," Juliet said, but her wry smile was fleeting. "Okay, Marc, I understand what you're saying, and I'll certainly take your advice. But . . . I get the impression you think I might get my first taste of intimidation on this assignment."

"I can't be sure of that, but it's fairly obvious that this isn't going to be an easy story to break. We're dealing with people who want very badly to keep the truth hidden," Marc told her candidly. "Our investigation scares them, and fear might make them try to intimidate us."

"Which, of course, would only make us more determined to get what we're after."

"Naturally. Now, let's forget about this assignment for a while and walk up to the top of the hill."

Marc took Juliet's hand as they stepped over a spill of rocks and resumed their climb and kept it clasped firmly in his when they reached the crest of the hill. Hearing her swiftly indrawn breath, he looked down and smiled at her expression of delight.

"It's so beautiful here," she almost whispered in awe, taking in the panoramic view of the tiny valley below and the taller majestic peak that rose up on the other side of it. It was as if the loveliness of the scene itself infused her with renewed energy and, slipping her hand from Marc's, she ran lightly across a low grassy knoll to the lone cedar that stood sentinel over the valley. In the shade of needle-laden branches, she sat down, resting her back against the huge furrowed trunk, and gave Marc a blissful smile when he joined her.

"Listen to the silence," she murmured, then joined him in muted laughter when an ill-tempered bluejay squawked and shattered the illusion. A smile lingered on her lips and a dreamy luminosity darkened her eyes to pools of forest-green as she gazed out at distant mountain peaks encircled by wispy mist against a background of sky that seemed as blue as Marc's eyes. "I was born in a place not too very far from here across the line in Tennessee. The mountains are lovely there, too, just like this," she found herself telling him but didn't confide that she had lived there only until she was three. Her father had died when she was barely two, and within a year her lonely mother had met the unfaithful man who had become Juliet's stepfather, and they had left the beloved mountains forever to live in Nashville.

Her stepfather was an aggressive, insensitive man who had hurt and humiliated her mother for years by flaunting his affairs with other women in her face. As she grew older, Juliet could understand less why her mother remained in this destructive relationship. But she could understand more the reasons behind her own cautious, perhaps even inhibited response to men. It was painful for her to visit her mother and though they kept in close contact, she hardly ever made the trip down to Nashville. Any place where her stepfather lived was not home to her.

To Juliet the word *home* would always mean the Appalachian Mountains, although in reality she had spent very little of her life there.

Vague, fragile but warm memories of her earliest childhood brought a dampness to her eyes, but a couple of discreet blinks dried them again, and she half turned to smile at Marc, who was sitting beside her. "Where were you born? In a big city?"

Shaking his head, he smiled. "Hardly. I grew up on a farm in Upstate New York. Lots of fresh air and sunshine and many cold mornings out milking cows when the automatic milking equipment broke down."

"I guess you don't miss having to do that?"

"Oddly enough, sometimes I do, though I guess it's the farm itself I really miss. My parents still live there, and I go home fairly often. It's my retreat."

Juliet's expression mirrored her feeling of slight surprise. "I wouldn't have thought you'd ever get tired of the city or the fast pace of reporting."

"The fast pace can become extremely boring sometimes. When it does, I go back home and bask in the quiet for a while."

She nodded understandingly. "I love to spend time in the country too."

"Mmm, then we have something else besides our work in common; that makes it even better," murmured Marc, his deep voice suddenly growing husky. And before Juliet could imagine what he was about to do, he reached for her, large hands spanning her waist, pulling her to him and turning her so she was partially reclining across his thighs. One hand lifted to cup her face and his thumb played over the full curve of her lower lip. "God, that mouth, Julie. . . . Do you know how often I looked at you today and wanted to kiss you?"

"Don't," she breathed, excitement and an inbred cautiousness battling fiercely within her as she gazed up into his eyes. "This won't do, Marc. I told you already I don't —"

"You already are involved," he whispered, strong arms almost effortlessly lifting her up against his hard chest as he lowered his head. Firm warm lips brushed teasingly back and forth over hers while he swiftly slipped the pins from her hair and murmured against her mouth, "I've wanted to do that all day too."

"But it's cooler up," she uttered, saying the first thing that came to mind in an attempt to defend herself from him. Her heart was pounding and her stomach fluttering while he watched her hair tumble down in a flow of molten gold and copper. When he gathered the silken swathe in one hand to lift it away from her neck and aside then gently blew on her heated nape, she was shocked by the force of the tremor that plunged through her. Her breathing quickened, making her voice revealingly shaky as she whispered, "No, don't, Marc."

"Don't talk," he commanded gently, silencing her compulsive response with a light kiss that lingered and lingered before his hardening lips took devouring possession of hers, exploring their soft shape almost intimately.

Juliet's soft moan opened her mouth to his, and when his tongue entered to taste the moist sweetness within, tension drained from her, she became all warm and fluidly pliant in his arms. Somehow Marc was robbing her of the ability to think rationally, and when the tip of his tongue grazed the sensitive flesh of her inner cheek, her own tongue playfully parried his.

With a muffled groan he molded her slender form to him and the electrically charged meeting of their bodies forged them together. Her arms wound around his neck as she reveled in the awesome power that crushed her against him. A wondrous weakness was invading her limbs, and she no longer could control her response to him; yet right then she didn't care. It was as if they were hungry for each other, and she couldn't resist the dizzying pleasure of his kisses or prevent herself from brushing her parted lips invitingly against his.

She sensed smoldering fires of passion flaring up just beneath the surface in him—fires that threatened to blaze out of control and consume both of them; yet that threat aroused her own desires rather than frightening her. Afloat in sensual pleasure, she enjoyed the feel of his hand sweeping over her, as it followed the contours of shapely calves, slender thighs, and rounded buttocks, then grazed upward along incurving waist and fully uprising breasts. And she liked touching him. She slipped her hands beneath his shirt to run them over the masculine hard heated flesh of his broad back, and she didn't resist—even when he tugged her blouse from beneath her waistband, swiftly unbuttoned it, and slipped it off her shoulders. Although she trembled when his fingers sought the hook of her bra and unclasped it, she allowed him to slowly peel the lacy garment off her and drop it beside her blouse on the grass. When he raised his head, her eyes fluttered open. Her heart raced. His eyes were like glinting blue fire as he gazed down at the rapid rise and fall of her bare breasts. Afraid, yet not afraid, she tentatively lifted a hand to brush her fingertips across his sensuously shaped lips.

"Julie," he whispered roughly, and bore her down onto the grass, partially covering her body with his. His weight pressed her down against the springy turf, and the grass cooled her naked back—but only for an instant—as a feverish warmth suffused her throughout. Marc's firm marauding mouth plundered the soft sweetness of hers again and again and her lips clung to his while she pushed his shirt far up his back, seeking the smooth taut texture of his skin.

With a muffled urgent whispering of her name, he broke off the kiss to rise up and strip his shirt off completely but as he knelt beside her, his gaze roaming hungrily over her, he suddenly became very still.

Some shyness and compulsive instinct caused Juliet to cover herself hastily. When his mesmerizing eyes captured and held her own, she saw in the clear blue depths something that caused a flutter to ripple over the muscles of her abdomen. She tried to shake her head as he simply smiled then leaned over her. "Marc, I—"

"Let me look at you, Julie," he coaxed. Gently uncrossing her arms, he extended them out beside her, exposing her completely. He held her wrists against the ground for only a moment, then trailed his fingers along her inner arms, tantalizing the nerve endings of sensitive skin.

Juliet could hardly breathe when Marc raised himself up again and his hot scorching gaze roamed slowly over her. The intense expression on his lean tanned face held her spellbound while he simply looked down at her for what seemed an eternity. She had never felt so erotically vulnerable in her life but vulnerability in this instance had a rousing effect. Normally modest to a fault, she realized with some surprise that this was becoming an increasingly pleasurable experience. Perhaps deep in her psyche there was a strictly suppressed fantasy of being an exhibitionist, but she was fairly certain that was not the explanation for what she was now feeling. She cringed at the thought of other men seeing her like this; with Marc it was different. She liked having him look at her, liked the emberglow in his eyes as they swept over her bare skin, liked the warm lethargy that spread through her entire being. Heightened color bloomed enchantingly in her cheeks as slowly building excitement accelerated her pulsebeat.

"Yes, you're so lovely, I have to look at you. And touch you," he at last said unevenly and reached down his hands. They clasped her waist then skimmed up across her midriff to cup full taut breasts, which swelled to his touch. He rubbed his palms over caramel-colored peaks, bringing them to ruched hardness with the caress. His eyes sought hers, and he murmured, "And taste, Julie. I have to taste too."

Juliet's breath caught when he leaned down. She trembled when his lips brushed the scented hollow between her breasts. Her hands came up to his broad shoulders, her fingertips tracing the contours of corded muscles, but her fingers tangled in his thick fair hair and she gasped softly as he began to encircle the twin mounds of femininely soft yet resilient flesh with devastating nibbling kisses that explored the rounded slopes and sought the summits. His lips aroused roseate tips to swift tumescence, then his mouth closed around one, gently imprisoning the tender morsel against his tongue, which exerted a slight pulling pressure that caused a soft moan to escape her parted lips.

"Oh, Marc, yes," she breathed, awakened to a desire more thrilling and all-consuming than she had ever imagined she could feel. The exquisite sensations that surged through her limbs as he took possession of first one nipple then the other were echoed in the deepest core within her. Emptiness, acute and aching, flowered open in her, a throbbing emptiness she wanted Marc to fill. At that moment she wanted everything from him. She wanted to give of herself and take from him. She wanted to know and possess every inch of him. He had kindled a fire in her that was becoming an inferno, a fire that burned away all thoughts of her job, of their associates, and even of the assignment that had brought Marc into her life. All that was forgotten, and she was lost in a world where only the two of them and the lovely countryside existed.

Juliet was a twenty-eight-year-old woman but because of the bitter lesson learned from her mother's experience,

66

she had always suppressed her sexuality—even though she had never wanted to be that way. But somehow Marc had found a key, unlocked a door, and freed the loving, sensuous woman she could be from her self-imposed captivity. And now Juliet was powerless in the grip of a real passion she was not accustomed to dealing with. Almost of their own volition, her hands glided over Marc's bare chest, her nails catching in the fine brown hair that roughened his skin. Then, feverish to be kissed again, she encircled his neck with her hands and urged his mouth back to her own.

Her lips opened to gently demanding pressure and moved caressingly over his, and when he caught the full lower curve of hers between tenderly nibbling teeth, the shattering sensations that rushed through her made her dizzy. Even when Marc pinned her legs beneath one of his, and she felt the indisputable evidence of aroused masculinity surge potently against her thigh, her sanity wasn't restored. And she was able to offer no protest as his knee pressed down and parted her legs.

It was the sound of movement in the trees she thought she heard at the same moment Marc unbuckled her belt that brought her back to reality at last. At the sound she tensed and comprehension of what she was inviting startled her out of passion-induced lethargy. When Marc began unbuttoning the waistband of her shorts, she stilled his hand.

"Marc, no," she murmured anxiously. "I know I've made you think I— I didn't mean— Oh, hell, I just can't."

Narrowed blue eyes searched her face. Marc sighed then smiled faintly. "You can't be rushed, can you, Julie? I knew that but . . ."

Juliet realized he was assuming they would eventually drift into an intimate relationship, and she shook her head. "You don't want to get involved with me. If you knew me better, you'd see I'm not—" She hesitated, then concluded in a subdued, almost sad, tone of voice, "I've been told by other men that I'm . . . cold."

"Cold! You?" Soft laughter rumbled up from deep in Marc's throat as he shook his head. "My God, Julie, if you'd responded with much more warmth a few minutes ago, you wouldn't have been able to stop me from taking what I wanted—what I know we *both* wanted." When she opened her mouth to answer him, he silenced her with the touching of a finger against her lips. "Julie, you're not cold. Inhibited, maybe; but I think we can burn away those inhibitions in time. Right now, we'd better get dressed and go back the inn before I change my mind about rushing you."

His teasing tone brought a wan smile to Juliet's lips, but it had faded by the time she had slipped back into her bra and blouse. As she walked with Marc down to the inn, a myriad of confusing thoughts bombarded her brain. Little Miss Cautious, her friends in college had teasingly called her. And she had been exceedingly cautious, always determined to create a life for herself that was predictable and safe. Then how in heaven's name, Juliet asked herself, had she managed to get in a situation like this—away on business, on a potentially dangerous assignment with a definitely dangerous man, a man she now realized could play havoc with her entire existence?

CHAPTER FOUR

Resigned but not defeated, Juliet hung up the phone, then looked up from her desk when Marc entered the temporary office and closed the door behind him.

"Still no luck, I guess?" he asked almost conversationally, dropping down relaxed and unperturbed in the chair across from her. Coatless, tieless, he rolled his shirtsleeves up to his elbows, observing her with a hint of a smile. "Have you been on the phone all day?"

"The biggest part of it, yes, and you're right—no luck at all," she told him, twirling a pencil between her fingers. "I know there are always snags in every story, but we're really batting zero right now. It's amazing that so many people were willing to talk to T.J. and his researchers, but now that we're here, they've just clammed up. Except for the D.A. and the police chief, nobody wants to say a word."

"It'll take some time. Everybody wants someone else to talk first. All we can do is stay in touch with them and try to gain their confidence. Eventually one of them will come through for us and most of the rest of them will follow."

"I certainly hope that happens soon," Juliet said wryly, "before the crew decides to mutiny out of sheer boredom."

"Grumble constantly, yes. Mutiny, no," Marc assured her, linking his fingers across his flat midriff, seeming to make himself quite comfortable. "But even though they

69

do complain, they all know that every assignment has its slow moments."

"Slow's the word all right. The most exciting thing I've done in the past three days was to try to lose the car that was behind me all the way to Trenton and back here yesterday morning."

Marc sat up straighter, his eyes narrowing. "The same sedan again?

Juliet nodded. "Same one, so I guess I am being followed. That car's been behind me too many times for it to be a coincidence."

"If you've seen it that often, you should be able to give me a better description than you did the other day," Marc declared solemnly. "Can you, Julie?"

"Well, not really," she admitted, wondering if he was about to read her the riot act again and quickly qualified her answer. "But that's not my fault. I have been keeping my eyes open. It's just that the car stays too far behind me for me to get a good look at it. I think it could be a Buick or maybe an Oldsmobile; I've always had trouble telling them apart. But I do know for sure that there are at least two people in the car."

"For now they're keeping their distance, but that could change very suddenly so stay alert, Julie," Marc cautioned, thoughtfully stroking his jaw. "Obviously someone's very interested in knowing exactly where you go and who you talk to. And since it takes either a great deal of power or money or both to have people systematically followed, we're probably dealing with someone who has a lot to lose if we get to the bottom of this story."

"Someone like the senator, you mean?"

"Velvy certainly would stand to lose more than anyone else if he was even remotely implicated," Marc speculated, then shrugged objectively. "Of course, I imagine the mayor feels he has a lot to lose too. Anybody else who was

70

involved and is afraid the truth will come out feels the same way, and right now it's impossible to know who's responsible for having you followed. Could be all of them agreed that the best way to handle this situation was to have you closely watched."

"Oh, I hope they're not that organized. If they are, we'll probably have a devil of a time getting our story," said Juliet, glancing at the list of people she had phoned in the past few hours. "We don't need to have our sources intimidated. They're reluctant enough to talk as it is."

"Intimidated or not, some of them won't ever tell us anything. The others will hedge awhile, then give us what we need, often simply because they feel that's the right thing to do."

"After you've pricked their consciences," she added, giving him a knowing smile. "I've heard you're a real pro at that. It must be nice to be so persuasive."

"It has its advantages," he replied, something more than mere amusement glinting in his eyes as they roamed over her in a deliberately provocative appraisal. "Now, if I could persuade you—"

"You're not only an incorrigible flirt—you're an incurable one," Juliet protested, laughing softly and shaking her head. But as he continued to watch her with that almost boyish half-smile that never failed to accelerate her pulse rate, she thought it wise to return to the original topic of conversation. "Anyway, I'll be relieved when we can move with this story again. I think I'm nearly as bored as the crew, and I find myself daydreaming about someday being given an assignment where everything progresses without a hitch from beginning to end. Of course, no such assignments exist. I imagine you even had some boring moments in Vietnam, didn't you?"

"Not nearly as many as the soldiers had. Many of them told me that war was about ninety percent excruciating

71

boredom and ten percent action, not that they were eager for action after being there awhile. Still, it was tedious and nerve-racking to wait in base camp, wondering when they would engage the enemy and watching the mosquitoes. But hell, maybe all wars are like that," Marc said, frowning. "It wasn't quite as boring for me because I had some freedom to move from unit to unit wherever there might be some action. And, more importantly, I had an option the soldiers didn't have: I could leave the whole war behind and come home if I wanted to."

"Could you have, Marc?" she asked. "Union sent you to Vietnam on assignment, and you couldn't really leave there unless they called you back."

"I could've quit my job. The soldiers couldn't. That makes a big difference, Julie."

Sensing that same inner turmoil she had detected the first time she met him, Juliet responded to it, wanted to help him release some of it by talking freely to her, if nothing else. She leaned toward him, resting her arms on her desk. "How long were you there?"

"About three and a half years, the last years. I got out during the evacuation of Saigon."

"Oh. I didn't realize. That was chaos, wasn't it?"

"Chaos is too kind a word for it," he answered with a bitter, reminiscent smile. "It was insanity."

"How old were you then?" Juliet murmured. "Weren't you very young to be a war correspondent?"

"I wouldn't say I was a correspondent. I was more like a stringer, one of several, sent out to find the news in the provinces and relay it to Union's major correspondent. And yes, I was young—much younger than I realized I was—and very impressionable."

"And did you go there believing you would see war in all its glory?"

"Probably. And I did see some glorious deeds done,

sometimes by young men, boys really, barely old enough to leave home," Marc said, his voice steel-edged, his jaw tight. "But I also learned the same lesson many people did during that time: There's no glory to war itself. It's just a horror, pure and simple. You can't reasonably call it anything else."

Juliet clenched her hands together on the desktop. "Would you ever go back there?"

"I want to go back. I had to leave friends there—Vietnamese who couldn't get out before Saigon fell. I need to know what happened to them, if I can possibly find out." Getting up, Marc thrust his hands into his pockets as he strode to the open French doors and stared at the peaceful mountains for several long moments before turning to face the room again. In silence he went to the easy chair and sat down again.

Seeing the play of various emotions on his tanned face, Juliet remained very still for a while, wondering if she had perhaps been wrong to question him. What horrible memories had she aroused? And what could she do now to help alleviate the pain that had come with them? Not sure what to do, yet needing to do something, she got up and went to him, hesitated, then brushed a gently soothing hand over his hair. "Marc," she murmured, a catch in her voice. "Maybe I shouldn't have brought up this subject."

"It's a subject we've all tried to avoid too long. It needs to be talked about," he said, a worn, rather tired smile moving his hard mouth. "I'm glad you were willing to listen to me."

When Marc slipped his hands from his pockets and reached for Juliet's, drawing her toward him, she went into his arms with no word of protest. A wealth of emotion surged up in her and she needed with every fiber of her being to hold him and be held by him. Clasping her hands together around the back of his neck, she touched her lips

73

to his once, then again, until he tenderly entwined his fingers in her hair and tilted her head back.

His eyes searched the depths of hers as he whispered, "Those war stories work every time—women can't resist them."

Gazing up at him, Juliet shook her head. "You can't fool me," she whispered back, easing her thumbs lightly across his cheeks. "I don't know exactly what your memories are, but I think I can imagine them a little. And imagine how you must feel. . . ."

He smiled again, this time warmly and without weariness. "You know, I think you probably can," he said softly, gathering her to him, his hard muscular arms conveying a rough urgency that was somehow also indescribably gentle. With the same spellbinding demand, his lips claimed hers, his teeth closing tenderly on the soft flesh, opening her sweet mouth to his.

Making a breathless throaty sound, Juliet molded her gently curved body against the irresistibly taut line of his and returned his deepening kisses with an ardor that might have shocked her had she been thinking clearly. But she wasn't thinking at at all; she could only feel the tingling, electric sensations that were shooting through her and experience the shattering effect of growing affection and most primitive desire as they became inseparably one. She was sharing a closeness with Marc that transcended the physical and made her feel, oddly enough, that with him she was where she belonged. Warmed by that sense of belonging and by the smoldering fire of his passion, she curled up closer to him, her shapely thighs tucked firmly against him.

Cradling her in the circle of one arm, Marc freed her hair from the loosely confining chignon on her nape then drew a silken swathe forward over her shoulder He ran his fingers through the sun-streaked strands until it was fanned out in glorious disarray over her, the lightly curled ends grazing the beginning swell of her breasts. He played idly with the curls, his hand heavy on her, and his hard knuckles rubbed gently into yielding but firm flesh.

Hearing the slight catch in her breath, he smiled intimately. "You can't fool me either, Julie," he murmured, looking into her eyes. "You try to hide a great deal beneath that cool professional exterior, but you can't hide the woman you really are from me. I'm starting to know you very well."

"Are you?" she asked huskily, wondering how he possibly could. Since meeting him, she hardly even knew herself; yet there was something exciting about the new uncertainty, something fascinating in the effect he had on her. Juliet felt as though she were being slowly drawn toward danger, but at that moment she could do nothing to escape the strong magnetic pull. Gazing at him from beneath the thick fringe of her lashes, she had to touch him and found herself teasing the corners of his mouth with a feathering fingertip. "And what kind of woman do you think I really am?"

"Warm. Arousing. Irresistible." Covering her hand with his, holding it still, he traced kisses across her palm, then slid the edge of his teeth over and over the mound of flesh at the base of her thumb until her fingers curled compulsively against his cheek. As he guided her arm around him once more, his lips descended on hers again, brushing their soft shape and exerting a slowly mounting pressure that elicited a warm response.

His subtle brand of male aggression was more than she could withstand. His mouth was too coaxing, the pleasantly rough tip of his tongue rubbing over hers too sensuously exciting, and his large questing hands wandering over her too masterly. Succumbing to seduction of the senses, Juliet allowed her own hands to sweep over him in a tentative exploration that became more emboldened with his impassioned response. His heated flesh seemed to burn her through the fabric of his shirt, and she wanted never to stop touching him. He was right. With him she did become warm, arousing, perhaps even irresistible, which was suddenly exactly what she wanted to be. She loved caressing him and delighted in his dramatically obvious need for her, a need that he made no effort to conceal. Her lips opened and closed over the lower curve of his, her kisses wildly tempting, inviting, provocatively feminine. And when he groaned softly, cradled the back of her head in one hand, and took possession of her mouth with a rousing thoroughness that made her weak and deliciously dizzy, she moved against him, pliant and warm.

She ran her fingers through his hair and played her fingers over his ears along his neck to the skin that hardened over his collarbone. When he drew the edge of one hand down into the hollow between her breasts, she waited breathlessly, content only when began rotating his palm slowly over the taut mounds of flesh. She covered his hand with hers, and pressed down harder.

"*Julie,*" he whispered, deftly undoing her blouse then the front clasp of her bra, baring her to his hot gaze and seeking fingers. He touched her almost reverently, playing with the rose-tipped peaks until they were erect and exquisitely sensitized. Then, cupping the weight of one ivory breast in his hand, his arm beneath her back arching her upward, he lowered his head and began exploring the uprising flesh with kisses.

A rush of heat flashed through Juliet as his lips grazed her nipple, but before he could close his mouth around the straining crest as she longed for him to do, what was left of self-control came to her rescue and she caught his chin in her hand, pressing a denying thumb firmly against his searching lips.

"No," she breathed. "You can't."

"You want me to."

"Yes," she confessed even as she shook her head. "But this is insane. We're in the office. One of the crew could just come walking in here."

With a slow smile Marc glanced at the connecting door opening to her room and his smile remained though she was shaking her head again. Watching as she fumbled with the hook of her bra, he finally eased her hands aside and fastened it himself. "You're safe this time," he murmured indulgently. "But be forewarned—I can't seem to keep my hands off you."

"This has to stop, Marc," she objected weakly, slipping from his lap to stand looking down at him as she hurriedly rebuttoned her blouse. "I've told you again and again that I can't get involved . . . like this."

"And I've told you you're already involved."

"Well, I *can't* be and that's that."

"Saying something's true doesn't necessarily make it true."

"Oh, hell, you just don't understand," she muttered wearily, wanting to throw herself back into his arms rather than argue with him. Yet she had no choice and tried again to explain without really explaining at all. "I simply cannot get involved with any man I work with."

"Oh?" he questioned curiously. "And why not?"

"It would be a mistake. A terrible mistake for me," she answered, wondering fleetingly if she should just tell him the truth about Henry Alexander and the scandal at Lancaster. But she simply couldn't bring herself to do it and added vaguely, "Professionally it wouldn't be the wise thing to do."

"You don't really believe that," Marc challenged softly, rising to his feet to grasp her shoulders lightly and pull her to him. He leaned down and brushed his lips over hers, yet she refused to respond, then looked at him, surprised, when he soon released her mouth and playfully stroked the bridge of her small straight nose almost as if he found her resistance rather amusing.

"And just remember, Julie. I'm a very persistent man," he warned softly, touched her shimmering tousled hair, then turned and left her alone in the room.

His softly worded warning echoed in her mind, and she spun around on one heel to stare out the window, gripped by a strange mixture of mild trepidation and slowly rising excitement. Part of her longed for an involvement with him, yet the more staid safety-conscious part of her feared him to some extent. He was the first man she had ever met who was so totally different from her stepfather that she could nearly trust him; however, if she trusted him, it would become far too easy to give of herself completely. She was, after all, a normal young woman with normal needs—needs she may have suppressed for years, but Marc had aroused them from their state of dormancy. And it was Marc, only Marc, that she wanted to fulfill those needs. He was everything she had ever expected to find in one man: caring, intelligent, witty, magnificently male, and—as she had seen today—just a bit vulnerable.

And she had lied to him. She was no longer afraid of becoming involved with him for strictly professional reasons. Her fear ran much deeper than that. Her feelings for Marc were too strong already and were growing stronger with each passing day. And she was afraid of the pain she would surely be inviting if she became involved in an intimate relationship that would probably be no more meaningful to him than a casual affair.

CHAPTER FIVE

The first part of the next week went incredibly well. Everything the *Perspective* team did clicked together to advance the story they were trying to get. The researchers picked up several valuable tidbits of information: the two interviews they taped were with minor county officals who showed little reluctance to talk candidly on camera, and the research team uncovered a couple more facts that served to strengthen the link between the U.S. senator, Mayor Haynes, and the district judge. The first three days of the week proved to be highly productive and exhilarating, but unfortunately Thursday turned out to be altogether different. It became one of those frustrating days when anything that could go wrong did go wrong. Although the county sheriff had finally granted Marc an interview, he had changed his mind at the last minute and canceled just as the technicians had arrived to set up in his office. Then, making the day a complete failure, Marc and Juliet had driven to a small town over a hundred miles away where they were supposed to be met by an anonymous woman who had called Juliet and sworn she could deliver documents that proved Mayor Haynes had been involved in bid-rigging. The woman had never shown, and after a three-hour wait Juliet and Marc had returned to Boone at about four in the afternoon.

When Juliet arrived back at the inn, she sensibly told

everyone to call it quits for the day, then atypically took her own advice and did the same. Shunning the work waiting for her in the temporary office, she went to her room instead and had a long soothing shower that washed away most of her frustration. Feeling greatly refreshed, she put on a cool blouse and shorts, then padded barefoot out onto the balcony. She leaned against the railing and surveyed the lush green slopes of the surrounding mountain with growing wonder as a sweet tranquillity settled over her.

"This really is amazing," Marc said softly behind her, his low voice rousing her gently from her reverie. When she turned around to face him, a teasing smile played over his firmly carved lips. "I can't believe what I'm seeing. You're actually out here enjoying the view when I expected to find you toiling at your desk, trying somehow to salvage the day."

Juliet lifted her eyes heavenward as if in dismay but smiled wryly. "Today was such a total washout that there aren't enough hours left in it for it to possibly be salvaged. And there's always tomorrow."

"Let's think about tomorrow later and concentrate on right now," Marc suggested, sweeping a gaze over her down to her bare feet. "All you have to do is put on shoes, and you'll be set for a game of tennis. How about it?"

"Tennis?" Juliet looked at him quizzically. "But I thought you always played with one of the cameramen. Eddie, isn't it?"

Marc grinned. "Eddie assured me he recently met a good-looking grad student who'll be willing to play with him today. If fact, I think he was glad when I told him I couldn't make our game this evening. And now that you don't have to worry about Eddie anymore, go get some shoes on, and we'll be on own our way."

Juliet grimaced. "Oh, I don't know. I—"

"Julie, you have to let yourself have some fun once in a while. Every evening, while most of us find some way of relaxing, you stay here in that office and work."

"Oh, I beg your pardon. That just proves you don't know everything there is to know about me," she retorted lightly. "It just so happens that many evenings—when the rest of you are working up a sweat on the tennis or handball courts—I'm doing laps in the pool on campus. If I do say so myself, I'm an excellent swimmer, and I've been to the pool every evening this week."

"My most humble apologies for my error," he quipped, bowing low with an exaggerated sweep of one hand. When he straightened to look at her once more, a mischievous light flickered in his eyes. "I should have known you couldn't keep that gorgeous body of yours in such terrific shape without some exercise. But I'd still like you to forgo the swimming this evening and play tennis with me instead."

"Swimming's cooler," she countered, pretending not to notice his provocatively appreciative gaze wandering very thoroughly over her. "Besides, I may very well be the lousiest tennis player in the eastern United States."

"I doubt that very much, because I remember that you brought a racket with you when we flew from New York down here."

"I did bring one along, yes," she admitted. "But only because I thought it might come in handy as a swatter if I happened to encounter any very huge flies or mosquitoes."

Laughing softly, Marc shook his head at the totally bland expression on her face. "Enough of this nonsense. I don't care how awful you are, he said, lightly gripping her shoulders to turn her toward the open French doors to her room. With a gentle little push, he provided impetus. "Put on some shoes, get your racket, and we'll be on our way."

"I'd still rather go swimming."

"Tomorrow we'll swim but today we play tennis," he told her firmly but with a smile. "You've aroused my curiosity, Julie. Now I have to see if you're anywhere near as bad a player as you claim."

"Okay, suit yourself. But you're going to be sorry," she warned half seriously over her shoulder as she walked toward the door. Smiling ruefully to herself, she stepped into her room and went to the closet to bring out her shoes and the racket, which was tucked away in the far back corner. *He may not believe I'm the worst tennis player in the East,* she thought, *but he'll be a believer once he's on the court with me.*

Twenty minutes later, on one of the courts on the university campus, Marc had to be beginning to realize Juliet hadn't completely exaggerated her lack of ability. In her first attempt to serve the ball it homed straight into the net as if some miniature guidance system had been planted inside it to take it there. On her second try she did manage to get the ball across the net, but when he lobbed it back to her, she leaped up, swung hard, and missed. Throwing a wan little smile in Marc's direction, she served again, and when he returned the ball, she actually managed to get it back over the net. To her surprise she was able to keep a volley going three strokes in a row before her lethal backhand sent the ball two courts away.

Naturally Marc won the game in short order, and Juliet was glad. Now it was his turn to serve. All she had to do was miss at least every other ball served to her. As it turned out, she did play a little better than that, yet it didn't take very long for Marc to win the second game, which made it her turn to serve again. She hesitated, ball in one hand, racket in the other, knowing very well Marc must be bored to death, and when she noticed four people had actually gathered courtside to watch this unmistakable mismatch, she bounced the ball a few times to stall for time. She simply didn't have the heart to humiliate Marc by serving to him again. She herself wasn't humiliated in the least. She was, she told herself, adept in several athletic activities; tennis simply wasn't one of them. She had always known that. Now Marc did, too, and she wondered if he might prefer not to be seen playing her since she was so obviously no match for him.

It was funny how even the best tennis players looked awful when they were matched against a total washout like herself, Juliet mused. And she had embarrassed some of the best, she recalled. Marc was no exception. He might even sprain something trying to get one of her crazy shots, she thought. After a few seconds of bouncing the ball, she glanced up and across the court at him, sighing with relief when he came around the net toward her.

"You don't really want to go on with this, do you? I tried to tell you I was a miserable player," she said quietly when Marc stopped beside her. "I really can swim though. I'm much better at it than I am at this."

"I'm looking forward to watching you swim tomorrow evening," he answered softly, his tone teasingly provocative as he stepped behind her. He lifted her right hand, which was gripping the racket, and brought her arm up and across her chest, his own arm curved over hers. "Much as I am looking forward to that, though, right now I want to give you a few pointers that might improve your backhand."

"Are you getting a little ahead of yourself?" she asked dryly, turning her head to look up at him. "Maybe you should start by giving me pointers that might improve my serve."

"Your serve's not that bad actually. It's just that you

don't play often enough to keep in practice. And you've never had lessons, have you?"

Juliet laughed softly. "Well, I did sign up for tennis as a phys. ed. course in college, but after only three days the instructor very gently advised me to transfer. He claimed that I turned a tennis racket into a lethal weapon."

"You could improve your game very much with some lessons then," Marc told her with a laugh. "Now, let's see what I can teach you."

Probably a great deal, Juliet thought, but her mind wasn't on tennis. As always, his nearness, the warmth of his hard body, was making her far too sexually aware of him; it took some concerted effort for her to be able to concentrate on the pointers he began giving her.

An hour later Juliet's game had improved a bit. At least she was able to win a couple of points, which to her was something of an accomplishment, considering the fact that Marc was unmistakably a good player. Of course, he didn't play all-out against her because she certainly couldn't have learned anything if he had aced her out completely. As it was, though, she really began to enjoy playing. She had always felt rather hopelessly inept on a court before, but today she didn't and she was somewhat disappointed when Marc decided to end the lesson.

When they met at one end of the net, however, he alleviated her disappointment by saying sincerely, "You learn very quickly. Your tennis instructor in college made a mistake when he advised you to transfer."

"Not really. You don't know what I was like then. In the water I could move gracefully, but out of it . . ." She smiled reminiscently. "I wasn't quite eighteen, and unfortunately, for some reason, I still hadn't grown out of that gangly stage. I was all arms and legs, not exactly clumsy but far from graceful."

"I can't imagine you ever being gangly," Marc said,

looking down at her face with a warm, almost promising gaze. His fingertips grazed the small of her back as he guided her along a path that widely bypassed the small knot of spectators who had been so curiously absorbed in watching them play tennis. Pausing at the edge of the asphalt parking lot, Marc smiled at her. "Ready to go back to the lodge now?"

Juliet wanted to say yes, but that overworked but ingrained cautiousness of hers wouldn't let her. She had tried to avoid being alone with Marc since Sunday night, and if she went back to the lodge with him now, and somehow did find herself alone with him . . . No. She didn't want to risk the possible consequences.

"Let's get something cool to drink before we drive back," she suggested, indicating with a gesture the small pizza parlor across the parking lot. "All right with you?"

With a silent nod he agreed to the plan, and as they walked across the lot, he stopped by his rental car to stow the rackets and balls they carried. A moment later Marc opened the door to the pizza parlor for her, and she stepped inside. The interior was adequately lighted, the atmosphere informal, and she didn't feel out of place dressed in tennis garb. But before she could proceed with Marc toward a vacant table, she began to realize it had been a mistake to suggest coming here. The place was filled with college students, and their previous chattering was swiftly fading away into a silence broken only by a few scattered whispers. Everyone was staring at Marc, but he seemed hardly to notice as he strode to the table and pulled out a chair for Juliet, who sank down, rather bemused by all the attention focused on them.

When Marc sat down across from Juliet, he gave her an easy unconcerned smile but they had no time to speak before a tongue-tied young waitress approached the table. And she barely had a chance to take their order before the other patrons in the pizza parlor were approaching Marc until there was a fair-size crowd around him. College students habitually try to act as laid-back as possible. Yet Juliet sensed in these young people a veritable groundswell of excitement; more than a few of them were unable to contain their exuberance at meeting Marc. Of course, he was known to millions of television viewers, and Juliet had seen people gather around him at Kennedy Airport in New York and Regional in Greensboro and even on the streets in Trenton, but somehow those episodes had seemed different from this. Sitting back in her chair, Juliet watched him autographing napkins, menus, and scraps of paper, and it struck her that he actually couldn't go to a restaurant without being mobbed or at the very least continually gawked at. It wasn't like this at the lodge, where *Perspective* crew members far outnumbered the other guests.

Although Marc accepted the adulation with friendly smiles and a warm manner, it seemed to Juliet that he was withdrawing a little into himself. He wasn't at all aloof, merely a bit detached. When the waitress served their drinks, he smiled his thanks—which seemed to please her enormously—but Juliet imagined he must be relieved when many of the people who were crowding around him drifted back to their tables until only three students still hovered near, two young men and a tall blond coed with an enchanting sprinkling of freckles across her nose. Journalism majors, they were more intensely interested in Marc than their fellow students were and they began firing questions at him and continued to do so even as he sipped the last of his stein of beer. He looked at Juliet as if to say, "This could go on forever. Time to stop it." And he did, adroitly sidestepping another question by glancing at the simple thin gold watch on his wrist.

"Maybe we can talk more some other time," he said to

the three, actually dismissing them but with a genuinely kind smile, a smile that didn't fade even when the blond coed stepped nearer the table instead of leaving.

"Mr. Tyner, I'm Chloe Spencer, editor of the university newspaper," she announced somewhat breathlessly. "I was wondering if I might get an interview with you while you're here on assignment."

"Sure. That can be arranged. Call Pine Lodge one evening next week, and we'll settle on a time to meet," he told her, then inclined his head toward Juliet. "Meet Juliet York, Miss Spencer. Juliet's my producer for this assignment."

Chloe Spencer's eyes widened as she stared at Juliet. "Really? I was wondering if you were anybody— Oh, dear, I didn't mean that the way it sounded. But aren't you very young to be a producer already?"

"Maybe you'd like to interview Juliet too," Marc suggested. "If you'll just call us next week, we can work something out."

"Oh, yes. Of course, I'll call. Thank you." Chloe's words tumbled out, then she hurried away excitedly to rejoin friends.

Juliet leaned forward in her chair. "I'm starved. How about you? Could we go back to the lodge now?" Marc's affirmative response hardly surprised her, since he had wanted to return there rather than come here in the first place. And now she certainly understood why he had as she also understood that the spectators on the sidelines of the tennis court earlier hadn't been interested in watching a mismatch. They had simply been interested in Marc, and incidents like that must often make him feel as if he were living in a fishbowl. That not very pleasant thought lingered in Juliet's mind while they paid the check and went outside. But when she saw the familiar car cruising to a stop in one lane of the parking lot, a momentary dread followed by resentment superseded all other thoughts.

"Looks like our friends in the dark sedan are getting restless," she said quietly to Marc. "Maybe they don't like waiting, just following."

Nodding as they reached his car, Marc opened the passenger door for her, then leaned down to look at her when she was settled in the front seat. "Dark sedan, Julie?" he questioned somberly. "Dark what?"

"Dark blue Buick. I even know the license plate number if you want to hear it."

"I already know it," he said, closing her door and going around the car to get in the driver's seat. He looked over at her, returning her self-satisfied smile. "I'm glad to know you took my advice and started being more observant."

"I've also noticed there are always two of them in the car. Both men."

"Yes, I know. When you and I aren't together, two of their cronies sometimes follow me."

"I'm beginning to feel like that sedan's my shadow. It's almost always behind me." Juliet sighed. "I'm not terrified, or even badly frightened, but it does make me feel very uneasy."

"You should feel uneasy; that way you'll be more alert," Marc said; his words sounded oddly clipped as he started the car and pulled out onto the road. He talked very little while driving them out of town up to the lodge, but his eyes often flicked up to the rearview mirror, which made Juliet realize the dark blue car was still behind them.

Later, after a shower, Juliet put on a cotton gauze dress of cool green and went downstairs to the cozy lodge restaurant. Marc was already there, and he stood up to beckon her to the table he was sharing with Paul Phillips. She joined them, and during the course of the meal they discussed Friday's schedule and—happily—various other topics totally unrelated to their assignment. It was an informal, relaxing dinner, and when it ended, Marc and Paul excused themselves to go chat a few minutes with several of the other *Perspective* team members who were also dining in the restaurant. Smiling to herself, Juliet watched as Marc laughed at something someone said, and she realized how much more comfortable he must be among people who were so accustomed to seeing him that they didn't crowd around or even stare.

When Marc suddenly glanced across the small room, met Juliet's gaze before she had a chance to avert it, and smiled at her, she felt a rush of affection for him so intense that her heart began beating wildly; she couldn't quite take a deep breath even after he looked away from her again. Hastily she pushed back her chair and stood, wondering if the two small glasses of white wine she'd had with dinner had made her a bit tipsy. It was either that, or she was a little crazy. Either way she was convinced that it would be wiser for her not to be at the table when Marc returned to it. Considering what she felt right now, she needed to get away from him. She threaded her way among the tables toward the doorway to the lobby but was stopped when Patty Clements, Paul's assistant, put out a hand and touched her arm.

"You're not going up to work, are you?" Patty asked, shaking her head disapprovingly. "Come on, give yourself a break. It was a rotten day, and you should compensate by staying here for a while to relax."

"Matter of fact, I wasn't going up to work. I think I'll walk outside for a few minutes and get some fresh air."

Patty frowned. "Should . . . I mean, maybe you shouldn't go alone. Even with those scattered floodlights, it's really dark out there."

"Oh, I'll stay close to the inn. I didn't plan to wander off anywhere."

"But—"

"See you," Juliet murmured, and walked away quickly, wanting to get out of the restaurant before Marc noticed she was leaving. She thought she had made it as she reached the bottom of the wide wooden staircase outside the lodge, but the sound of rapid footfalls on the planking behind and above her made her turn around. When Marc came running lightly down the steps to catch her right arm in a less than gentle grip, she gasped softly with surprise.

"What—"

"Dammit, you can't come out here by yourself at night," he said roughly. "Don't you have any sense?"

"Oh, for heaven's sake, let's not get melodramatic," she said, waving her free hand dismissively. "I'm sure that even our faithful escorts have to sleep sometime."

"I'm sure whoever hired them to follow you could easily hire somebody else for the night shift," said Marc, his hold on her wrist gentling, his tone becoming far less rough. He stepped closer to her. "Listen, Julie. You can't be sure someone's not out here right now watching. And I don't think you want to risk someone jumping out of the shadows at you and scaring you half to death."

"No, but I won't be intimidated, and I won't be made to feel afraid to take a breath," she replied with a defiant little uptilting of her chin. "And I also don't want you to try to coddle me. If I were a man—"

"If you were a man, and it was obvious most of the attempts at intimidation were going to be directed at you, Paul and I would still be extra careful with you."

"What . . . do you mean?" Juliet suddenly felt a little chilled. "Are you saying—"

"Paul and I decided it would be best not to tell you because if you acted frightened, whoever is behind all this might be encouraged to harass you even more." Laying his

90

hands on her shoulders, Marc began to massage her tense muscles. "But I want you to know that we're keeping a close watch over you. You never go out alone in your car without a member of the crew following behind you and the blue Buick. I don't think these people are ever going to try to really hurt you but—"

"Why do you think they're going to try to harass me more than anyone else?"

"Because I've been warned So has Paul," Marc said softly. "We've both received calls, Julie, and although there were vague threats made against the entire crew, the more specific warnings concerned you."

Juliet shook her head, more confused than greatly worried. "But why me?"

Marc shrugged. "You are the produce You're also a young woman. And sometimes there's a very vulnerable look about you, so I suppose the mastermind behind this amateurish plot thought you'd make an easy target."

"Then he better think again," Juliet declared. "We're going to get this story, no matter what. I'm even more determined to get it now, because whoever is trying to stop us is beginning to make me mad."

"But not so mad that you want to continue your walk in the dark just to prove you can't be intimidated? You wouldn't be foolhardy like that, would you, Julie?" When she shook her head, he smiled approvingly and turned her around to face the entrance stairs. "I'm glad to hear it. And if you still want some fresh air, which is why you came out here, according to Patty, you can get it from the balcony outside your room. But only if I go with you. Anybody can get on that balcony by simply walking up the outside stairs."

Juliet glanced quickly at him. "In other words you're volunteering to be my bodyguard?"

91

"I can't think of a body I'd want to guard more than yours," he drawled with a theatrically wicked inflection.

She had to grin. "And who will protect me from you?"

"No one. That's the most important part of my devious plan," he whispered villainously, but he was grinning, too, as they walked together up the steps.

A few minutes later Marc and Juliet went through her room out onto the balcony, although she knew very well she should have told him she had changed her mind about getting some air. After all, he was the reason she had gone out in the first place—the depth of her feelings for him had begun to concern her, and she had needed to be away from him for a while. Yet when he had suggested they come up here, she hadn't even tried to avoid doing that. Now she was alone with him and, dangerous as that could prove to be, she was unable to deprive herself of the pleasure of his company. With him she felt warmer, more alive, and happy. She was only human, she didn't want to try to escape such good feelings, and so she made her reckless decision.

Propping her elbows on the top rail, resting her chin in cupped hands, she gazed out at the rugged outline of dark mountains rising against a backdrop of lighter purplish sky. The soft light of a half moon gilded the topmost leaves of surrounding trees and lay like a shimmering coverlet over the slopes that descended to the lodge. The strange music of katydids floated along with a gentle breeze and lulled by tranquillity, Juliet pushed everything from her mind except the reality of the lovely night and of Marc standing beside her.

"I guess what happened today in the pizza place happens almost everywhere you go, doesn't it?" she asked suddenly but very softly, turning to gaze at his shadowed face as he looked at her. "Does it bother you a lot when people crowd around you like that?"

"It doesn't exactly bother me. After all, the people who

do crowd around are my viewers and because they like me, I can keep on doing the work I love. I think I'd have to be a fool to resent their attention," Marc said quietly, a warmth in his deep voice accompanying a slow, almost pensive smile. "But I have to admit there are times when I'd like to go anywhere at all I wanted without one single person noticing me."

"Instead, everywhere you go, almost everyone stares at you." Moving from the railing, Juliet faced him fully. "You must feel like you can't have any kind of private life at all."

"I don't feel like that in New York nearly as much as I do when I'm on assignment. New Yorkers are typically blasé about seeing celebrities in public places. They'll generally leave you alone. In New York I have friends who accept me as simply that—a friend. They aren't at all impressed by the fact that I'm on television, thank God."

"But when you're on assignment, almost everyone you meet is terribly impressed by Marc Tyner, the news media superstar," murmured Juliet. "Everybody knows who you are, yet nobody knows you—the real you."

"It's something like that, I guess." His hands in his trouser pockets, Marc stood facing Juliet but was staring over the top of her head out into the night. A short moment passed before he lowered his gaze to her face. He smiled. "Of course, it helps a great deal when some of the crew members are good friends."

Despite his words Juliet had seen something lonely in his smile, and suddenly her affection for him surged again, expanding like a living thing in her chest until it felt tight, and her heart was beating rapidly. It was as if the lonely part of Marc that she was sensing so strongly was beckoning her to him. She stepped nearer, astounded that the mere thought of his being lonely hurt *her* badly. Her hands drifted up to cup his face.

"Marc," she whispered, stretching up to brush her soft lips against the firmer shape of his. His hands left his pockets to span her waist and hold her gently as she kissed him once, then again and again, offering sweetness and incredible tenderness, and of course, arousing passion in him.

"Julie," he murmured gruffly, arms encircling and pressing her tight against him, lips hardening swiftly to part hers.

The burning heat of his desire kindled her own, and very soon they were both being consumed in the white-hot fires of their mutual passion. Marc's hands roamed with gentle urgency over Juliet's back, her rounded hips and the backs of her thighs before retracing their downward path up again to sweep her incurving waist. Then the heels of his palms were stroking the straining sides of breasts pressed hard against his chest, and Juliet felt she could never get close enough to him. She wrapped her arms around his neck, and her warmly malleable body yielded to the tauter, straighter line of his. She was on fire for him. The aching emptiness inside her was becoming so intense that she wondered how much longer she could bear it. Her senses had been aroused to a fever pitch so swiftly that she felt magnificently dizzy and she clung to Marc; their kisses became more deeply seeking, more ardent, and more and more a delightfully dangerous prelude to complete intimacy. Marc's warm, sensuously firm lips were exerting a slightly twisting pressure on the soft shape of hers, and she was kissing him back with a hunger that matched his. And when Marc started lowering the back zipper of her dress, she could barely drag her mouth from his.

"Not out here," she breathed against one finely sculpted cheek. "Take me to my room." And after he did, while he shut the French doors and drew the drapes closed across them, she watched him, eyes soft green with desire, the

94

color in her face heightened by the liquid fire flowing through her veins. She was waiting for him, and Marc diminished the short distance between them with one long stride. He took her hands in his and pressed them against his chest. No words were needed. As Juliet unbuttoned his shirt he slipped the pins from her hair, and it tumbled down to her shoulders in a golden-red spill like the finest silk.

Juliet's wandering kisses explored the muscular contours of Marc's tanned chest as he removed her dress, slip, and lacy bra. Yet when he slid his fingers beneath the waistband of silken panties and she trembled lightly, he relented, touched her full creamy bared breasts, and kissed her with rousing demand before putting an arm round her waist and drawing her to her bed.

Juliet stepped out of her sandals and lay down, her breathing quickening as she reached her arms out to Marc. When he lay down on the mattress beside her, her slender delightfully curved body turned to meet the raw power and male tautness of his. She moaned softly, and her mouth opened to the sweet onslaught of his like a flower opens to the warming sun. When he guided one small hand to his belt, she unbuckled it but the moment he began slipping her panties off, she trembled again, though not with fear. She trembled with the clamoring need so soon to be fulfilled. But Marc had tensed and was pulling away from her despite her soft sound of protest.

"God, you're not ready for this," he muttered huskily, looking deeply into her opening eyes. "I knew that, but damn, everything just happened so fast."

"But, Marc, I—"

"Hush," he whispered, silencing her with a lean finger touched to her lips. His warm gaze searched her face, and he almost smiled. "How sweet you are, Julie, but what you don't realize is that your eyes tell me nearly everything.

And a few minutes ago on the balcony, I saw as much compassion as passion in your eyes. You think I'm lonely and you're half right. Sometimes I am. But, Julie . . ." He gently brushed a tendril of hair back from her cheek. "I'm not so lonely that I'm ready to accept sympathy sex. Oh, I do want you, but not like this. Not until you're really ready. Not until you want me as much as I want you. And for the same reasons."

Juliet was stunned. He was so wrong about what he thought she was feeling! Before she could begin to tell him that, however, he swung off the bed and picked his shirt up off the chair where she had dropped it. At that moment she needed so badly to be close to him that she thought she might die if he left. "Marc, don't go," she whispered. "Stay with me."

"I will—the first night you really want me to. But not tonight, not like this," he said quietly, looking back at her for only an instant before walking toward the door that opened onto the inner hallway. "Good night, Julie."

"Marc!" Juliet sat up, wanting to go after him, longing to entice him into staying. But she had not yet lost all inhibitions and those that remained held her back until it was too late. Marc was gone; the door was closed behind him. And Juliet was alone in her room, her entire being, body and soul, still achingly in need of him. She fell back on the bed.

"Oh, dammit to hell," she muttered, her voice muffled as she turned her face into the soft pillow under her head. If Marc only knew how wrong he was. . . . Apparently her eyes, expressive as he said they were, didn't tell him everything. If they did, he would know without a doubt that she hadn't been offering herself to console him. She had been surrendering herself completely to him because, in the past few days, she had somehow committed the ultimate folly and fallen in love with him.

CHAPTER SIX

Marc's strategy with the mayor worked. After the taped interview with Trenton's police chief, who colorfully provided additional details about the corruption scheme, Mayor Haynes had a change of heart. When Juliet called his office immediately after the chief's interview and requested an appointment, one was finally granted for ten o'clock Friday morning. Juliet's diplomatic ultimatum that Marc would not come unless the mayor agreed to a taped interview met with resistance, but she was firm and he, through his secretary, capitulated in the end. When Juliet hung up the phone, she sat back in her chair with a satisfied smile. It was obvious Mayor Haynes was very reluctant to face the cameras, but because they had interviewed his critics, he now had little choice in the matter.

Friday morning was hectic, and Juliet had no chance to talk to Marc before their appointment with the mayor. While she was busy conferring with the research assistants who were investigating the allegations that there was a link between the United States senator and the state judge who had handed down ridiculously lenient sentences in the earlier corruption trial, Marc was taking calls from New York. He was still on the phone when Juliet left to join the camera and sound crews who had gone earlier to set up their equipment in Mayor Haynes's office, and it wasn't until later, after the hour-long interview had ended, that she had the opportunity to speak to Marc.

"I imagine he feels like he's been put through a wringer after all the questions you hit him with," she commented offhandedly while she and Marc walked away from the old courthouse. "But I have to admit he handled himself pretty well. Didn't you think?"

Marc shrugged. "He had his answers down pat. Probably rehearsed them, but that's not unusual. I never expected him to fall to his knees and pour out a confession," he said coolly. "Did you?"

"No, of course not," Juliet said softly, rather taken aback by his chilling tone. But when she said something else and he didn't answer her at all, she decided he must be lost in serious thought and hadn't even heard her, so she didn't speak again while they were walking to their parked cars.

Half an hour later, back at the inn, Juliet met with Paul and Marc in the temporary office adjoining her room. It soon became apparent to her that something was still on Marc's mind because he contributed very little to the discussion, and for that reason the meeting didn't last long. Even after Paul left the office, however, Marc made no move to go and Juliet gave him an expectant smile, assuming he had stayed to talk about some phase of their assignment that didn't require Paul's involvement.

But Marc said nothing at all. For a full minute—which seemed to tick by with excruciating slowness—he simply sat in the chair across the desk from her, his chin resting on steepled fingers as he looked at her.

Juliet fidgeted with a pencil. Again and again she glanced up at him, trying to analyze the expression lying over his carved features but she couldn't decipher it. There was such a fathomless look in his blue eyes that uneasiness began to steal over her, and at last she could bear the silence no longer.

"I've been thinking about Mayor Haynes," she began with an abruptness that nearly made the sound of her own voice startle her. Thoughtfully tapping the pencil eraser against her lips, she continued despite her growing discomfort. "He did give some rather convincing answers to your questions this morning, and I wonder a little about the possibility that the 'evidence' we have against him might be misleading."

Marc's eyes narrowed. "There's always that possibility, but in this case it's very slim."

"Yes, I guess it really is," Juliet conceded, and smiled rather sheepishly. "It's just that the mayor is, or seems to be, such a courtly old gentleman. During the interview, he was so gracious and charming that I found it hard to believe he could be involved in anything corrupt."

"Was that just a case of innocent sentimentality overriding objectivity?" Marc asked coolly. "Or do you just have this thing for older men?"

Juliet bit back a sigh as her heart seemed to leap up into her throat only to plunge down into the pit of her stomach. *Someone had told him the lies that circulated about Henry Alexander and me,* she thought. And judging by the derisive twist of his lips and the hard set of his facial features, he believed them. An aching knot seized the center of her chest, but she ignored the inconvenient pain she felt as defensive pride stiffened her spine, lifted her chin, and made her hold her head high as she met Marc's cold stare.

Determined to make him voice the lies if he was so ready to believe them, she challenged, "Tell me exactly what that little remark was supposed to mean."

"You know damn well what it meant," he replied, his voice icy, his words clipped. His feet were planted wide apart on the floor, and when his arms dropped down to

99

lie along the chair's armrests, there became something menacing in the way he was sitting. He exuded an aura of threatening power, and he looked as dangerous as a predator about to pounce. His gaze raked over her as she sat straight and stiff behind the desk and he smiled unpleasantly. "Or have you already forgotten your affair with Henry Alexander now that it's gotten you what you wanted?"

"I did not have an affair with Henry," she muttered through clenched teeth, angry defiance flashing in her eyes. "And I must say I never would have believed you would put much stock in gossip. I thought reporters at your level were scrupulous about verifying hearsay. Most —if not all—of what you hear on a corporate grapevine is untrue, and what you heard about Henry and me is a ridiculous lie."

Marc's dark brown eyebrows lifted mockingly. "During one of my calls from New York this morning, I mentioned your name and someone I consider very reliable was convinced enough that what he'd heard about Henry and you was true that he decided to tell me all about the two of you."

"Well, your 'very reliable' person was wrong, and he passed along some very *un*reliable information."

"Did he? I've never known him to do that before. Researchers get in the habit of being certain of their facts," Marc stated bluntly. "And he didn't seem to have any doubts that you used old Henry as a rung up the ladder of success."

"And you believe that?" Juliet exclaimed softly as the knot in her chest expanded in a fiercer tighter grip. Looking at Marc, seeing the implacable set of his jaw, she shook her head. "I don't understand how you can believe that."

"Why shouldn't I? After all, you lied to me when I asked you why you left Lancaster Broadcasting. You said

100

it was because you get better money and more prestige with Union."

"That happens to be the truth."

"No. That's a half truth, which can be worse than a lie," Marc ground out, moving his upper body forward so swiftly that Juliet's heart stopped a second because she thought he was coming up out of his chair. But he only leaned toward her, his face hard-planed and unyielding, his elbows on his knees, and his hands clasped and extended toward her as if he were pointing an accusing finger. He had become the ruthless interrogator she had seen occasionally in taped interviews, and there was nothing gentle about him as he shook his head. "No, Julie. You didn't leave Lancaster for more money and prestige with Union. You left because your affair with Henry had become common knowledge."

She wasn't going to be able to make him believe her; Juliet knew that, and with the realization a strange numbness spread over her. Rising as majestically as she possibly could from her chair, she walked around the desk and started past Marc's chair toward the door to her room. She didn't give him so much as a cool glance as she stated proudly, "I don't have to listen to this."

"Oh, yes, you do. I'm not through yet." One large hand grasped one delicately boned wrist, stopping Juliet as he stood with lithe muscular grace. He pulled her closer to him, his eyes glinting icy shards as he muttered, "Before I let you go, tell me if it's still going on between you and old Henry. I know he used his influence to get you this job. Are you still prostituting yourself in appreciation?"

Juliet's nostrils actually flared. She had endured weeks of frustration and humiliation, knowing that accusation was constantly being whispered behind her back. But no one had dared call her a prostitute to her face—until now, when she had to endure hearing the very man she loved

101

call her that. Horrible pain and anger combined explosive-
ly, and her reaction to his cruel mockery was immediate
and reckless. She swung up her free hand, palm flat, and
brought it forcefully toward his cheek. But before she
could deliver the slap, he caught hold of that wrist also
and jerked it down to clasp it with the other he held in one
hand. Juliet trembled violently, overcome with hurt and
defensive rage.

"I wouldn't advise you to try that again," he warned;
his deep rough voice sounded threatening. "If you do, you
might get more of a response than you bargained for."

"Let go of me," she commanded coldly. "Right now."

"Not yet. You still haven't told me if you and Henry
still—"

"I'm not going to even bother trying to defend myself
to you!"

"Maybe that's because you don't have any reasonable
defense."

"And maybe you've just been digging up other people's
dirty little secrets too long," she snapped at him, trying to
twist her wrists free from his powerful grip. "Maybe you
can't trust anybody anymore. Maybe you're too jaded.
Ever thought of that?"

"No. And we're not discussing me. We're discussing
you. I'm curious, Julie. Was it really worth it to let an old
man make love to you, a man you had no real feeling for,
just to become an associate producer?"

"How dare you ask me that?" Her glare was so cold, he
should have been able to feel its chill. "I didn't have to let
anybody make love to me to get where I am! I worked
hard, and the work I did was *excellent*. I deserved the
promotion I got. You even admitted as much yourself. Or
were you trying to flatter me then? Part of your own
seduction plan?" She laughed bitterly as Marc's expression visibly paled. "You men are all the same. If a man

102

makes it before he's thirty, he's a genius—a boy wonder! But a woman only makes it to the top on her back. Well, I've got news for you."

Marc's answering smile was sardonic and unpleasant. "Come on, Julie. You're only twenty-eight. How many other associate producers your age are there in this business?"

"I don't particularly care," she spat out. "Maybe there aren't *any*. Maybe I'm the exception to every rule or maybe I just got lucky and one day Henry Alexander decided to reward me for the damn hard work I did for him. He recognized some talent in me—and not a talent in *bed*, because I never slept with him. If you think I sleep around to advance my career, how do you explain my not falling over myself to hop into bed with you? You have enough clout at Union to get me promoted to senior vice-president in no time flat, and I know it—so why haven't I let you make love to me?"

Marc paused and averted her eyes before he spoke.

"You could just be a very shrewd lady. You wouldn't want to appear too eager."

"You're determined to believe the worst of me, aren't you?" It was a statement of fact instead of a question. Juliet's voice was hushed, and as she uttered the words her fist came down hard against the tabletop. She had been absolutely stunned when the unwarranted gossip about her had started, and some of that sense of disbelief lingered even now.

She looked up at Marc almost incredulously but her tone was flat when she added, "You're so convinced that I wouldn't have been made an associate producer if I hadn't . . . put out for Henry Alexander that you *must* have some complaint about the quality of my work. Well? I'm waiting," she said in a shrill voice. "Have I completely botched this assignment? Are we wandering around in

103

circles trying to get this story? Are the technical crews being sent off in one direction while the editorial staff goes in another? Is everything in chaos? If you think I've made such a shambles of this assignment that we'll never be able to put together a segment we can air, then you know what you can do to get rid of me. Call Pete Webster and tell him how incompetent I am. He can fire me and send someone down here to do this story who has the ability to handle the production of it."

There was a subtle change in Marc's expression. Apparently he understood her exactly. He had no reason whatsoever to complain about the quality of her work, which meant no one could say with honesty that she had been made an associate producer even though she was totally lacking in ability. Watching Marc, Juliet gained little satisfaction from the expression of uncertainty that seemed to flit across his face. She was so thoroughly sick of the gossip about her, sick of the accusations Marc had made, and at that moment even sick of him. Once more she tugged the hands he held imprisoned, and when he released her wrists, she started to walk away only to be stopped by him again. This time, however, his touch was gentler, the heels of his hands light on her shoulders. Assuming the most indifferent expression she could muster, Juliet simply stared at him.

"All right, Julie, you've made your point. I do know you're a very competent producer," he said, searching her face as if he expected to find some great truth there. "But the fact that you're amply qualified doesn't prove you didn't sleep with Henry so he would promote you sooner. I like to think that isn't true but . . . convince me you're telling the truth, Julie."

"I wouldn't waste my time trying to convince you of anything."

His hardening gaze raked over her. "I don't have much choice except to believe what I've heard then."

"Believe whatever you damn well please and go straight to hell while you do it," she said icily. With the backs of her hands she brushed his off her shoulders, stepped around him, and walked through the adjoining doorway to her room. *Make me believe you,* he had said. He had actually expected her to defend herself to him! Angry despair erupted in her again, and she slammed the door behind her. Yet the moment she closed herself into her room away from him, the strength born of her anger deserted her. She buried her face in her hands and began trembling all over. She was stunned, scarcely able to believe what had just occurred. She would never have imagined Marc could be so unfair and unyielding. So quick to condemn her without considering—even for a moment—that she might be telling the truth; that all he had heard was a lie.

He had betrayed her, betrayed all the love she felt and all the trust she had had in him. In that moment it didn't matter at all that her defense against his accusation had sounded pitifully weak, even to her own ears—he should have believed her anyhow, he should have trusted her. Even if the whole of New York City believed she had been Henry's lover, Marc should have believed her!

But now he did not, and Juliet was astounded by the crushing pain in her chest. The hurt was excruciating and seemed to drain away all physical strength. And pressing her fingertips hard against her temples, she mentally railed herself for ever becoming so vulnerable. *She had known she shouldn't fall in love with him.* Yet who can destroy love when—with little warning—it enters the soul in silence, flourishes like a secret garden, then suddenly becomes the most vital aspect of existence? Juliet didn't know. She only knew she loved Marc, he had betrayed her, and she wasn't sure she could ever forgive him. Yet as she trudged across the room to drop down on her stomach across her bed, she felt less inclined to curse him and more inclined to cry. But tears were a luxury she rarely allowed herself and, by sinking the edge of her teeth into her trembling lower lip, she managed to avoid giving in to them this time.

Throughout the weekend Juliet stayed as far from Marc as she could. She saw him only when she had no other choice and never spoke to him at all because that was how she wanted it. And judging by his indifference, that arrangement suited him too. When Monday came, however, she knew that despite their personal feelings, they were on this assignment together; gathering her most professional demeanor around her like a magically protective mantle, she plunged into the fray. It wasn't easy. Simply being around Marc hurt. And when on occasion, he would accidentally touch her or she him, she would feel as though she were shriveling away inside herself, remembering what their touches had meant. Now he was indifferent, and she was polite. There was nothing personal between them except a widening rift, and although they had to work together, Juliet tried as often as possible to address herself to Paul rather than directly to him.

The days crept by; the nights were longer and added insult to injury—Juliet couldn't get much sleep. Although she purposely manufactured work and stayed at it from early in the mornings to late in the evenings simply to wear herself out, she didn't succeed in getting more rest. The moment she dropped into bed physically exhausted, her mind would leap into action, a tangle of thoughts weaving endlessly through her consciousness, driving her crazy. She missed Marc. That was the problem and she knew it. She missed feeling at ease with him, missed being with him, and most of all missed talking with him. At times she felt so lonely, she contemplated going to him and trying to explain more convincingly what had happened at Lancaster. But she had tried once and she had no idea what else to say to him. She had told Marc the truth once, but he had chosen not to believe her. Now there was nothing left for her to do.

By Thursday lack of sleep, disillusionment, and lingering angry resentment combined to exhaust Juliet by early afternoon. Paul seemed to recognize her weariness, and when they went into Trenton to tape a transitional scene with Marc addressing the cameras from the courthouse steps, she called Paul aside. Although she usually spoke to him and the crew together, she talked to him alone this time. After telling him how she wanted the scene shot and giving him a few specific instructions to relay to Marc and others, she gratefully withdrew to the background to watch the taping.

Back in the office in the lodge two hours later, she sat staring blindly at some papers on her desk when Marc swept the door open and strode into the room. She glanced up at him, then back down.

"Yes?" she mumbled.

Marc stopped directly across from her, feet planted apart on the floor, hands on his hips. "We'd better smooth out our working relationship," he announced bluntly, his words clipped. "I see no reason why you can't talk to me directly. When we're taping and you have instructions for me, I'd like you to tell *me* what you want and not Paul. You've never relied on him as a spokesman before. Why start now?"

"Why not?" she drawled, her southern accent slightly more pronounced as she gave him a pretty but fraudulent smile. "Some producers relay all their instructions through their directors."

"You don't work that way though. You always speak to the crew and me yourself."

"And I plan to go on doing that. But sometimes, like this afternoon, I might have Paul speak for me. I think that's my decision to make."

"Enough, Julie," he commanded softly, leaning over the desk, palms flat on the top as he looked squarely into her eyes. "This is getting ridiculous."

Rolling back her chair, she stood, turned her back on him and moved a few steps away. "Ridiculous, Marc?"

"Yes." He came around the desk, stopping close behind her. "Up to now, we've worked extremely well together, and it isn't necessary to let our personal differences change that."

"I wasn't aware that our working relationship had changed all that much. We're cordial to each other, compromise when we have differences of opinion. You certainly can't complain that we're at each other's throats."

"No, but I am complaining about the tension that could start affecting the entire crew."

Turning around, Juliet looked at him evenly, lifting her delicately arched brows a fraction of an inch. "Some tension's inevitable under the circumstances, don't you think?" she asked coolly, trying to ignore the raw pain that clutched her chest. This close to Marc, looking at him, she wished with all her heart that it had not turned out this way between them, that she could turn back the clock to the time when he had at least respected her. But it was impossible to do that and, determined to salvage her pride if nothing else, she gave him no indication of what she really felt. She shrugged rather carelessly instead. "But I'm sure it's not enough for the crew to notice."

"But *I* notice it," Marc stated tersely. "And I prefer to work with a producer I can communicate with."

"Well, short of asking Pete Webster to replace me, I

don't know what you can do," Juliet replied, keeping her tone cold even as she wondered bleakly if that was what he was planning to do. She paused a moment, giving him the opportunity to express that intention. When he didn't, a tiny unreasonable hope rose in her, and she added, "Unless, of course, you've changed your mind and decided I was telling the truth about Henry Alexander."

Hope was immediately dashed. Ignoring her last remark as if she hadn't made it, Marc took another step in her direction, towering over her and thrusting his hands into his pockets. "I'm sure we can resolve this with a little extra effort," he said, glacier-blue eyes boring into hers. "I don't have to approve of how you conduct your personal life to respect your work, just as you don't have to approve of how I conduct mine. As long as we're working together, we can be friendly."

"Friendly but not friends. Fine, that arrangement suits me." Unknowingly Juliet raised her chin as she looked right back at him. "I'm pretty choosy about who my friends are anyhow. They all trust me."

"You must not have very many of them in this business then."

Juliet swallowed hard. "Probably not," she answered at last, maintaining a steady voice, valiantly concealing the deep wound the words had inflicted. "But the ones I do have are worth having because when I tell them the truth, they believe me." She glanced past him at her desk. "Now, I'm busy, and since we seem to understand each other, I don't think we need to discuss this further."

"I hope not, Julie," he murmured, a hint of warning in his low tone. "We have enough on our hands trying to get this story, and I don't want us wasting any time not communicating with each other."

"Right. From now on, we'll be *friendly*," she said with

109

some sarcasm, then shrugged. "I don't know how convincing I'll be at it though. I'm not much of an actress."

"Don't underestimate yourself" was his caustic retort, and he stared down at her for several long moments before he turned and walked out the door.

The following four days were even more difficult for Juliet. Dealing with Marc completely without relying on Paul as go-between made her feel she was constantly on stage, acting out a play—though she didn't know any of the correct lines to say. As a producer, she had long since learned how to be diplomatic and highly professional. But as a woman, she had never had to learn how to pretend to herself that she wasn't in love with a man who didn't love her, and now no longer even respected her. During every minute spent with him, she was overwhelmingly aware of her love for him; each time she had to seek him out, she had to force herself to endure the inevitable pain. Yet she had little choice. After all, he had told her in no uncertain terms that he expected direct communication between them, and she was unwilling to cross him, remembering always in the back of her mind that he could possibly cause her problems with Pete Webster if he chose to do so. She didn't think he would, but unsure of that, she knew she couldn't take any chances with her career. Besides, she would survive; she knew that and the hope that dealing closely with Marc would become easier with each passing day sustained her through the worst of it.

To some extent the passage of time did help Juliet. At least she became more adept at willing away the hurt she felt when Marc was with her and also more adept at pushing thoughts of him to the back of her mind when she was alone. Late Monday afternoon, after a reasonably productive day, she was concentrating exclusively on the story and going through her files when Paul paid her a visit.

"Got a minute?" he asked, pausing in the office doorway. "This won't take long."

"Oh, I have time. Don't worry about it. I was just glancing through these files, hoping to catch something we might have missed anyway," she told him, waving him toward the chair across from her, smiling as he sat down. "Okay, I'm listening."

"It's just this: Are you satisfied with the way this assignment's going?" Paul asked straightforwardly, jerking at his tie. "Or more specifically, are you satisfied with the crew's work and mine?"

"Of course, I am. You would have heard about it if I weren't," Juliet assured him, baffled by the question. "Why do you ask?"

"I just got the impression things might not be going the way you'd like them to."

"Well, all stories have their ups and downs, and maybe this one does have a few more downs than usual, but we knew it would be a tough story to get. And I'm pleased with our progress so far. I think this will turn into a piece we can all be proud of. What's the matter, Paul?" she asked with a grin. "Have I been snapping at you and the crew lately? If so, I didn't mean to."

Paul shook his head. "No, no, it's not that. It's just that you've seemed a little preoccupied recently."

"Ah, well, you know how easy it is sometime to get bogged down in details."

"Are you sure there might not be something else bothering you? If you don't mind my asking, have you and Marc had a disagreement about how to go after this story? He's been acting slightly impatient and I just wondered. . . ."

"Maybe he's just eager to wrap up this assignment."

111

"Maybe. But I don't think that's it. To be honest I've noticed that his relationship with you has been somewhat strained lately," Paul stated candidly, his expression earnest as he leaned forward in his chair. "And I thought if the two of you had had some disagreement about how to treat this story that I should have a talk with you. If you wouldn't mind some advice, that is?"

"I don't mind at all," Juliet told him, watching him speculatively, wondering what he was getting at. "I'm always willing to hear your advice, Paul."

"Good, because I like you, Juliet. I think you're an excellent producer and have a great future in this business. And I'd hate to see anything happen to change that," Paul said with quiet emphasis. "That's why I have to remind you that Marc is one of the most valuable correspondents in broadcasting today, and Union would bend over backward not to lose him. And they expect his stories to reflect his style of investigative reporting, so he's used to having some say in the way they're produced. Not that he would ever try to take complete control. That's not his way. But if you've had a disagreement with him, Juliet, I advise you to try reach a compromise. Someone in his position can refuse to work with you. I've seen it happen, believe me, and it's the producer who doesn't last long."

"I see," Juliet murmured, her eyes widening slightly. "Are—are you saying Marc has told Pete Webster that he doesn't want to work with me again?"

"No, no, no. I'm not saying that at all," Paul exclaimed, shaking his head vehemently. "I'm just trying to tell you what could conceivably happen."

Juliet breathed a silent sigh of relief. "But Marc and I haven't disagreed about this story, and I would always be willing to listen to his ideas, not least because they're usually good ones."

"You have nothing to worry about then. Glad to hear

it," Paul declared, smiling widely, as if greatly relieved. He jumped to his feet. "I just thought it wouldn't hurt if you got a little advice from an old man who's been in the business since you were a baby."

"Not *quite* that long, I'm sure," Juliet countered, giving him a grateful smile. "And thank you, Paul. It's nice to know you're concerned."

"Good producers don't come along every day. I like to hold on to the ones I find," he explained, giving a jaunty wave back over his shoulder as he left the office.

Unfortunately as soon as he was gone, Juliet discovered that her relief was short-lived as it occurred to her that Marc could still refuse to work with her. His reasons need not be professional. He could blacklist her simply because he believed she had slept with Henry Alexander in order to get her job at Union in the first place. Groaning softly at the mere thought, she lowered her forehead on her folded hands upon the desk only to sit up straight several minutes later. Anger at herself flashed in her eyes. She was sick and tired of brooding, sick and tired of worrying, sick and tired of just about everything. Thrusting out her chin, she reached for the phone, asked for Patty Clements, Paul's assistant, and suggested a movie and a bite to eat when the woman answered her phone after one ring. Happily Patty thought it was a fine idea.

The theater in Boone was relatively uncrowded for a seven o'clock showing, and fortunately the movie was a riveting mystery which allowed both Juliet and Patty to lose themselves in the scenes portrayed on the screen.

Hungry afterward, they stopped in a diner for hamburgers and spent a pleasant hour or so chatting over their late dinner. It was after ten when they returned to the lodge, and Juliet felt more relaxed than she had in days.

"Well, I have some letters to write," Patty said, stopping by her room in the upstairs corridor. "But that was really fun. We'll have to do it again sometime. Okay?"

"I'd like that," Juliet said honestly, then exchanged good-nights with the other woman and started toward her own door, searching through her purse for her key. But just as her fingers closed around its sharp edges, she became very still, hearing heavy footfalls approaching her quickly along the corridor. Her heart leaped; she spun around and gasped sharply when large hands suddenly seized her shoulders.

"What are you doing, Marc?" she squeaked, staring up at his grimly lined face. "You nearly scared me right out of my skin."

"Where the hell have you been?" he muttered furiously, dropping one hand to take the key from hers and unlock her door. Then he swept her into her room, pushed the door shut again with his foot, and stood glaring down at her. "You know you're supposed to tell Paul or me whenever you go out. I have the entire crew out searching the county for you right now."

Juliet winced. "Oh, I'm sorry," she uttered sincerely, shaking her head. "I really just forgot to tell you or Paul I was going out."

"Going where? Where *have* you been, Julie?"

"To a movie," she said softly. "In Boone."

"At night? When you know those men follow you everywhere you go, you still went out alone at night and didn't even bother to mention you were going. What were you trying to prove?"

"Nothing. I just wanted to go to a movie. And I didn't go alone," she informed him, flexing her shoulder, trying to escape his binding grasp. "Patty Clements went with me, so I was perfectly safe."

"Two women alone aren't necessarily safe," he said harshly, his expression darkly thunderous. "What would you have done if those two men in that sedan had finally decided to do more than just follow you?"

"I don't know," she admitted stiffly, resentment beginning to rise up inside her. What right did he have to interrogate her this way, believing what he did about her? Deciding she had had enough of his abuse, she glared up at him. "And who made you my keeper anyway?"

"I did. You certainly seem to need one."

"That doesn't mean you had to volunteer for the job," she replied, her eyes and voice cold, her delicate features incongruously hard. "Frankly I can't believe you really give a damn about where I go or what I do."

"For God's sake, Julie," he muttered, his hands gentling on her shoulders. "You think I don't still care what happens to you?"

"It doesn't much matter to me whether you do or not," she lied, driven by pride. "As long as you believe I'd go to bed with anybody just to get a promotion, I don't need your concern or your protection. I don't want it."

"Dammit, Julie," he said roughly. "Did you sleep with Henry Alexander or not?"

"Did I?" she drawled provokingly, finding some perverse pleasure in sounding every inch the femme fatale. "Why ask me that, Marc? I thought you already knew the answer."

Uttering a muffled curse, he released her abruptly. "We'll discuss this again sometime, when you're in a more reasonable mood."

"I think not. I think we've said all there is to say on the subject."

"Too bad. We'll discuss it anyway," he replied, a tight smile touching his carved lips. "As for now, I want you to remember to never leave this lodge again without telling Paul or me where you're going. Understood?"

"I understand, and I'll think about it."

"Don't push me, Julie or—"

"Or what?" she challenged recklessly. "You'll tell Pete Webster to fire me?"

"Hardly. I don't need Pete's help to handle you, love. I can handle you just fine by myself," Marc said softly.

And before Juliet could respond, he turned around and strode out the door, closing it noiselessly behind him. Juliet was alone. She stared at the door and then the floor, wrapping her arms tightly around her waist, her thoughts in turmoil. She wanted so badly to believe that Marc would still care if something happened to her; wanted to believe she had actually detected some doubt about Henry and her in the depths of his azure eyes. And she wanted to believe she wouldn't forgive him if he were, by some miracle, to ask her to. But deep down inside, she knew she would.

CHAPTER SEVEN

Marc flew to New York late Saturday afternoon, planning to return to Boone Sunday evening. In his absence Juliet was busy rescheduling the itinerary for the next week, conferring with the chief technicians, and answering Tom's seemingly endless list of questions. Tom was a fine worker, not long out of college, a very bright and personable young man. Six years Juliet's junior, he was everything she would have wanted in an assistant. She admired his swift mind and enthusiasm and believed he was headed for a brilliant career. She was also quite fond of him. While his fondness for her seemed to border on adoration, it was the adoration he might feel for an older sister. Juliet knew that he must have heard the gossip about Henry Alexander and her although he never mentioned it, yet in the weeks they had worked together, she had sensed his feelings for her had become strongly protective. She suspected if anyone ever unwisely sullied her name in Tom's presence, he would defend her with a vengeance. He seemed to believe in her completely both as a person and a professional, and that gave her a good feeling, especially when she had to consider what so many other people in the business thought of her. And because Marc's lack of faith in her had hurt her to the quick, it was comforting to spend Sunday working with someone as supportive as Tom.

Around eight in the evening Juliet called it a day, thinking she and Tom had accomplished a great deal. Closing a folder, she smiled appreciatively at her assistant. "Thanks for volunteering to work today," she told him. "I needed your help, but I wouldn't have insisted you stay here. You could have gone with some of the other crew members to the lake. Or found someone to play tennis with."

"Oh, I can play tennis tomorrow evening," he told her, shrugging carelessly. "Besides, I learned a few new things today."

"Even so, work isn't everything, and I can see you're getting a bit restless." Grinning, Juliet consulted her wristwatch. "Yes, it's about that time, isn't it? So go on and call your girlfriend. Mary Ann, isn't it?"

"Yes, Mary Ann." Tom grimaced comically. "Although I wouldn't have missed this assignment for anything, I do miss Mary Ann. She really was disappointed that I couldn't get back to New York this weekend so . . ." He shifted his feet uncomfortably while clearing his throat before finishing in a rush of words, "I was hoping you might not need me here next weekend and I could go then. Just to spend Saturday night, of course."

"Sure, I think you should go. Pete Webster wants us to wrap up this story as quickly as possible so he can air it soon, but everyone needs a break," Juliet told Tom. "You can leave here Saturday afternoon early."

"What a relief. Now I can tell that to Mary Ann when I call her, and maybe she'll stop worrying about—"

When he broke off abruptly, Juliet lifted gently arched brows. "Worrying about what?"

"To tell the truth she's jealous of you," he blurted out. "She works at Union and she's seen you. She says she'd be a fool not to worry about me being with such an attractive woman."

118

"Well, I appreciate the compliment." Juliet smiled wryly. "But I'm sure you can convince her we're only co-workers and friends, of course."

Tom shook his head. "I've been trying to convince her of that, but she can't seem to believe I'm not going to fall very hard for you."

"Remind her that I'm six years older than you are."

"She just figures that might make you appeal to me even more."

"Then I think you're going to have to do some very persuasive wining and dining next Saturday night. Let her know how much you care about *her*," Juliet advised. An indulgent smile warmed her eyes. "Tell her the truth, Tom—that as far as you're concerned, I'm the older sister type." She waved him toward the door. "Now, go call her and let me finish in here because I'm dying to get into a hot bath."

After Tom had gone, Juliet smiled ruefully to herself. Probably Mary Ann had heard the gossip about her and feared that Tom was in the grasp of one of those predatory females who specialize in stealing men away from other women. "You're getting paranoid," she muttered aloud, knowing that everyone who heard gossip didn't necessarily believe it. But Marc had believed the lies about her. She pushed that thought from her mind the moment it popped up, cleared the desk, and went into her room for the night.

Thirty minutes later, after a soak in a bath oil–scented tub, Juliet slipped on a wonderfully soft pearl-white silk Charmeuse chemise with an edging of real Venetian lace that grazed her thighs. Luxurious lingerie was her weakness and although silk Charmeuse was ridiculously expensive, she had been unable to resist the chemise and short matching robe. She splurged occasionally on extravagantly priced undergarments and nightwear simply because she loved the feel of silk or satin against her skin. Lazily

119

stretching her arms above her head, she yawned, then walked to the bedside table where she surrendered to another weakness—a family saga filled with romance. She tossed the book on the bed, plumped the pillows against the headboard, and settled herself.

Juliet was still reading when, around ten o'clock, she heard the door to Marc's room open then close and she knew he was back. She took a deep breath, dreading tomorrow morning when she had to see him again, then nibbled her bottom lip and forced herself to concentrate on the book she was holding. After almost another hour of reading, she was sufficiently sleepy to switch off the bedside lamp and curl up beneath a sheet.

Awakening from a sound sleep to the shrill ringing of a telephone makes the heart pound, and Juliet's seemed to be hammering as she sat up straight in bed sometime later. She reached toward the phone on the night table, grabbed up the receiver midring, and muttered a none-too-encouraging hello. There was no response, only silence for several seconds. Then a muffled male voice began speaking, and Juliet didn't listen long before slamming the receiver down hard on some degenerate's ear. Hastily she switched on the bedside lamp.

"You son of a—" The descriptive expletive trailed off into silence before completion as sheer amazement at what she had just heard washed over her. She had just been threatened for the first time in her life, and she could hardly believe it. She stared at the phone, half expecting it to ring again; when it didn't during the following slow two minutes, she lay down again, leaving the lamp on.

Her stomach began to flutter, and her entire body started to tremble. She couldn't relax and knew falling back to sleep for a while would be an impossibility. Someone had actually called and warned her to pack up the crew and equipment and get back to New York, describing in no uncertain terms what would happen to her if she didn't. It was now perfectly clear that the production of this *Perspective* segment was making certain people very nervous indeed—nervous enough to make ridiculous threats. Resentment coupled with journalistic tenacity heated the nape of her neck. Stubborn resolve had merely been intensified in her because of that phone call. She wasn't about to chuck this assignment. Her jaw tightened. If those people thought she—

The muffled ringing of a phone nearly made her jump out of her skin. Even when she realized the ringing was coming from next door, Marc's room, she couldn't stop shaking. She sat up, tense and alert, and when the shrill pealing ceased after two rings, she began to wonder if Marc's caller could be the same as hers had been. No more than a half minute later she heard his door open; muffled footfalls in inner hallway; then two soft raps on her own door. Grabbing her robe, she got out of bed and went across the room.

"Marc?" she called cautiously, and when the deep familiar timbre of his voice answered, she turned lock and knob and opened her door. Earlier she had dreaded having to seeing him again but now he was a blessed sight. His feet bare, his sandy hair sleep-tousled, he stood before her in a short brown terry robe he had thrown on over cream pajama pants.

"I just had a phone call, then stepped out on the balcony and saw your light was on. He called you, too, didn't he?" Marc asked briskly, and when she nodded he stepped into her room, flicking a quick glance over Juliet's short silk robe. "When?"

"Not more than five minutes ago," she told him, her voice a bit quavery. "Then when I heard your phone ring, I thought it might be the same weirdo who called me." A tiny frown of concern notched her brow when Marc went to the French doors that opened onto the balcony, parted the closed drapes a few inches, and tried the door handles. A shiver ran over her as she watched him. "You don't think—"

"No, I don't think anyone will try to break in, but I'm glad to see you lock your doors at night. It can't hurt to be careful," Marc said, coming back to where she stood. His piercing blue eyes bored into the soft depths of hers. "What did our caller say to you, Julie?"

She shrugged lightly. "Oh, you know, it was a typical threat, I guess: 'Forget about trying to get this story and go back where you came from or else.' "

"Or else what?"

"I didn't listen long enough to hear all of it," Juliet murmured, her fingers shaky as she fidgeted with one silk-covered robe button. "The best way to take the fun out of one of those calls is just to slam the phone down. And I hope his ears are still ringing."

A grim sort of understanding smile touched Marc's hard mouth while he allowed his narrowed gaze to wander swiftly over her. "It isn't very pleasant to wake up to a call like that, is it?" he asked softly, bringing one large hand up to lay it gently against the side of her slender neck. "Did he scare you very much, Julie?"

"I think I was more shocked than scared. I've never been threatened before, and though you'd warned me it might happen, I was still a little surprised."

"You're trembling. Come here," he commanded gently, drawing her against him, putting consoling arms around her. "I can't really say you'll ever become accustomed to this sort of thing. None of us do, but after a while it does get a little easier to take it in stride."

With a sigh Juliet allowed her head to rest in the hollow of his shoulder, moving her cheek against the soft terry fabric, needing to be held by him again and knowing she

122

shouldn't give in to that need. Yet she couldn't help it and allowed herself to relax against him, grateful for his reassurances. She was glad he had come to her room because, after the threatening call, she had needed to talk to someone to begin to relax again. Now the warmth that emanated from him eradicated the sense of aloneness she had felt and started slowly to ease her of tension. Her hand clenched against his chest began opening. She felt so amazingly secure and content in his arms that she tilted her head back to smile up at him almost dreamily.

The smile he gave back to Juliet was tenderly sensuous, and the embrace that had been merely comforting for the past several seconds was becoming something altogether different. And he led her into the altered mood of the moment with endearing patience. He freed her shimmering hair from the clip that had confined it on the back of her head, and when it fell softly, he gathered it forward across her left shoulder and buried his face in the glorious thickness. His warm breath stirred scented strands before he kissed her temples, the high curves of her cheeks and the hollows beneath her ears. As he playfully nibbled one soft lobe Juliet's arms glided around him, and she stretched up on tiptoe to rain kisses over the tendons of his neck.

She pressed closer to him. The feel of his firm male body was an enticement she couldn't resist. They seemed to fit so perfectly together, like matching puzzle pieces. His lithe subtly muscled lineation yielded little, while her softer, superbly curved form was more pliantly accommodating to him—and she liked it that way. She in no way felt intimidated by his obviously superior strength. Instead, she felt fantastically feminine, inviting him to enjoy her womanly softness as much as she enjoyed the taut powerful feel of him. It was an invitation he didn't refuse. He untied the silk ribbon on the waist of her robe. His hands went inside to caress her hip and silk beneath his fingers moved sleekly against her equally smooth skin.

"Julie," he murmured, his arms swiftly going around her, tightening, bringing her closer to him. His hands wandered over her back, his fingertips exploring the fine bone structure and firm warm flesh down to the base of her spine and the gentle outsweep of rounded hips. When Julie responded by pressing nearer, he trailed a strand of lingering kisses along the slope of a shoulder, the curve of her neck and the fragile line of jaw and chin. His lips, firm and warm, touched hers, brushing with featherlike strokes over their perfect fullness until they parted with the quickening of her breathing. As he arched her gently against him, his mouth took possession of hers with such a swift rush of intensity that she kissed him back passionately, caught up in a sweet uninhibited expression of needs, both emotional and physical. Exquisitely acute sensations, deep-throbbing and thrilling, swept through her. Marc's very touch on her bare skin was like a stimulus to her every nerve ending, and her shapely arms went up round his neck as she succumbed totally to aroused desire.

Several minutes later Juliet involuntarily murmured soft protest when Marc moved away from her but he held on to her hands, sat down on the edge of her bed, and drew her between his parted legs.

Juliet went willingly, longing to be in his arms again and unable to tear her gaze from the smoldering emberglow promise in his eyes' dark blue depths. Standing very still, she allowed him to slip her robe from her shoulders, down her arms, and off completely. He let it slide from his fingers to drift down and settle with the softest whisper around her bare feet. Marc looked deeply into Juliet's lambent emerald eyes, and the slight smile that touched his lips was a promise too. His intent gaze lowered to her slender body, scarcely concealed by the thigh-length che-

124

mise. In the glow of lamplight behind her the silk became almost transparent, silhouetting her every curve for him. He put his hands on her hips, fingers spreading possessively over her firm buttocks. He drew her to him. His lips sought the rounded curves of her breasts, pressing with easy demand into cushioned flesh and Juliet felt his small smile against her sensitized skin when he heard the soft but audible catching of her breath. Her fingers slipped into his thick sandy hair as she gazed down at him. Waves of heat were already coursing through her and he set her ablaze with fiery desire as his mouth sought the darker aroused peaks of her breasts, outlined moistly against fine silk.

Through the delicate fabric of the chemise Juliet felt as if he were tasting bare flesh as his lips teased the tingling tips of her nipples. With a throaty moan and a rush of warmth that weakened her legs, she couldn't resist as he pulled her down onto his lap, wound her hair around one hand, and tilted her face up to seek her mouth. His lips were firm, possessive, insistent; she responded with an ardor that matched his own. But when he lowered her back on the bed, his long lean body partially covering her and their kisses deepened and his caresses verged on the intimate, she came slowly but irrevocably to her senses.

What she was doing was insane! She knew it even though the passionate woman Marc had awakened in her didn't want to admit it. Yet common sense and a lifetime of being cautious still ruled her existence. She knew she could not make love with Marc. Not only because he believed the worst of her, but because she would truly be involved emotionally, while he wouldn't be, not really. Already she was too much in love with him. She didn't dare risk an intimate relationship that would certainly deepen that love. The very thought of that happening frightened her, and in the split second all those considera-

125

tions were clamoring in her mind, she pulled away from Marc on the bed, her hands catching both of his.

With a muffled curse Marc sat up, raking his fingers through his hair. His eyes bored into hers as she raised up also, tugging at the hem of the chemise, which had twisted high up around her thighs. "If you were faking that response, you've missed your true calling," he muttered, his expression dark as he surveyed her face. "Somehow I don't think you were faking though. Am I right, Julie, or am I wrong? Are you warm, yet cautious? Or are you simply cold and calculating as rumor has it?"

"I see you caught up on all the gossip while you were in New York," Juliet replied icily, the softness in her eyes being replaced by cold hardness. "Did you manage to dredge up all the sordid details about my 'affair' with Henry Alexander?"

"No, I didn't," Marc answered, scrutinizing her closely. "There just seems to be a general assumption that the two of you had something going but the story is peculiarly lacking in specific details, like so-and-so saw you and Henry at such-and-such hotel checking in together. Or someone else saw you and him kissing in his office or in the park—there's none of that. No one who talked to me seemed to have any idea when or where or how often you two saw each other. Either you were very discreet or, as you said, the whole story is a ridiculous lie." He paused, and when he began to speak again she sensed his hesitancy. "I believe you're telling me the truth about not being involved with Henry."

"Oh, you do, do you?" She sat up abruptly and crossed her arms over her chest, glaring at him across the wide bed. "It's about time, dammit." Her tone was hard and unyielding. As unyielding as he had been when he'd unjustly condemned her. He believed her now and probably expected an unqualified and instant forgiveness for all his harsh, insulting accusations. Forgiveness for a betrayal of trust that had hurt her most of all.

"Yes, it is about time," he echoed softly. "I am sorry. Please believe me when I say that."

"But why should I *believe* you, Marc?" Her tone was laced with bitterness, and she felt herself on the brink of tears. "Did you believe me when I asked you to? When I all but begged you to listen?"

She turned her face away from him, not wanting him to see how much it still hurt to recall his scornful words.

She heard him rise off the bed with a sigh—a mournful, desperate sound. He came around to the other side of the bed and stood beside her. Before she could speak, he knelt down and took one of her hands gently into his own, willing her to look at him. "I'm sorry. So sorry, you'll never know. But if you tell me that my words have come too late, I'll go." He stared down at her hand, and absently stroked the sensitive flesh of her palm with the ball of his thumb. "Is it too late, Julie?"

She looked down at him in silence. Perhaps it was the husky tenderness of his plea that had melted the last of her resistance, and smoothed away the last of her anger. Or perhaps it was the fact that she knew full well deep in her heart she had already forgiven him. She didn't stop very long to analyze her feelings. The man she loved was reaching out to her, begging her for reassurance, and she couldn't bear to make him wait an instant longer.

"It's not too late," she barely whispered, laying her other hand on top of his. "I do believe you . . . please don't go."

She could only feel relief and warmth inside again and as she looked up at him, her slow smile widened just enough to create tiny dimples in her cheeks. But Marc didn't smile back. "God, you do have the most beautiful mouth," he murmured abruptly. His voice was rough and sensuous and almost irresistible as he rose to sit beside her and reached for her with an appealingly urgent *"Julie."*

For an instant, seduced by his voice and his warm hands around her waist, Juliet swayed toward him, but her earlier resolve still surged strongly enough through her to prevent her from giving in to temptation. Although it was difficult, she resisted as Marc started pulling her to him. Her hands came up against his broad chest and, denying herself the pleasure of tracing the muscles rippling beneath her fingertips, she shook her head. "Marc, this is so crazy," she whispered. "You have to understand now why this can't go on between us. I'd just be asking to be gossiped about more than I already am."

"Henry's married, Julie. I'm not. The circumstances aren't at all alike."

"In one way they are. You have so much influence at Union Broadcasting that people would assume I was using a relationship with you to further my career, just as they assumed I was using Henry. I can't risk starting the tongues wagging full speed again. I'll be lucky if I ever live all this other gossip down."

Bringing a hand up from her waist, Marc traced the slight downcurving of her mouth with one fingertip as his penetrative eyes seemed to try to plumb the depths of hers. When her lips parted at last to his grazing touch, he gave her a slow indulgent smile. "Julie, no matter how afraid you are of possible gossip, you must know you can't fight this. We want each other too much. It's inevitable that—"

"No," she murmured, shaking her head once more. "No, nothing is absolutely inevitable."

"This is," was his low, compelling reply, and as if to prove his point, he lifted her chin with one finger and lowered his head.

The moment his warm lips brushed her own, Juliet's mind was waging a losing battle with her traitorous body and emotions. Passion, piqued by their earlier embraces, was too near the surface to be suppressed. She felt consumed in a blazing sheet of flames when his palms, curving around the straining sides of her breasts, recalled his mouth's possession of the still-sensitive peaks through the delicate silk. Suddenly she needed desperately for him to do that again, and this time to skin bared for his kisses. She was caught up in a longing like no other she had ever experienced—even that first night when she had realized she loved him and had come so close to giving herself in love to him. Now they had been apart too long, and all her pent-up desire overpowered her and as they kissed, she opened his robe. She swayed against him, her warm lissome body inflaming his own needs, and he bore her back down on the bed with an urgent swiftness that brooked no denial.

When Marc lifted Juliet's chemise off over her head and tossed it aside, she had already pushed his robe from his shoulders, urging him to discard it. Now she was running her hands over him, wanting to possess as much as to be possessed. She couldn't get her fill of touching him, of playing her lips against his. And when he wound her hair around one hand, holding her still as his mouth sought first one breast then the other, she lay making soft pleasured sounds and lazily drew her fingernails back and forth across his own hard nipples.

Trembling with her caress, Marc teased the tips of her rounded flesh with his tongue, his teeth, and his breath. He tenderly caught the firm budding nubs between the edges of his teeth and flicked his tongue over and around them, tasting their sweetness, exploring their texture. His breath feathered her skin, and when he closed his mouth around one throbbing circle then the other, drawing at her with thrilling pressure, she took his lean face in her hands,

129

holding him to her as she slowly flexed one leg, brushing it between his.

Marc's wholly masculine response was a promise that made her feel faint with rushing delight. She moved beside him on the bed until they were in each other's arms, their lips meeting again. He trailed his hand down her side, charting the curve of her waist and rounded line of her hip, exploring with a gentleness that also conveyed a near-ly intolerable passion as her fingers plied the heated flesh of his chest, sides, and naked back with soft arousing caresses.

"Julie," he whispered, parting her knees with a hand that glided steadily upward between satiny thighs, upward to irresistible warmth. His spellbinding gaze enslaved hers.

"Oh," she breathed ardently when his fingertips moved over her, warm and rousing through a gossamer-thin bar-rier of fabric. As she looked at him a drowsy sensuous smile graced her lips. She lovingly touched his face even as danger signals went off in her head, telling her she would be courting pure emotional chaos if she submitted to her desires and his. Although the warning registered in her brain, she was prepared to ignore it but apparently part of what she was thinking was reflected in the depths of her luminous eyes. She heard Marc's slowly indrawn breath, felt the gradual tightening of his entire body, and saw him shake his head.

"When are you going to stop being so unsure of me?" he asked almost indulgently, stroking her arms. "When we make love the first time, I want to see certainty instead of uncertainty in your eyes. I won't settle for less than that, Julie."

Disappointed? Relieved? Juliet didn't know which she was feeling. She wanted to say something to him but couldn't and merely lay there watching him. Her thoughts

130

were a riot of sheer confusion; they seemed to race in circles round and round inside her head. She wanted to make love with him, wanted to give herself to him and attain the fulfillment of love for herself, yet he was right—she still had lingering doubts. Bewildered, she drew in a long tremulous breath and almost wished he had simply taken what she had been offering and thus put an end to all this maddening indecision.

He hadn't, however. Nothing important is ever easy and this quandary wasn't going to be solved easily for Juliet. Facing that fact, she accepted her chemise when Marc pressed into her hands and sat up on the edge of the bed to turn it right-side-out.

"You won't always be unsure though," Marc said softly, moving behind her to press a kiss into the enticing arch at the small of her back. "Somehow I'm going to make you sure of me, and I'll wait as long as it takes. That's how much I want you, Julie. Remember that."

The teasing, feathery lightness of his warm breath on her skin was more than she could withstand at the moment; it was as if his promise were branding itself in her memory. She would remember what he said all right. A woman in love never forgets such provocative words, but right then she was swamped with confusion, unable to deal with his touch or even the well-loved cadence of his deep voice. And, needing time alone, she moved beyond his reach and wriggled into the chemise while he got up from the bed, thrusting his long arms into his robe. Her eyes followed him to the door, where he paused a moment, hand on the knob, and looked back at her with a reassuring smile.

"I'll ring the desk and tell them not to put any more calls through up here tonight," he said quietly. "You try to get back to sleep now."

Nodding silently, Juliet watched him go and when he

closed the door behind him, automatically locking it, she breathed a deep sigh. Sleep wouldn't come easily—and she knew it—but it wasn't the threatening phone call she had received that would disrupt her night's sleep. Marc was quite capable of doing that all by himself. Pensively nibbling at her lower lip, she slipped between the sheets again and switched off the lamp but lay awake for long tedious hours, trying to sort out all her contradictory emotions.

CHAPTER EIGHT

The following Monday night Juliet wrapped her arms lightly around her pillow and drowsily burrowed her cheek deeper into its softness. Curled up in the center of her bed like a lazy cat, she was pleasantly drifting closer and closer to that point where she would actually fall asleep. Fragmented thoughts of Marc spun vaguely in her head, receded sometimes, and were replaced with less and less distinct thoughts about the story they were seeking. It was that spiraling-down time that comes just before actual sleep and brings with it a sense of well-being. As Juliet floated peacefully nearer the edge where conscious thought would cease, however, she reluctantly became aware of a faint but annoying scratching sound. Though she tried to ignore it, the noise was naggingly persistent, dragging her back toward fuller awareness, though she longed for sleep.

The scratching became more distinct in her ears, sounding more like a faraway scraping of metal on metal. Her mind automatically increased its level of alertness and delivered a swift message to her body. Juliet felt herself tense and as her heart seemed to pick up a few extra beats, she cursed mentally in sheer frustration. After she had come to bed, it had taken an hour of tossing and turning for her to come this close to going to sleep and now, she thought, some damn irritating little noise was rapidly bringing her awake again.

What was that blasted sound? Juliet knew if she could identify it, she could maybe get up and put an end to it, then climb back into bed with perhaps some hope of not having to endure another hour of tossing and turning. She lay very still, listening. After a short moment, she realized the scratching was coming from the closed balcony doors —outside the balcony doors. It wasn't the wind, because the wind rattled doors; it didn't scratch at them. Her body tensed with alarm. Perhaps the small branch of a tree was scraping one of the glass panes? No, it couldn't be, her still somewhat fuzzy brain chided itself. There was a balcony out there, not trees. But if not the wind, if not the branch of a tree . . . what then?

Uneasiness crept over Juliet, and she opened her eyes for the first time. She propped herself up on her elbows. The ceaseless scratching was sounding increasingly more ominous with each passing second of time. Her heart gave a little lurch as she swung her feet off onto the floor and rose silently from the bed. She started toward the French windows, compelled to go even though the shadows in her room seemed to be crowding in on her. *Nothing but my overactive imagination,* she told herself in a fit of bravado, because by now she was a little scared. But of what? Planning to find out, she stepped up to the doors. The drapes were closed, and as she lifted a hand, intending to part them and peek out, the bank of clouds that had been passing front of a full moon drifted on. Pearl-white moonlight showered down onto the balcony and silhouetted the hunched figure just outside the French doors. An instant later the figure moved, straightened up, and became unmistakably a man!

Juliet stifled the gasp that rose rapidly in her throat by slapping hand over hand across her opening mouth. She felt as if the bottom had been knocked out of her stomach. Her insides, as well as her arms and legs, became weak and for the merest fraction of a second her mind mixed signals in a frenzy, then fought for control of itself but only met with partial success. Juliet knew that the man was trying to break into her room, but she also knew that only a distance of about two feet—and two not particularly substantial doors—separated her from him and she could only stare out, wanting to believe she was only dreaming. She finally realized that she could see the man because he was in the light, but she wasn't, and he couldn't possibly see her standing only feet from him. That realization comforted her very little. Then there came the grating sound of the door handles turning, slowly turning! Her heartbeat bombarded her ears. Feeling as helpless as a rabbit in a trap, she froze there, unable to move until the doors didn't swing open and the man bent down. Metal began scraping metal again. Momentary relief flowed over her. He hadn't unlocked the doors yet.

And she couldn't continue to stand here in a panic. Scream, something told her. But no, she didn't want to scream because the man would only run away then, and she wanted him caught. She had enough presence of mind to know that. Slowly she started backing toward the door to the inside hallway, afraid to take her eyes off the French doors for fear the man would suddenly slam them open, burst into the room, and grab her from behind if she didn't keep watching him. Her progress toward the door possessed a nightmarish quality. She felt as if she were caught up in a slow-motion videotape. *Stop thinking like a television producer! Just get the hell out of here!* Juliet kept moving.

Her hand held out behind her touched the door at last. She found the knob and turned the lock as quietly as she could. When she opened the door, the light from the corridor was going to spill into her room. The man would see it even through the drapes. But who gave a damn? By the time he did see it, she would be at Marc's door, and that's all she really cared about. She wanted the man caught, but if he wasn't, she couldn't help it. She certainly couldn't stay in there.

With a quick shallow intake of breath Juliet turned the knob, jerked open the door, and bounded out, imagining she heard the sound of cracking glass behind her as she leaped forward. That made her feet fairly fly down the hallway, and she didn't wait to come to a complete stop before Marc's door before she began banging with her fist, then turning the knob back and forth urgently as she called his name.

When it opened almost immediately, she moved into the room, grasping a muscular forearm with one hand while the other gestured expressively. "A man on the balcony, outside my door," she whispered, breathing fast. "He's trying to break in."

Marc broke her grip on his arm effortlessly and, for a man who had just been awakened, he moved with incredible sureness and speed, striding across the room to his own French doors. Silently he unlocked and opened them.

"Be careful, Marc, please," Juliet called softly after him as he stepped out on the balcony, but the words were so low and rasping as they came out of her dry mouth, she was sure he couldn't have heard them. Fear squeezed her throat again, fear for Marc this time rather than for herself. Without conscious thought she closed the door to the inside hall without making a sound, then rested back against it, her palms pressed flat on the lower hardwood panel. She waited, but the need to know what was happening outside was agonizing; she listened, but the dragging silence roared horribly in her ears. And when she heard something thud against the balcony's floor planking, she

136

propelled herself toward the French doors, terrified Marc might have been knocked down and hurt. Then there was the sound of running footsteps. The man was trying to get away. But what about Marc? Unable to bear the dreadful suspense any longer, she stepped outside and nearly sobbed with relief when Marc walked back to her.

"He was starting to creep away before I got out there, and when he heard me, he bolted. I went after him, but barefoot I didn't have a chance of catching him," Marc explained calmly, taking Juliet's arm to lead her back into his room. He stopped inside, turned her to him. "Are you all right?"

"What was that thump I heard?" she exclaimed softly, wide emerald eyes searching him for possible injury. "I thought—"

"During his getaway, he knocked over one of those potted trees on the balcony. Unfortunately he kept his balance. If he'd tripped, I might have caught him."

"If you had, though, he might have gotten violent. Maybe it's just as well you didn't." Juliet shuddered and chewed her lower lip. "If . . . he had gotten into my room . . . What do you think he meant to do?"

"I don't think he intended to hurt you. I really think this was just another attempt to intimidate you, Julie. Maybe he just broke in to steal something, so you would know someone had been in your room while you were sleeping."

"He just kept picking at the lock," Juliet murmured. "Obviously a determined man."

"Also a man who won't get caught for this, I'm afraid. I didn't see his face but I did see he was wearing gloves. No fingerprints. And I'm sure he's long gone from here already," said Marc, reaching for the phone. "Better call the sheriff anyway."

It only took a short time for a deputy sheriff to arrive

quietly, and he left less than fifteen minutes later, carrying with him a wire left in the door lock, though he said he doubted it was worth much as evidence. After he was gone, Marc walked over to where Juliet was standing beside his bed, his expression gently compassionate when she looked up at him.

"You know, I still can't believe this is happening," she told him bewilderedly. "Someone wanted me to realize he had broken into my room just to try to scare me away. It's almost ludicrous. These people must be crazy. Don't you think so?"

"You were very scared," Marc stated perceptively, his brilliant blue eyes impaling the soft green of hers. "Weren't you, Julie?"

"Yes, I was," she admitted in a whisper, then stepped into his arms and clasped her own around his waist. He enfolded her in a light embrace and she leaned against him, happy to be close to him again. He stroked her back and his hands warmed her skin even through the thickness of her gown and the robe he had brought from her room for her to wear. She could almost imagine she could feel the pleasant masculine rough texture of his fingertips, and slowly but surely the fear that had lingered in her was coaxed from her by his ministering hands.

With the fear vanquished at least for the present, only need remained, a need to stay with him. Warmed to the bone and totally relaxed by his nearness, Juliet lifted her head from his shoulder and looked up at his beloved face. She felt no apprehension, only wonder, as her eyes met his, and she saw what she wanted to see in the depths—a faint glint of light that suddenly flared brighter. When he leaned down, she pressed closer against him and her parted lips met the masterly touch of his. The kisses she gave him were meant to tease and arouse—and they succeeded. With a deep-throated murmur he gathered her tighter to

138

him, arching her slender, lushly curved body over the supportive arm around her back. He kissed her more demandingly, opening her mouth beneath his to explore its sweetness, and when the tip of her tongue played along the edge of his, he curved a hand over the rise of her hips and held her lower body against hard muscular thighs.

There is a theory that danger shared between a man and a woman has an aphrodisiacal effect. But Juliet knew what had happened tonight had little to do with her present response to Marc. He simply hadn't touched her since he had left her bed Thursday night and, because he hadn't, she had felt bereft. Now she was in his arms again; hers were around him; and she felt too gloriously alive to consider the consequences of what she knew very well she was inviting. Later she might regret her actions, but she seriously doubted it. She loved Marc, and it felt right for her to want to give all of herself to him and take what he would give. Tonight loving sensuality held sway; she reveled in her femininity and ached to share it with him. And as his hard but tender hands swept over her with increasingly persuasive demand, the need to know Marc as only a woman can know a man could no longer be denied; her need and his had to be fulfilled. With caressing hands she pushed aside the lapels of his robe and sought his bare chest, feathering evocatively light fingertips over the hard nubs of his nipples. She took one between her teeth and nibbled gently, desire surging hotly in her as he shuddered with the caress.

"Julie," he groaned, tilting her head back in one hand to search her eyes. "You know where this is leading?"

"Yes," she murmured, playing her fingers teasingly over the fine hairs on his chest, pressing her softly parted lips into the hollow at the base of his throat. "Yes, yes, I know."

139

"And you're sure it's really what you want?" he muttered roughly, arms tightening around her. "Is it?"

Juliet leaned back in his arms to look at him. Her soft smile beckoned. "Take down my hair, Marc," she whispered and, watching the blue fire ignite in his eyes, knew that he understood as well as she did that now there could be no turning back. She visually explored his face while he undid the clasp that held her loosely upswept hair. She saw the intensity of his expression and recognized passion enhanced by an endearing tenderness. For her, he was the perfect man to love. Perhaps she hadn't really been suppressing her sexuality until now after all—perhaps she had simply been waiting for someone as special to her as Marc was with whom to share an intimate involvement. Other men she had kept at a distance had accused her of being cold—some had even said frigid. She had almost begun to believe they were right, but that had been a mistake because those men had been wrong. She wasn't frigid in the least. She was simply selective, and now that she was in the arms of a man she could like and respect and even love, all her intrinsic warmth enveloped him. When her hair cascaded down over Marc's hands, she reached out to untie his robe, her gaze softly seductive as she pushed the terry fabric off his broad, sun-browned shoulders.

Marc's smile was sensually exciting. He returned the gesture, hands warm as he removed the satiny forest-green robe that accentuated the color of her eyes and matched the floor-length gown that sleekly clung to her every curve. His gaze traveled over her. "You wear very sexy nightgowns, Miss York," he said, his tone softly playful. "You obviously enjoy looking irresistible."

"Am I?" she responded as playfully. "Irresistible, I mean."

"Shall I show you how irresistible?"

"I'd like it very much if you did," she murmured,

putting her hands in his when he held them out. A shivery little thrill of delight danced over her as his thumbs moved in light circles over the pulses in her wrists. Marc sat down in the chair behind him, silently pulling her to him. With a warm rush of anticipation Juliet moved gracefully onto his lap.

Thursday night Juliet and Marc had been swept up swiftly in whirlwind of passion but this night was to be different. Desire would arise steadily but more slowly, allowing them to savor fully every exquisite touch, every dizzying kiss.

Marc watched her face as she settled warmly in his lap. His arms encircled her gently. "You have such a lovely mouth," he murmured, his smile soft. "Have I ever told you that?"

Juliet smiled back. "Uh-huh, but tell me again. I like to hear it."

"You have the most beautiful mouth, Julie," he complied, rubbing the side of one lean finger across her lips. "So soft and sweet and incredibly kissable."

"You happen to have a very terrific mouth yourself." Lifting a hand, Juliet stroked first one corner then the other with a fingertip before tracing the firmly curved outline of his lips. When, without warning, he caught the tip of her finger between his teeth and nibbled tenderly, an tremor of excitement rippled through her, and her free hand drifted over the expanse of his chest to his neck. Her fingers pushed under the clean crisp ends of his sandy hair on his nape, tangling in the thickness, exploring the vi brant texture. Marc stopped nibbling her fingertip only to cover that hand with his to press her palm against his lips. He found the mound of flesh at the base of her thumb. His teeth sank gently into it, and when she trembled with the powerful sensations he evoked, the tip of his tongue tasted her skin.

Closing her eyes, Juliet stroked his face, her fingers brushing the line of his brow, the bridge of his nose, the smooth taut skin over his cheeks, and the firm line of strong jaw and chin, as if she were committing the exact contours of his features to memory. For a long time Marc simply held her, allowing her tactile exploration to continue. Then, at last, he touched her, too, his curved hand grazing upward along her slender neck and cupping her face before his own fingers began a slow exploration of her features. When he feathered a fingertip along the ends of her long thick lashes, she caught her breath. She had never imagined how rousing his simple touching of her face would be. Her eyes opened. In the blue depths of his, she saw both sensuality and sensitivity, and in that moment she had never loved anyone in her life more than she did him. She turned her head and pressed a kiss into the hollow of his shoulder as she inhaled the heady, spicy, clean male scent of him.

"My sweet Julie," he whispered, one arm still supporting her back. The hard edge of his hand moved with evocative slowness over the front of her gown, resting heavily for a tantalizing moment in the valley between firmly uprising breasts before continuing the downward journey past her waist to her abdomen. His fingers spread apart and slipped lower. Breathless, Juliet awaited an intimate touch, and there was an empty throbbing deep within her when, instead of touching, Marc's hand trailed back up her body again.

Fascinated with the muscular curvature of his free arm, Juliet ran a hand around and along the sensitive inner surface and up over the ball of his shoulder. She skimmed her thumb around the hard edge of his right ear, delighted as a light shudder of excitement went over him. Her drowsy eyes sought his. "Kiss me, Marc," she whispered. "Now."

142

A half smile moved his carved lips. "You kiss me, Julie."

She did. Curving a hand around the back of his neck, she urged his head down while raising herself slightly. When he cooperated by tightening his embrace, holding her securely against him, she turned. Her breasts were warm and resiliently soft against his chest as her full lips began to part and close teasingly on the firm shape of his. Her heart jumped with a surge of happiness when Marc made a low sound and claimed her mouth with a gentle but swiftly intensifying kiss. Strong arms across her back molded her supple form to him, and his fingertips stroking the straining sides of her breast seemed to sear her skin. Emboldened by their kisses and rising desire, she moved the tip of her tongue playfully over his lips. His impassioned response inflamed her senses. As his mouth hungrily possessed hers, thrills rushed in waves through her, intensifying the central emptiness she was feeling. Her slender arms were around him, her hands moving feverishly over his broad back, and she was warmly weak and acquiescent against him.

Marc laid a hand on Juliet's right hipbone, silently urging her to lie flat across his thighs again. When she moved with graceful fluidity and a soft whisper of satin, he pushed the gown's thin straps off her shoulders and down her arms, then lowered the top of her gown until it draped around her waist. Smouldering passion glowed in his narrowed eyes as he surveyed creamy, smooth bare skin.

"God, you're beautiful," he murmured, meeting her gaze. "I could look at you forever."

"I wish you would," she whispered, an almost tremulous smile touching her lips in response to his. "I . . . like for you to look at me."

"And do you like for me to touch you too?"

"Yes," she breathed. In both her hands she took one of his and brought it up between her breasts, sighing her pleasure when he cupped first one then the other. His thumb played over and around one hardening peak while his forefinger caressed its equally aroused twin as he asked of her, "And would you like for me to kiss you here . . . and here?"

She felt she was melting under his mesmerizing gaze. Somehow unable to answer his last question in words, she did so with action. When he lowered his head slightly, her fingers tangled in his thick hair and she guided his lips to a throbbing nipple.

"Julie," Marc whispered huskily, flicking his tongue over the upsurging and sensitized tip. "You taste like honey."

And when he suddenly closed his mouth around softly resilient flesh, Juliet's hushed gasp of delight accompanied the slight upward arching of her body. She had reached the point where all she cared about was that he go on touching her. And during the following glorious minutes as he kissed and caressed and tasted her breasts, she rubbed a hand slowly back and forth against the firm plane of his flat abdomen then traced the circle of his navel with one fingertip until he groaned and moved to cover her mouth with his own.

"Julie, now I have to see all of you," he muttered after several lengthening heat-inducing kisses that had been delightful yet not enough for either of them. Cupping her jaw in one hand, he looked deeply into her eyes. "Take off your gown for me."

As Marc lowered her feet to the floor and she stood, she felt dizzy in the grip of emotions more intense than she had ever known. And it was her own need for intimacy as well as Marc's that allowed her to overcome her basic shyness and slip her gown down over her trim hips, then

144

step out of it after it rustled down onto the floor. She glanced up at Marc and saw his scorching gaze roam over her. Although she felt she was suddenly being consumed by a fire that was burning her, she slipped her thumbs beneath the elastic of her bikini panties. Then she stood very still, hesitating.

"Yes, those too. Let me, Julie," Marc commanded softly with a hint of an understanding smile. Putting his hands on her hips, he eased her a step closer to the chair. Then his long fingers glided beneath the elastic, and he slid the panties down her long shapely legs.

Juliet stepped out of them as Marc's hands returned to span her waist. She was already trembling slightly, but her knees felt as if they might buckle under her when Marc leaned forward to trail lazy kisses along the length of her right thigh and across her fluttering abdomen up to her navel.

He stood. Juliet could hardly catch her breath as she gazed up at him towering over her, yet when he swiftly took her into his arms, she knew she was where she belonged.

"I'm going to explore every inch of you," he promised, his warm breath tickling in her ear and sending a sensual shiver over her. He nibbled at the tender fleshy lobe. Juliet moved sinuously against him, her bare, heated flesh pliant and tempting, inviting his touch. His hands drifted over her, following every enticing curve. Juliet stroked his lean taut sides. She slid her fingertips beneath the elastic of his pajama pants, following the waistband around to the center of his back. Slowly, provocatively, she gently drew them down, her touch lingering along each of his lean legs. Muscles rippled in his thighs at her touch then became like bands of steel as Marc lifted her up in his arms to carry her to bed.

When he laid her down, her head nestled into the

depression in the pillow that his head had made. Bathed in soft lamplight, she watched as Marc came to her; she was fascinated by the bronze glow of his skin and the masculine lineation of his tapered waist, lean taut hips, and long strong hair-roughened legs. When he simply stood by the bed, looking down at her for several seconds, her wandering gaze at last drifted upward to met his. Juliet pulled the sheet up over her but turned down the corner nearest Marc invitingly and smiled softly at him. A pleasant weakness dragged at her lower limbs, and her heart began to beat even more rapidly when Marc came into the bed beneath the light cover with her. Inwardly she trembled a little, though she wasn't at all surprised when he slowly drew the sheet down to the foot of the bed, uncovering her and himself at the same time.

Resting on one elbow on his side, he ran his fingers through her hair, which was fanned out on the pillow beneath her head as he murmured, "You don't mind the light?"

Feeling lost in the depths of his incredibly azure eyes, she shook her head. How could she possibly mind? Marc was the man she loved and now that the time had come for her to give freely of her love, she wanted to experience every moment to its fullest. In the light she would be able to see each movement of his lithe naked body; she would be able to see his face.

Almost as if he could read her thoughts, he added huskily, "I want to be looking into your eyes when we—"

"Oh, Marc," she whispered tremulously, turning to kiss him, afraid if he finished saying what he had been about to say that she would want him to take her quickly. And instinct told her it would be better later—all the better for the waiting—and as Marc responded to her kiss by pulling her closer and holding her fast against him, she breathed his name again and again.

146

Passion seemed to rise to a nearly intolerable level in Marc, but he held it in tight rein even as he swiftly bore her back down on the mattress and imprisoned her slender body beneath the partial weight of his. Firm, commanding lips lightly twisted the soft shape of hers and Juliet responded ardently as wild sensations plunged with stiletto sharpness through her. Marc lay over her as their mouths met and parted repeatedly in languid yet deeply searching kisses. Swept up in a world where only feelings and her love for him existed, she was swiftly losing any inhibitions that had lingered in her. This was the night of her complete sexual awakening, and she felt she was freeing both body and soul to bask in the pleasure of it all. Cupping Marc's face in her hands, she urged a more poignantly demanding possession of her mouth. As his lips moved maraudingly against hers she entangled her legs with his, rubbing a silky smooth thigh along the rigid column of aroused masculinity. Marc groaned softly, and her heart seemed to leap in delight as his hand, playing over her round breasts, squeezed and massaged her before gliding down to slip between her thighs. Juliet's pulses pounded in hot anticipation as she slowly moved her legs apart and, with Marc's first touch, pleasure rushed through her with such force that she moaned softly.

Juliet feathered a hand down his body and a smooth hardness stirred potently against her stroking palm as Marc's fingers moved gently over her, probing her most secret femininity with such rousing caresses that she felt almost faint with desire. Soon, when his exploration became even more intimate and he sought ultimate inner warmth, Juliet's softly encouraging sigh accompanied Marc's swiftly drawn breath. Opening her eyes, she looked into the tanned face so near her own and met his somewhat loving gaze.

"Julie, relax," he said unevenly, lowering his head again

147

almost at once to continue scattering warm nibbling kisses over the creamy skin of her neck, murmuring between them, "I want you so much. I want it to be wonderful for you."

He couldn't see the anxious light in her eyes. She brushed a hand over his sandy hair and asked quietly, "Do you mind very much that I . . . I'm rather . . . inexperienced?"

"Mind?" The kisses had ceased. He had lifted his head and was staring at her. "Do *I* mind?"

"I mean, I just don't want this to be a disappointment to you." she whispered, hesitancy in her voice and in lambent emerald eyes.

Her experience with men was limited, to say the least. Though she had cared and had wanted to be close to one or two men in her past, no man's touch had ever aroused her like Marc's. Men had turned away from her, calling her unresponsive, cold—or worse. But no one before Marc had ever approached her with such patience and tenderness and passion. In answer she seemed to come alive in Marc's arms. Now she was desperately worried if she would be able to express all the love and longing she felt for him; to please him, as she was sure he would please her.

The smile tugging upward at the corners of his mouth was followed by his low soft laughter as he shook his head. "No, I doubt very much you'll be a disappointment," he whispered back. "After all, experience and technique aren't nearly as important as feelings."

"Well, then we shouldn't have any problems," she said, lifting her head off the pillow a couple inches to touch her lips to his. "This is what we both want, isn't it?"

Without answering, Marc regarded her closely, searching her eyes as the backs of his curved fingers brushed over the rapid pulsebeat in her throat and his thumb pressed gently over her chin, tugging her mouth open slightly. His lips descended onto hers with an initial gentleness that lingered even as his kisses became passionately insistent again. When Juliet wrapped her arms around him once more and arched against him, he wound her hair around one hand and tilted her head back slightly on the pillow as his mouth sought the gentle curve of her neck.

Moments later he was kissing the taut opalescent skin of her breasts, then tenderly nibbling each desire-tipped nipple in its turn until Juliet's breath was coming in soft quick little gasps. "God, yes, this is what I want," he muttered roughly, lips seeming to sear her flesh. "I've never wanted anyone as much as I want you, Julie."

"Then love me, Marc," she whispered, her hands tightening over his shoulders. "Love me now."

"Soon. Very soon," he promised, his warm minty breath filling her throat as his lips tasted the honeyed sweetness of hers again.

Shivery delight raced over her when he lowered his head and trailed lingering kisses around her narrow waist. The skin there was so sensitive, his mere touch would have been rousing enough; the feel of his firm lips and warm breath on her nearly drove her crazy. Her hands moved in circular strokes over his broad upper back, and his chest and his shoulders began to shake slightly but not from fear when slowly he drew a hand upward between her thighs.

Her eyes tightly closed, Juliet caught the curve of her bottom lip between her teeth as she waited, waited, feeling she might faint if he touched her that way again or die from longing if he didn't. Then, when at last the touch came, it was more exquisitely pleasurable than the first had been, his caressing fingers exploring more gently, in obvious consideration, yet also moving more possessively with a surer knowledge of her responses.

As he had obviously meant to do, Marc succeeded in

149

arousing her desire to a feverish pitch and as sensations rushing through her became both ecstasy and torment, he slipped an arm round her waist to bring her directly beneath him. His hand glided down to cup her hips and lift them and Juliet could feel the pulsating pressure of him against her. Her eyes fluttered open, dreamy green and warm with love as they looked into the fathomless depths of his.

When he smoothed her tousled hair, she brushed a kiss against his cheek and whispered, "Now, Marc."

"Yes. Now," he whispered back, the pressure of him against her increasing slowly until, with a wondrously gentle penetrative thrust, he entered her.

Juliet pressed her nails into the corded muscles of Marc's shoulders as his lips swooped down on hers, catching up the first soft sound she made while the warmth inside her flowered open to welcome his filling hardness. His lips brushed hers tenderly; his tongue opened her mouth, and as his kiss lingered, a melting warmth gave way to the tingling awareness of partial fulfillment. Her hands relaxed on his shoulders; her fingers caressed smooth sun-bronzed skin as he scattered kisses across her cheek up to her temple.

"All right?" he asked, his deep voice hushed.

"Ummm, I'm just fine," she murmured, becoming lost in the tiny pleased smile that moved his hard mouth, seeing affection in it. Marc was fond of her; she knew that, and because she loved him so much, this intimate merging of their bodies touched her very soul. Sheer joy flowed in her, and with an emotional whispering of his name she brushed her lips over his, kissed him, then kissed him again and again until he began to move within her. Soon she was moving with him, and they were creating ever-increasing delight for each other as she met each of his deliciously slow rousing strokes.

An aggressive yet incredibly patient lover, Marc introduced Juliet to the delights of lovemaking with extraordinary finesse. Every kiss, every caress, every movement of his lean muscular body was tenderly insistent and heightened her responsiveness. Although she was normally a rather reserved person, her feelings for him allowed her to become an uninhibited lover. Feminine instinct guided her, and she felt she had become all woman: warm and enticing and tempting. Yet, despite his obviously intensifying need to seek total satisfaction, Marc held at bay his nearly uncontrollable passion, and she loved him all the more for caring enough to do that. Together they swirled slowly up in a sensuously misty world of their own making; each plateau of pleasure they reached more keenly irresistible than the one before.

Alive with nerve-shattering sensations, the fires inside her stoked by Marc's tenderly masterly thrusts, Juliet clung to him, her hands sweeping lovingly over his bare back, feeling she would cry out if completion didn't come soon. And, in that moment, she was borne swiftly up to a piercing pinnacle of ecstasy beyond expression.

"Oh Marc, yes! Yes, *yes,*" she gasped as tidal waves of rapture pulsated deeply in her: physically exquisite, emotionally fulfilling. Her heart was pounding. She was trembling. The waves receded only to surge to the finely honed crest of delight again and, as she moaned breathlessly, she wound her long legs around Marc, pressing him against her, compelling him to join her at the keenest peak of completion. And he took her with such tender fierceness that she felt infinitely desired and precious and found an ultimate emotional joy in the giving.

Afterward Juliet lay, warm and replete, in Marc's arms, her legs still sinuously entwined with his. Her head rested against his chest and beneath her ear; his heartbeat was slowing to a normal rate as hers was. Love for him and blissful contentment filled her very being. She breathed a long shuddering sigh, massaging his shoulder gently as his fingers toyed with that notorious tendril of her hair that was always too rebellious to be confined.

"I suppose I should be sorry for being the scoundrel who robbed you of your innocence," Marc murmured after a while. "But I'm not sorry, Julie, and I hope you're not."

She shook her head. Regret was not what she felt now. Later she might be sorry she had committed herself to him so completely, but at the moment she didn't think so. Moving slightly so she could see his face, she smiled faintly and saw the rather wicked teasing glint in his blue eyes as he smiled back.

"You are delightful," he whispered, touching the end of her nose with a fingertip. "Besides being intelligent and lovely, you're also terrific in bed."

Juliet's smile deepened as she playfully prodded his side with her elbow, but as she gazed at him for several moments, her expression became more serious. "I'm glad it was you, Marc," she said softly, coming as close to a declaration of love as she could. "Very glad."

"God, I am too," he answered, his low tone warm and sincere as he gathered her closer to him. "What we shared was very special to me, Julie."

Afloat in the warm afterglow of love given and need fulfilled, Juliet snuggled lazily against him, finding sweet contentment in the words he had said as she drifted gently off to sleep.

CHAPTER NINE

Marc's kisses awakened Juliet Tuesday morning. His warm lips, firm yet coaxingly tender, nuzzled the hollow just beneath her left ear, tantalizing sensitive skin and sending a pleasant shiver of awareness over her. Despite her extreme drowsiness, the memory of the night she and Marc had shared was arousing. Still relaxed in the glow of a supreme sense of physical well-being, she turned lazily beneath the arm flung across her waist and ran a hand over his chest up to the ball of his shoulder.

"Ummm, morning," she whispered throatily, still half asleep. Struggling to open her eyes, she peeked at him through the thick fringe of her lashes, just able to see his tanned face clearly in the pale gray light. She smiled dreamily. "What time is it?"

"Early, very early," he murmured, touching his lips to hers. His hand moved up to rub feather-lightly over full taut breasts, then he pressed her lithe pliant body against the hard length of his. "Sweet, sweet Julie. You're very cuddly when you first wake up, so cuddly in fact, I'd like to keep you in bed with me all day."

"Unfortunately we have to work," she reminded him softly. Capturing his hand in hers, she drew it up from her breasts to her collarbone, trying to ignore the thrill of excitement his caress had evoked in her. Her eyes opened

153

wider, looked in to his. "And I have to go back to my own room, Marc."

Smiling provocatively, he shook his head. "Why in the world should you want to do that? It's much too early to get up and stay up, so why leave this warm bed to go back to that cold one of yours?"

"Stop trying to tempt me into staying," she chided lightly, scooting a few inches away from him, toward her side of the bed. "I can go back to my room now without having to worry about anybody being up to see me leave yours."

"Well, if that's all that's bothering you, I can set your mind at ease. It's only five thirty," he whispered coaxingly, moving toward her on the mattress. "You'll have plenty of time later to get back to your room without being seen."

"But, Marc—"

"That's why I woke you this early—so we would have plenty of time before we had to think about getting up," he continued, reaching out one hand to gently grip her waist as she inched further away from him. "Come on, Julie. You know you'd rather stay with me the next couple of hours than leave."

"Maybe I would, but I'd be crazy to stay with you that long," she argued breathlessly, slipping from beneath his light grasp. With lissome swiftness she rolled to the edge of the bed and off to stand naked in the pink-gray light of dawn. She looked down at Marc, saw his gaze roam freely over her, and shook her head. "No. I just can't stay. By seven thirty, three fourths of the crew will be up and around. Someone would be bound to see me leaving your room and you really wouldn't want that to happen, would you?"

Raising up on one elbow in the bed, Marc quirked a

dark brown eyebrow. "Frankly I don't really care what the crew knows about us and last night."

"But *I* do! I have to care. I get talked about enough already, and for no good reason. I certainly don't want to give anybody a valid excuse to talk about . . . our relationship."

"*Julie.*" Crooking a finger to beckon her to him, Marc swung off her side of the bed and stood no more than two feet away from her. "Come here."

Taking an involuntary step backward, Juliet shook her head. But a not unpleasant excitement was rising in her at the sight of Marc's virile body—his skin cast in copper in the early morning light—and even as she held out a restraining hand, an unsuppressible smile tugged at the corners of her mouth. "Marc Tyner, don't you dare come near me or I'll—"

"Or you'll what?" he challenged, wicked amusement flashing in his blue eyes as he took one long step then another toward her. "You can't scream for help, can you? How could you ever hope to explain what you were doing in my room naked at five thirty in the morning in the first place?" He chuckled deep in his throat. "It seems, my sweet, that you're at my mercy."

"You should have been an actor. You've got that villain's part down pat," she retorted, taking another step. She glanced behind her, realized she was about to back herself up against a wall, and quickly sidestepped Marc as he took one long stride toward her. A strange exhilaration accelerated the beat of her heart as she darted around him, narrowly escaping capture when his left arm shot out in her direction. As it was, when she moved past him, his fingertips grazed her bare side, and with a soft little gasp she dashed across the room, executing a perfect pirouette when she stopped, in order to keep her eye on Marc. He remained where she had left him, but he was watching her

155

through narrowed eyes, his expression deliberately threatening. She moved one hand in a dismissive gesture. "Stop this nonsense, Marc. I do have to get to my room."

"Not yet, my lovely Julie," he murmured, his eyes wandering over her. "Not until I've had my way with you."

Stepping back as he advanced toward her, Juliet caught sight of her own reflection in the dresser mirror and stopped dead, hardly able to believe what she saw. Naked, her skin ashimmer in the pale light, her coppery gold hair tumbling in disarray around her shoulders, she was laughing—almost giggling actually. Oh-so-serious and sedate Juliet York was frolicking around in the nude in her lover's room and almost laughing out loud. It was incredible, and Juliet's reaction to the entire situation surprised even her. Yet she was not so surprised that she was caught off guard when Marc stepped close enough to touch her. Willowy, with the natural grace of a deer, she escaped once again, putting some distance and the wooden valet between him and herself.

"Ah, you want to play games," he said, the near growl of his deep voice convincing to make her spine tingle despite the laughter glinting in his eyes. He came after her. "You may be quick, but I'll catch you soon, love. There's really nowhere to run to in here."

He was right. For the next two or three minutes Juliet was able to maneuver well enough to avoid capture but there was really nowhere to run. Finally, weak with laughter and breathless from the thrill of the chase, she faced Marc as she stood between the back of the easy chair and a wall. His eyes were locked on hers; his hands lightly gripped the arms of the chair as he leaned toward her, ready to pounce with the first move she made. Juliet took a deep breath, feigned to the right, intending to dash away to the left, but Marc wasn't taken in by her diversionary tactic. He moved in the same direction she did, caught her up in his right arm around her waist, and effortlessly and unceremoniously tossed her onto his bed. Dropping down beside her, he pinned both her legs beneath the weight of one of his and, catching both her wrists in one large hand, lifted her arms above her head, holding her in a way that made it virtually impossible for her to move.

"That's better," he growled. Amusement and a hint of triumph shone in his eyes as he smoothed back her rumpled hair. "Now I have you where I want you."

"Under you, you mean?" she questioned breathlessly.

"Or on top," he countered casually, rolling over and taking her with him to lie above him. "Whichever position you prefer. I'm a flexible man."

"You're also a crazy one," she answered, laughing down at him, shaking her head. "Instead of chasing me around your room, you should really let me go back to mine."

"Why? This is more fun, isn't it? I'm enjoying it thoroughly. Aren't you?"

"Yes, but—"

"Relax," he commanded softly, massaging her bare back with strong but gentle fingers. "You worry too much about what other people think. You need to learn how to have some fun."

"I know how to have fun!"

"Not fun like this."

"No, not fun like this," she admitted, a slight catch in her voice as she recognized the desire slowly replacing the amusement in his eyes. Fascinated by the emberglow in the clear azure depths, she was unable to look away and gave him a soft somewhat hesitant smile. "Marc, I—"

"Don't talk. Just kiss me," he whispered, cradling the back of her head in one hand to bring her face down close to his. His lips passed over her cheeks and chin and temples with the light touch of a breeze, then brushed each corner of her mouth until her own lips parted and swiftly met his.

Juliet heard the low groan of satisfaction that rumbled up in his throat and then he was kissing her back, the tip of his tongue opening her mouth to seek hers, his fingers moving evocatively as they probed the flesh of her back. Beneath her, Marc's lean body was growing tauter with each passing moment and he throbbed rigidly against her smooth thighs, arousing a flash of hot corresponding desire in her. Her mouth opened wider to his. She cupped his face in her hands and with slightly shaky fingers, traced the contours of his ears as the kiss they shared deepened to convey their insatiable hunger for each other. Delighting in the clean male scent of him, delighting in the touch of his hands and warm lips, delighting in the hard strength of his body beneath her, Juliet felt the fires inside her and inside him blaze up in flames on the surface of their skin, as if to forge them together as one being. She relaxed fully against him, her lower body invitingly soft and yielding on his muscular thighs.

"God, I *want* you, *need* you," Marc whispered urgently, holding her fast in his arms as he turned onto his side and molded her slim firmly curved body to the long line of his. "I can't ever get enough of you, after last night." His breath fanned her cheek. "You were so sweet, Julie."

"Was I?" she whispered back, mesmerized by the hot demanding searching light in his eyes. "I've never really thought of myself as sweet."

"Oh, but you are. Take my word for it," he counseled, an endearing smile etching attractive indentations into his cheeks beside his mouth. "And besides being sweet, you're incredibly passionate. Of course, that doesn't surprise me. I always knew you were a fiery little Rebel."

"And I always knew you were a Yankee marauder."

"Well then, are you ready to surrender?" he asked,

caressing the firm flesh of her breasts, his fingers feathering over and around her erect nipples. And as Juliet breathed a long tremulous sigh, he caught it up in his lips as they covered the parted softness of hers. The slow kisses they exchanged grew more impassioned, more heated; yet after several intense moments, Marc drew back slightly to look at her while running his fingers through her hair. "Why no other lovers, Julie?"

"My career's kept me too busy, I guess; there's just never been much time left for men," she murmured, telling him only part of the truth, then confiding a secret she had never shared with anyone else. "But maybe I never tried very hard to make time or to make a relationship work . . . because of my stepfather. My mother has remained married to him—despite his affairs with other women. Growing up around that kind of relationship didn't do much to bolster my faith in men in general."

"I see." Marc's darkening gaze searched her face. "In other words you don't trust men. Don't you trust me either?"

"In some ways I do," she told him honestly. She had trusted him to be a gentle, considerate lover, but she didn't trust him never to cause her pain, simply because she was in love with him. Loving someone makes any person vulnerable, especially so when love isn't returned. She knew that and had to accept it as a fact of life that could not be changed. If she stopped loving Marc, she would no longer be vulnerable where he was concerned, but she had an intuitive feeling it wasn't going to work out that way for her anytime in the near future. Yet, as she looked deeply into his eyes, she didn't want to think about the future. Only the present mattered—this time, with him. Touching the lock of sandy hair that had fallen forward across his forehead, she gave him a faintly wry smile. "Oh, well, that's better than if I didn't trust you at all, isn't it?"

"It's a beginning," he replied. "But you can trust me, Julie. Completely."

He doesn't understand. He has no idea how much I love him, Juliet thought. Her smile became a little wistful.

"Well, maybe not completely," he amended his statement with a teasing grin. "I'll admit I can't be trusted to keep my hands off you, ever, anytime. I'll try to behave when other people are around, but when we're alone like now. . . ."

"Show me," she whispered, love and desire inseparable as that teasing grin of his won her heart irrevocably. Slipping an arm round his waist, she trailed kisses over the spice-scented tan skin above his collarbone. "Touch me and kiss me; love me now."

"I intend to. For a very long time," he vowed, gently catching her chin between thumb and forefinger to tilt her head back. His eyes were closing as hers were when his warm coaxingly firm lips met the more tender texture of hers. Words hadn't dimmed the passion between them; it flared up now as white-hot and intense as before, and as Marc's teeth gently nipped at the full curve of Juliet's lower lip, she moved silkily against him, responsive, in love, and eager to give. At that moment she scarcely remembered she had ever told Marc she didn't want to get involved with him.

It was Wednesday night, and Juliet looked across her desk at Paul Phillips and Marc. "If either one of you has any ideas that might help us deal with this problem, please speak up," she said hopefully. "I'd be more than happy to listen to any suggestions."

"Hell, that's the trouble. There's really only one way to handle a situation like this, and that's the way you just mentioned, Juliet," Paul muttered, disgruntled but obviously resigned. "We just have to keep digging for new information while waiting and hoping our sources will finally agree to talk on camera. It's always a wait-and-hope game when sources have been intimidated and are suddenly too scared to tell what they know. Don't you agree, Marc?"

Tapping his steepled fingers against his chin, Marc nodded. "We always hope, of course, but in this case, I'm not too optimistic about our chances of convincing these sources to talk on camera. They've both been threatened and they're scared. While we're waiting and hoping, we'd better be scouring the hills for new sources."

Resting her elbow on the desktop, Juliet planted her chin in her palm and raised her eyes heavenward. "Come on, you two, you're old pros at this game. I was counting on you to bail me out of this mess."

"Sorry, but ideas are your department, not mine," Paul gibed, a twinkle of amusement in his brown eyes. "You're the producer and I'm only the director."

"But it's your story too."

"Only when it's going smoothly," Paul countered wryly. "Now that it's getting bogged down, it's all yours with my compliments. I'll just get the film and soundtrack and put it all together any way you want it back at the studio."

"Your loyalty is overwhelming," Juliet retorted, but with a smile because she knew Paul hadn't meant a word he'd said. She looked at Marc, realizing as she did that her smile softened, became something more than friendly. She doubted either Paul or Marc could see the subtle change in her expression although she was overwhelmingly aware of it herself. But that was because she knew how much she loved him; she felt it anew every time she looked at him. She was feeling it now, but only for the split second it took for her push all things personal to the back of her mind in order to continue with the business at hand.

"You mentioned finding new sources," she said to Marc. "I have one idea, but it's very iffy, and to tell the truth, I hate losing the sources we thought we could count on. Oh, the law clerk from the judge's office didn't really know a great deal but the dispatcher from the sheriff's department knows even more than she's told us off the record. I'm sure of it. You saw how startled she looked when I mentioned the senator's possible involvement."

"I saw but I also saw that she's too scared to talk to us now. At the very least she's been told she'll lose her job if she says anything on-camera. We can keep trying to convince her to talk, but I doubt we're going to have much luck." Marc shrugged, as if those were the breaks of the business, while regarding Juliet speculatively. "What's your iffy idea?"

Her green eyes brightened with some enthusiasm even as she admitted, "It isn't much really. But remember the woman who called me and said she had documented proof of the mayor's involvement in bid-rigging, then never showed when we went to meet her? I keep thinking about her voice on the phone. There was something very familiar about it, but I can't connect a name or face to it . . . yet. But I feel sure I'd talked to her before she called about that. If I could just remember . . ."

"You probably will some time when you're not even trying to remember," Paul said. "Usually happens like that."

"I hope it does this time. If it doesn't . . . God, I can just see myself now," Juliet drawled, smiling dryly. "Eighty-one years old and still trying to wrap up this story."

"Oh, it won't come to that. You might just feel older than eighty-one by the time this assignment ends," Paul joked, laughing as he rose up from his chair. "Well, I'll

162

just leave the two of you alone now, unless you had something else to discuss with me, Juliet."

Although a barely discernible frown touched her brow, she simply shook her head. "No, that's all for tonight. Thanks, Paul." Watching him cross the room, she saw him toss up one hand in an acknowledging wave, but when he pulled the door of the temporary office shut on his way out, she stared down somberly at the top of her desk and strummed her fingers restlessly. "Wonder what he meant by that?"

"Meant by what?"

Juliet looked up at Marc. "He said, 'I'll just leave the two of you alone now,' and I wonder what he meant by that."

"I assume he meant he was leaving and when he did leave, the two of us would be alone. In other words he didn't mean anything by it."

"Then why would he say it like that?" Juliet asked quietly. "Unless he has some reason to think we might want to be alone together. Do you think he has?"

"Could be. Paul and I have known each other for years," Marc said, leaning forward in his chair, resting his elbows on his knees. "He probably has noticed my interest in you is personal, as well as professional. He may even have guessed how involved we are. Does it bother you that he might have?"

"No, I don't really mind if Paul knows about us. I just wondered how he knew. But you've explained that," she said, hesitated, then shook her head. "But that doesn't explain how some of the crew know, too, and I'm sure some of them do, Marc. And you know how gossip like that flies. Some people know today, and tomorrow everybody knows everything."

"They can hardly know everything, Julie," Marc said

with a faint indulgent smile. "Unless someone's bugged my room in the last two nights."

"You know what I mean," she murmured rather bleakly. "They might not know everything, but they know enough—and they're talking about it."

"And obviously that *does* bother you?"

"It has to. Oh, Marc, you don't know how it feels to be accused of getting ahead in your career by lying on your back in somebody's bed," she said softly but with strong conviction. "I despise being talked about like that."

"I really don't see how anyone could talk about you and me that way. You couldn't advance your career by sleeping with me. I'm not your boss."

"You have so much influence at Union Broadcasting, you might as well be."

"That's neither here nor there. The point is this: The crew's either talking about us or isn't. And if they are, there's nothing we can do about it," Marc told her, getting up and stepping over by her desk. Reaching down, he took her by the hand and drew her up out of her chair, his smile comforting. "You have to stop worrying so much about what people say about you, Julie. Worrying never changes anything anyway. You know that. Besides, all that matters is that you and I both know our relationship changed because we wanted it to, not because you thought I could help your career."

"Unfortunately we're the only two people who do know that," Juliet murmured somberly. "And when it comes to gossip, I'm not usually given the benefit of the doubt. I guess the only answer for me is to be certain I don't give people any reason to talk about me."

"Meaning?"

Looking up at Marc, Juliet sighed inwardly as her personal needs warred mightily with her commonsense knowledge of what other people probably considered proper behavior. Much as she wanted to continue this new relationship with Marc, she knew she would almost assuredly be judged harshly if she did; all day long, the glances she had noticed crew members exchanging and the whispering that had stopped when she had approached had served as reminders of how much she loathed being judged that way. Pulled between what she wanted to do and what she thought she should do, she sighed again, audibly this time and with some impatience at the ludicrousness of the situation.

"Marc." She spoke at last, her voice low, meeting his eyes in order to gauge his reaction to what she was about to say. "I've decided that since someone obviously saw me leaving your room yesterday morning or this morning and started all this talk, I can't take the chance of being seen again. I'm going to stay in my own room tonight."

His expression didn't change. "If that's what you want to do."

"I didn't say that's what I want to do," she said quietly, incongruously disappointed that he wasn't even attempting to change her mind. She gestured vaguely. "It's just that I know how harmful gossip can be. If the whole crew wasn't staying here in the same lodge with us—"

"You wouldn't have to worry so much about people finding out you were sleeping with me. Right?" he questioned rather sardonically, releasing her hand. "Well, it's up to you, Julie. But I wonder how much sleep you'll get in your own room if you start wondering if your would-be intruder could make a return visit."

"I guess I'll find out how much, won't I?" she replied, a sudden coolness in her voice and her eyes. Even if he was annoyed by her decision, he didn't have to retaliate by reminding her of the intruder. Disappointed in him, disappointed in the lousy kind of day it had been, and somehow, disappointed even in herself, she glanced at her wristwatch, then back up at him. "It's after eleven and I'm tired. I'm going to my room." Picking a key up off her desk, she handed it to him. "Would you mind locking the door on your way out?"

"Not at all" was his quick answer.

But as Juliet walked to the connecting door to her room, she detected the hint of mockery in his voice and didn't even say good night as she left.

Maybe it was better this way, Juliet considered glumly while trying to find relaxation in a long hot bath. She had got far more seriously involved with Marc than she had ever intended but that fact was beyond changing and she was now coming to the realization that the longer their involvement lasted, the more difficult it would be for her when it ended. Perhaps it was just as well her hatred of gossip, rearoused today, had compelled her to end this madness with Marc after only two nights with him. Surely two nights would be somewhat easier to forget than many.

Finding cold comfort in such rationalization, Juliet finished her bath and got ready for bed. Wandering out of the bathroom, she tried not to think about Marc's comment about the intruder. Yet she couldn't forget it, not least because the remark had been surprisingly unkind and callous, as if he only cared about getting back at her for not continuing to be his bedmate. Perhaps she had never been much more to him than an attractive young woman with whom he could while away the free time during this assignment. Perhaps he found someone convenient like her during each of his assignments. Because he had acted genuinely fond of her, Juliet had never considered this possibility seriously before, and to do so now was disturbing and painful. Reaching for her hairbrush on top of the dresser, Juliet sighed and began brushing her hair with brisk vigorous strokes until a quiet knocking at the inside entrance of her room interrupted the procedure.

When Juliet opened her door and found Marc standing in the corridor, her heart reacted predictably by beating faster, to her dismay. Her eyes widened. "Oh. I didn't expect—"

"I'll sleep in here tonight, Julie. You take my room," he said quietly, stepping inside uninvited, his dark, thoughtful gaze never leaving her face. "I shouldn't have said what I did about the intruder possibly coming back. It was an absolutely unnecessary remark and I'm sorry I made it."

"It was rather like something my stepfather might say. But then, he wouldn't ever apologize for it either," Juliet accused then relented in the same breath, simply glad that he at least cared enough to try to make amends. She smiled faintly. "All right, apology accepted. And you don't even have to trade rooms with me."

"But I'm going to," Marc declared firmly. "I'll feel better if you're in my room and I'm in here."

"But I don't see—"

"I've already told Paul and most of the crew that we're switching rooms because the intruder could possibly come back," Marc interrupted tersely, impatience hardening his jaw. "You don't have to worry about anybody thinking you're spending the night in my room, *with* me."

"Actually that thought didn't cross my mind until you mentioned it," Juliet replied blandly, concealing the distress she felt because he wouldn't try to understand her fear of gossip. "I was simply trying to say that I don't see any point in our switching rooms. I really don't think that intruder will be back so I'm not afraid to stay in here."

"And what if you're wrong and he does return?" Marc questioned. "*I* don't see any point in taking that chance."

"But I—"

"For God's sake, Julie, there is such a thing as being too independent," he nearly growled. "Try not to be boring

167

about it. Just go sleep in my room tonight and tomorrow we'll move your things in there and mine in here permanently. All right?"

After a short moment's hesitation fueled by sheer stubbornness, she nodded, realizing it was useless to argue with him. This was one battle he fully intended to win. She could tell by the expression that mantled his carved features, the same expression that he wore during difficult interviews. Besides, it was nearly midnight, a very silly time to be arguing about something as relatively unimportant as which room she should stay in.

"Okay, I'll go," she said and after getting her toothbrush and hairbrush and after saying a rather strained good-night to Marc, she went.

Five minutes later, in Marc's room, Juliet switched off the lamp and settled down in the middle of the bed, wrapping her arms around her pillow. As her eyes became accustomed to the dark, she could see moonlight peeking in around the closed draperies covering the French doors. The memory of seeing the would-be intruder outside her own door suddenly made her shiver. Marc was right. She did feel safer in his room. Yet she felt lonely, too, in his bed without him. For several confusing minutes she wished she were one of those people who could throw caution to the wind and live life dangerously. If she were, she would get up, go next door, and spend tonight with Marc because she loved him and wanted to be with him. But she wasn't much of a risk-taker. Despite what she wanted, she didn't get up and go back to her room.

"Little Miss Cautious," she called herself regretfully and with some impatience as she nuzzled her face in Marc's pillow, detecting the lingering fragrance of spicy after-shave. Yet she still spent the night alone in his bed and lonely without him.

CHAPTER TEN

"I'm still not crazy about this plan," Paul complained the following Monday morning, while watching Juliet put on her suit jacket. "I can understand why the mayor's secretary won't talk on-camera but, since she's willing to hand over this so-called documented proof of his involvement in the bid-rigging, why can't she drop it someplace where either Marc or I can pick it up, instead of you?"

"The ladies' room in the Trenton post office seems like an ideal drop site to me," Juliet said, glancing up to find Marc simply staring at her in silence as she sorted through her purse for her car keys. Unsure of what his rather brooding expression meant, she hastily looked away and gave Paul a reassuring smile. "After all, everybody goes to the post office, so after my convenient little chat with the district attorney, I'll just drop by there and mail something. My shadows in the blue sedan won't suspect a thing."

"Your shadows in the blue sedan are exactly why I feel uneasy," Paul muttered, adjusting his glasses on the bridge of his nose as he often did when displeased. "If they realize somehow that you're picking up evidence against the mayor, I doubt they'll hesitate in trying to take it away from you."

"How could they realize that? The mayor's secretary certainly isn't going to tell anybody she's supplying us with information. She isn't exactly thrilled by this whole situation, and we'll probably be lucky if she actually goes through with the drop," Juliet told him. "She was pretty upset when I called her at home last night and told her I'd finally placed her voice and knew she was the woman who'd phoned, offering to meet Marc and me. It's obvious she wishes she didn't have to get involved in any of this and if she leaves the proof in the ladies' room for me, she's hardly likely to go around town blabbing about doing it."

"Exactly why *is* the formidable Miss Duncan even thinking of giving us information?" Marc asked abruptly, his gaze capturing and holding Juliet's when she quickly looked over at him. "When we taped the mayor's interview, she seemed like the classic fiercely loyal secretary to me."

"Frankly I think her conscience is bothering her. She knows she should hand this information over to somebody, much as she hates doing it," Juliet explained, dragging her eyes away from his after several long moments to look at her watch. "I just hope she hasn't changed her mind since last night. We'll soon find out, I guess. If I go to Trenton now, I can leave the district attorney's about the time Miss Duncan is getting back from the post office. She made me promise to wait until she's left before going in."

"I still don't like this," Paul reiterated gloomily as Juliet stood up behind her desk. "I think I'll go with you. Or Marc can. One of us should."

"Why?" Juliet asked, smiling wryly. "I assume you'll have one of the crew tagging after me as usual, won't you?"

"As a matter of fact, yes," Marc answered flatly before Paul could. "Unless Tom's going with you."

Juliet shook her head. "I sent Tom out on a few errands."

"I'd feel better about it if he were going with you but as long as one of the crew is keeping an eye on you, I guess it'll be all right," Paul said without much enthusiasm, and when Juliet picked up her briefcase and started toward the door, he called after her, "But be sure you come right back here after you make the pickup."

"Right back, I promise," she called back cheerily as she left the room.

An hour later, in the Trenton post office ladies' room, Juliet found a manila envelope behind the paper towel dispenser as prearranged. Breathing a heartfelt sigh of relief because Miss Duncan hadn't failed her, she quickly dropped the envelope into her briefcase. Though curiosity was practically killing her, and she could hardly wait to see what the envelope contained, this wasn't the time and certainly not the place to find out. She left the ladies' room and after mailing a couple of letters she went outside, directly to her car.

Negotiating the narrow winding road that led back to the lodge was challenge enough under the best of conditions, but today the weather was drizzly and beneath gray overcast skies the dark pavement looked menacingly slick. Juliet maintained a moderate speed, and on occasion after rounding a steeply inclining curve, she glanced up in the rearview mirror and saw exactly what she had expected to see—the dark blue sedan following close behind her. Wondering which crew member was making up the rest of the little parade, she felt comparatively safe but knew she wouldn't feel entirely secure until reaching the lodge.

For the next several minutes Juliet concentrated fully on following the serpentine road until she came to the point where it became an unusually long straight stretch of pavement and she was able to look up into the mirror again. Her eyes widened as suddenly the sedan gained on her with breathtaking speed, pulled out into the opposite lane, then veered sharply toward her car as if the insane driver intended to broadside her. With a gasp Juliet involuntarily jerked the steering wheel to the right. Gravel on the shoulder of the road clattered against the underside of her car as it flew up from beneath the right wheels. In the misty gray, Juliet saw the mountainside drop steeply away outside the right window and felt as if the bottom were falling out of her stomach. Pressing her trembling lips firmly together, she tightly gripped the wheel and eased the car completely onto the road again.

The sedan dropped back behind Juliet but almost immediately pulled around and cut sharply toward her once more. This time she cursed the driver under her breath and kept all four wheels on the asphalt until she saw a scenic overlook just ahead. Barely slowing down, she veered off the road completely, only aware that the sedan was speeding on. Hitting the brakes, she came to a complete stop in the parking lane.

"Oh, my God," she breathed, leaning forward to rest her forehead against the steering wheel. And she was so relieved she hadn't gone careening off the side of the mountain that it didn't occur to her that the men in the other car could turn around and come back—until she heard the throbbing of an engine. Jerking her head up, she saw the blue sedan turn onto the overlook and start rolling directly toward her. Her heart was beating like a triphammer as she slammed into reverse. But before she had time to take her foot off the brake and hit the accelerator to back up and try to escape, another car swept onto the overlook and came to a sudden stop in front of Juliet.

Marc was out his door in an instant. The sedan came to a screeching halt, its back wheels skidding on the wet pavement for several moments before the driver was able to regain control. Then, jerking the steering wheel hard around, he spun out onto the road and roared away.

After switching off the key in the ignition, Juliet sank down in her seat, suddenly limp and weak-kneed. The thunderous beating of her heart was slowing somewhat, but her breathing was still too shallow and too quick. When Marc walked over and opened her door, she tried to stop trembling, but that was a feat she was unable to accomplish, though she managed a shaky welcoming smile when he leaned down to look in at her.

"Are you okay?" he asked roughly, concern and anger glinting in his eyes. When Juliet laid a visibly unsteady hand on his left arm, he caught her fingers in the strong tight grip of his. "I would've been here sooner, but another car pulled out between me and your friend and didn't turn off again until a minute ago."

"But why were you following me yourself? I thought one of the—"

"Paul and I decided one of us better tag after you this time."

"Thank God you did. I've never been so happy to see anybody in my life," Juliet murmured, her free hand touching her throat as she stared disbelievingly at Marc. "That man who was driving today must be out of his mind. He nearly—"

"Their little game seems to be getting out of control, but at least we're not in Talbot County. The sheriff here won't be pleased when he hears about this," said Marc, his features tightly drawn. "But I imagine our friends will dump the sedan then lie low for a while to avoid being caught. You'll probably have to get used to somebody else following you now."

"Terrific," Juliet mumbled, unable to prevent herself from pressing her cheek against the back of his hand as it brushed across her creamy skin, finding both pleasure and pain in the first caressing touch she had received in days.

173

But, realizing Marc was only offering comfort, she soon drew away to smile wanly up at him.

"Did Haynes's secretary leave the information?" Marc asked. When Juliet nodded and gestured toward the briefcase on the seat beside her, he reached around her to take it out. "Maybe it would be better if I carry this with me then. I doubt our friends . . . knew you had it—harassing you today was probably just coincidence. But just to be on the safe side . . ."

Actually Juliet didn't feel truly safe, even after they arrived back at the lodge five minutes later. Although Marc had offered to take her with him and send someone back for her car, she chose to drive herself, insisting she was fine. She wasn't really. She was still trembling when Marc and she entered the temporary office where Paul awaited them.

"Why are you so pale?" Paul asked her immediately, a deep frown furrowing his brow. "What's happened?" After Marc told him about the incident on the road, he shook his head and cursed quite profusely. "This harassment is getting out of hand, isn't it, Marc?"

"Marc called the sheriff from downstairs, and he'll have his deputies watching for the car. That's the best we can do for now, so let's forget all about it for a while," Juliet suggested, tiring of all the fuss and trying to ignore the residual shakiness in her hands, which she clenched together atop the desk after sitting down. She moved one finger in the direction of the briefcase Marc held. "Let's see Miss Duncan's 'proof' of the mayor's guilt."

Several moments later photocopies of statements from the mayor's out-of-town bank plus a typed list of county bid-letting dates were laid out on Juliet's desk. Her eyes darted over the papers for a minute or so before she beamed a smile up at Marc, who smiled back. "Thank goodness for Miss Duncan's conscience," she said. "This isn't absolutely conclusive, of course, but it's very close to it."

"It's very strong circumstantial evidence all right," Marc agreed. "These dates of deposit are always a day or so after bids were taken for county projects. And where does a small-town mayor get five thousand dollars every few months to salt away in an out-of-town bank? A jury might well believe he was being paid off to keep quiet about the bid-rigging."

"Quite a little operation they had going here," Paul commented with a humorless smile. "The mayor and a town councilman get payoffs, and two deputies and probably the sheriff himself harass contractors who don't want to be involved in the bid-rigging. And naturally the taxpayer foots the bill for the whole deal."

"Ummm, but it looks like at least one more of them will have to pay some price for being corrupt. The mayor," Juliet mused, tapping the eraser of a pencil lightly against her chin as she looked at the papers in front of her. "I know the D.A. will be overjoyed when he sees this evidence, but before we turn it over to him, I'll call in and see how Pete wants us to proceed. I've heard he wants the legal department to review any information that might be turned over to the authorities."

"Yes, you'd be wise to call. Pete's a very cautious man. Never likes leaving anything to chance," Marc said tonelessly. "But you can understand someone like that, Julie, since you aren't willing to take chances either. Are you?"

Juliet looked up at him, ready to meet the challenge she expected to see in his eyes but there was only a mysterious darkness in the usually clear blue depths, a darkness she was unable to analyze. The expression on his suntanned face was unreadable and after several long nerve-fraying moments of stillness between them, she directed her gaze away from him and toward the phone on the desk.

"I guess I do tend to believe it's usually better to be safe than sorry," she admitted with quiet dignity as she picked up the receiver and began dialing directly to New York and the Union Broadcasting offices.

"I understand Pete being cautious but I really didn't expect him to want a meeting with us early tomorrow morning," Juliet said that evening while preceding Marc into a small but elegant Manhattan restaurant. "It's logical for him to want the legal department to review our evidence against the mayor, but I am a little surprised he had us fly back here right away so we could discuss the situation with him personally."

"As I said this morning, Pete leaves little to chance," Marc reminded her as the maître d' showed them to a corner table and they sat down. After unbuttoning his jacket, Marc tugged lightly at his tie, loosening it a bit before casually relaxing in his chair. "When you called his office this morning, I suspected he might tell us to fly up to see him. Maybe he just wants to be sure we haven't done anything illegal—like bribe a bank employee to steal the mayor's records."

Wrinkling her nose at Marc's less than serious tone, Juliet moved one hand in a dismissive gesture. "I'm sure Pete realizes neither one of us would be foolish enough to do anything illegal—which makes me wonder even more why he insisted on seeing us."

"He's just being his overcautious self. Don't worry about it. I can't think of any reason he wouldn't let us use our evidence against the mayor," Marc assured her. Resting one arm on the small round table between them, he leaned toward her, touching pleasantly rough fingertips against the back of her right hand and looking deeply into her eyes as they met his. His tone of voice deepened. "Relax, Julie. I'm glad Pete did call us in. His timing couldn't have been better. I have to tie up some loose ends from my last assignment anyhow. More importantly you needed to get away from Boone for a while, especially after what happened this morning."

"That was a rather disconcerting experience."

"Terrifying is more the word for it."

"I have to admit I was scared."

"I know. I saw how your hands were shaking when I arrived at the overpass."

Nodding, Juliet gazed down at the lean sun-browned hand next to hers. Compulsively she slipped her fingers between his, seeking the security that came with touching him and breathing a soft sigh. "I'm not sure what frightened me more—nearly being run off the road into a ravine or seeing that car coming back toward me when I stopped on the overpass." Remembering, she caught her bottom lip between her teeth for an instant, then asked, "Marc, what . . . do you think those men were planning to do before you spoiled all their fun by coming to the rescue?"

Marc's jaw hardened, making his expression somewhat grim while strong fingers tightened perceptibly, squeezing hers. "Hopefully they just wanted to scare you a little more than they already had. Unfortunately we can't be sure that's all they had in mind."

"You . . . don't think they'd ever get really violent, do you? I mean, physically hurt. . . ."

"Hell, Julie, who can predict what thugs like that might do? Like Paul said this morning—this situation seems to be getting out of hand. You, especially, have to be very careful," Marc said almost roughly, his brilliant blue eyes piercing the depths of hers. "You do understand that?"

"Completely. After what happened on the road today, I won't be taking any foolish chances when we get back to Boone," she promised, giving him a little smile. Though his answer had been more honest than reassuring, she

177

realized very well he had been wise to tell her the truth. He wouldn't have been doing her any favors by making light of a situation that could be more potentially dangerous than she had previously imagined. Now she had been forewarned by both Marc and the unpleasant events of the morning and she took the warnings seriously even as she decided to relegate such uneasy thoughts to the back of her mind for at least a few hours. Suddenly, Boone was far away and she was unwilling to spend the entire evening with Marc, fretting about thugs and their methods of intimidation. She settled back in her chair, started to tuck back that unruly strand of hair, but dropped her hand and allowed the wispy tendril to continue to graze her cheek when she glimpsed the knowing glimmer of amusement that appeared in Marc's eyes as he watched her. She half smiled. "I'm ready to talk about something more pleasant for a while."

"Good, because that's precisely why I made reservations here. It's quiet and I intend to wine and dine you and make you relax and forget our assignment for the rest of the evening," Marc told her with a devil-may-care wink while discreetly beckoning a waiter. "Any objections, Julie?"

"I can't think of any offhand," she murmured, smiling softly at him, feeling happier in that moment than she had in several days.

Dinner was delightful. Over the main course of succulent lemon sole, which was more delicious than any Juliet had ever tasted, she and Marc lost themselves in engrossing conversation. One subject led swiftly into another as they discussed books and music and art and even indulged in a good-natured stimulating debate on politics. After declining dessert, they sipped dark aromatic coffee from delicate porcelain cups and continued talking, barely noticing the frequent curious glances tossed at Marc by peo-

178

ple at nearby tables. Juliet realized she was becoming accustomed to the fact that his was a familiar face, and that it was only natural for many people to stare at him—and thereby at her—when she was with him. Tonight she felt completely at ease, despite the unbridled interest of some of the diners around them. Even when she laughed at yet another of Marc's witty comments and he suddenly moved one large hand over her smaller one on the table, she didn't pull hers away. Forgetting all the curious eyes that might be watching the two of them, she simply smiled and basked in the warmth that accompanied his gentle touch.

Marc's gaze was darkening. His fingertips played over hers. "Julie . . ."

The moment he said her name Juliet's attention was abruptly diverted by someone coming to a sudden halt beside the table. Involuntarily she looked away from Marc and up at a tightly drawn face of a woman she immediately recognized. Biting back the groan that rose in her throat, Juliet looked beyond that face at the tall, handsome man with a mane of silver hair who was with the woman. *Henry Alexander and wife.* At once she felt her emotions were being pulled in two opposing directions. In spite of all that had happened, she was still fond of Henry, and in a way was glad to see him. Yet . . .

"Henry, it's nice to see you again," she murmured after the briefest of hesitations. She tried to smile naturally. "How have you been?"

"Busy, as usual. And you, Juliet?" Henry responded, his tone friendly yet more subdued than it might have been had his wife not been with him. "How's it going at Union Broadcasting? Between assignments at the moment?"

"On assignment actually. In North Carolina. We're just in town to check in with the boss," Juliet told him, quickly

179

including Marc in the conversation by smiling at him. "I believe you two have met."

"Henry and I have known each other for years," Marc said, rising lithely to his feet to extend his hand to the older man while giving Mrs. Alexander one of his most irresistible smiles. "But I've never met your wife, Henry."

After promptly making the introduction, Henry cupped Mrs. Alexander's elbow in one hand and turned her slightly toward Juliet. "Vivian, dear, I can't recall whether or not you and Juliet have ever been properly intro—"

"Yes, we've met," his wife interrupted, her expression stony, her words razor-edged. "You introduced us yourself."

And under far more pleasant circumstances—before that ridiculous scandal had spread like a disease, Juliet mused, but tried not to think about that. She smiled faintly at Vivian. "Hello, Mrs. Alexander."

The older woman didn't speak. She merely bobbed her head in the curtest of nods, then spun around and walked away.

"The maître d' is waiting to show us to our table. Nice seeing both of you again," Henry said with a rather worn smile before following his wife.

"Oh damn," Juliet muttered as Marc took the chair across from her once more. Sighing, she twirled the wayward strand of hair round and round one finger. "It's obvious she still thinks Henry and I had an affair."

"That's not too surprising, Julie," Marc commented softly. "There have been rumors about Henry and other young women."

"I know. And those rumors, true or false, didn't do a thing to help my reputation. When the gossip about Henry and me started, everybody just assumed . . ." Juliet's shoulders rose slightly and fell in a resigned shrug. "Of course, it was no use trying to convince those people they were wrong. But I did hope Henry would be able to convince Vivian nothing happened between us. Obviously he hasn't succeeded."

"Obviously not."

An almost wounded expression flitted like a shadow over Juliet's features as another, softer, sigh escaped her lips. Bending her head, she stared morosely at the fine linen cloth that covered the table. "Knowing what Vivian thinks really makes me feel terrible. I just wish there was something I could say to her that would make her realize how wrong she is."

"Maybe I should go tell her you couldn't possibly have had an affair with Henry since you were a virgin until . . . just recently."

Responding to the lean finger that slipped beneath her chin and lifted it, Juliet looked up swiftly and saw the wry indulgence gentling Marc's face. Her lips twitched then curved into an irrepressible answering smile. She shook her head at the deliberately preposterous suggestion. "Somehow, I don't think Vivian would believe you even if you did tell her that."

"I'm sure she wouldn't even if I volunteered to sign a sworn affidavit, and that's exactly the point I'm trying to make, Julie. There's nothing you could say to Vivian that would change her mind. If she doesn't trust Henry, that's a problem he has to solve with her. You certainly can't solve that for them. Right?" When Juliet nodded, he smiled. "All right. Now I suggest we get out of here so the Alexanders can have dinner in peace, and you can begin to relax again." And lifting one finger to gain the waiter's attention, he signaled for the check.

Outside on the well-lighted street a few minutes later, Marc stopped on the sidewalk to look down at Juliet. "Anywhere special you'd like to go?" he asked. "If not, my apartment's not far. We could walk there."

"I don't know, Marc. It's already after ten, and it's been a long day for both of us. Maybe I should just go on to my place."

"Scared, Julie?" he whispered provocatively, his warm breath stirring her hair as he slipped an arm round her waist to draw her close against his side. "Afraid to be alone in my apartment with me?"

"No, not at all," she answered, sliding her own arm around him because it made walking easier and also because touching him was suddenly something she wanted very much to do. She smiled at him. "Is there some reason I should be scared?"

He shook his head. "No reason whatsoever. That settles it then. I'll take you to my loft and show you my etchings."

Juliet laughed even as she realized for the first time how seductively appealing humor could be in a man. "Marc, that *is* a line that's older than the the hills," she chided teasingly. "I know you can do better than that."

"I'll try harder next time," he promised with an endearing grin. "But my lack of originality tonight isn't going to cause you to refuse my invitation. Is it?"

"No. I accept. I like very much to see where you live," she answered, impulsively surrendering to what she wanted to do rather than what her mind told her she should do. And with that decision, a thrilling shiver scampered over her skin, a shiver that couldn't be attributed to the gently flowing breeze that was cooling the balmy night air.

CHAPTER ELEVEN

Moonlight silvered the leaves on the tall trees in Gramercy Park. A cool oasis of calm and quiet in the hot bustle of the city, the park was enclosed by a wrought-iron fence and seemed to Juliet reminiscent of the common of a small village that surrounding residents could share as a community. Gramercy represented the ultimate in urban living, providing solitude and serenity, and tonight Juliet was as impressed by the charm of the area as she had always been. The golden glow of lamplights mantled the sidewalks; a soft wind whispered among the leaves and the blocks of stately old homes that stood sentinel around the square had lost none of their former dignity since being converted to apartments. Enjoying the peaceful atmosphere, Juliet smiled appreciatively when Marc opened an ivy-festooned gate, then escorted her along a short brick walkway and into a foyer of one of the buildings.

"I didn't realize you lived here. Gramercy Park is such a lovely place, I've always thought," she told him as they stepped together into a small elevator with an intricately carved wood-paneled interior. When the doors glided shut and the car began a sedately slow and smooth ascent, she turned to Marc, a somewhat mischievous sparkle in her eyes. "Very impressive so far. And I suppose living here even entitles you to a key to the gates of the park?"

In response Marc tucked a hand into a pocket of his

trousers and extracted just such a key. "We might have the park to ourselves this time of night. We can go back down and take a stroll through if you'd like, although I think you'd enjoy a daytime walk even more."

"I'm sure I would, too, especially after what happened this morning. At the moment I'm feeling just a little too cowardly to risk walking through a dark park, even a private one. Besides, we must be here," Juliet said as the elevator slowed easily to a halt and the doors slipped open. Realizing that Marc's apartment obviously covered the entire third floor, she stepped out into a high-ceilinged entrance hall where light through small prisms of a crystal chandelier reflected in rainbow hues on a highly buffed dark wood floor. Seeing the spacious living room beyond opened double doors, she walked in that direction, stopping at the threshold to look inside with great interest. "Marc, this is so nice. I really like it."

"So do I," he answered, gently curving a large hand into the small of her back to urge her into the room where he reached for a switch and brightened the lights slightly. "It's not an opulent place but I prefer keeping home neat and simple."

Simply elegant was a more apt description for what Juliet was seeing. Around a magnificent vibrantly colored Persian rug, antique furniture covered with pearl damask graced the center of the expansive polished floor. Mahogany pieces placed here and there around the remainder of the room prevented it from appearing too empty, though there was a simplicity to the decor that bordered nearly on the Spartan. Accents had been limited to several fine paintings on the oyster-white walls and a few creations of shimmering lead crystal; yet the total effect of the room was warm. After the first quick glimpse around, Juliet nodded, smiling at Marc. "Yes, this suits you; I imagine you can feel relaxed in here."

184

"It's comfortable, but to tell the truth, I spend more time in my study. Come on, I'll show you," he said, taking her hand in his to lead her to a side door which he pushed open. He reached in to switch on a light in the smaller book-lined room dominated by a sprawling oak desk and a royal blue plush sofa with matching chair and ottoman.

The study was less orderly than the living room, but that merely made it cozier. Drawn to the overstuffed sofa without waiting for an invitation, Juliet settled herself on the cushion at one end, slipping her feet out of navy kid pumps and tucking them up beside her.

"A fireplace," she murmured, gazing dreamily at the hearth inlaid with black marble. "Does it work?"

"Perfectly, and I use it whenever possible. Too bad the weather's too warm tonight to have a fire," said Marc, crossing behind the sofa to a small built-in bar. "But I can offer you brandy. That all right?"

"Ummm, I'd love some," Juliet replied, smiling her thanks when he brought it to her a moment later and joined her on the sofa. During the following several minutes, they spoke very little, both of them content to share companionable silences until Juliet noticed an oval china paperweight, hand-painted in an unusually intriguing design sitting atop his desk. She leaned forward to pick it up for a closer look. "How beautiful. It must be an antique."

"I think maybe it is, but I'm not sure." Crossing his outstretched legs at the ankles, Marc intently surveyed the object Juliet held for an instant before his gaze wandered to her face. He shrugged. "I didn't buy that myself. My ex-wife gave it to me on our first . . . and last wedding anniversary."

"Oh, I see." Replacing the paperweight on his desk, sat back again and unconsciously began to twirl the short stem of her glass between her fingers as she added, "I didn't know you'd ever been married."

"Sometimes it's difficult for me to remember I ever was. It was a long time ago. Beth and I were both too young to get married, and we stayed together less than a year and a half. It just didn't work out the way we'd expected," Marc stated candidly, the half-smile that moved his firmly shaped lips reminiscent and somewhat regretful rather than bitter. He sipped the last of his brandy. "We didn't really know each other very well; that was the problem. I didn't realize what a strictly traditional life-style Beth wanted, and she didn't realize how much my work meant to me. I was away on assignment a great deal. She hated that and told me repeatedly before, during, and after the divorce that marriage just wasn't for me; that I cared more about my career than I ever would any woman." His broad shoulders rose and fell in a shrug again. "That's the way it ended, and it was better for both of us that it did."

"The breakup of any marriage has to be painful though," Juliet said softly, probing gently, wanting him to talk to her, confide in her, and perhaps exorcise completely any lingering hurt that might accompany his memories. After placing her empty glass next to his on a side table, she met his open gaze and deeply searched the dark blue depths of his eyes. "The divorce couldn't have been easy, because you must have loved Beth at one time."

"I think I did . . . but obviously not enough. I'm not proud to admit it, but I didn't miss Beth much at all after we broke up. Oh, at first, between assignments, the apartment seemed empty; but I can't even pretend that I was excessively lonely without Beth, because I wasn't. I was always thinking about the next assignment so maybe she was right—she never was quite as important to me as my career."

Would any woman ever be? Juliet wondered. She dismissed that insidious question the moment it popped into her mind because she had no right to ask it, even to herself.

Marc had made no commitment to her; she had known from the first day she met him that investigative journalism was the most consuming aspect of his life. Deep in her heart she was more than a little relieved that an undying love for his ex-wife and sorrow because of their parting didn't torment him and that realization bothered her to some extent. Fear that he could love no woman as much as he did his work and joy that he had never truly loved Beth were conflicting reactions that Juliet's brain couldn't quite reconcile although her heart could easily do so. She watched Marc stand up, shed his jacket, and lay it across the chair beside the tie he had previously removed. When he put a record on the stereo and came back to her, she recognized the twinges of jealousy that were still lingering within her.

"Do you . . . see Beth often now?" she found herself asking on impulse. "Does she still live in New York?"

"Far from it—she never cared much for the city and lives in Wyoming now, where she married the principal of the school where she teaches. She has the traditional family life she always wanted, two children, and another on the way the last I heard. She's happy and I'm glad," Marc said with what seemed to be sincerity while his gaze traveled slowly over Juliet's face. "Why do you ask?"

"Just curious," she lied, taking a hasty look at her wristwatch. Her small straight nose wrinkled slightly. "It's getting late. I should call a taxi although I'm sorry to say that my adventures down in Boone have managed to make me reluctant to be alone, even in my place here. I know that's silly but—"

"It isn't silly. Don't dismiss those men and their actions so quickly. You're wiser to feel uneasy," Marc muttered, his eyes a stormy gray for an instant before becoming their normal less ominous shade of blue again. His expression became gentle once more. "But there's no need for you to

187

go to your apartment tonight anyway. You could stay here with me."

Faint pink color rose in Juliet's cheeks. "You don't have to offer sanctuary, Marc. I didn't say what I did because I was fishing for an invitation."

Suddenly the hand lying over the back of the sofa behind her swooped down to gently cup the nape of her neck beneath her hair. A slow indulgent smile spread over Marc's face as he shook his head and said in a near whisper, "Julie, you have the craziest notions sometimes. Why should I think you were fishing for an invitation? I thought you realized my bringing you here *was* an invitation. Isn't it obvious that I want you to stay?"

"You didn't say. . . ."

"Words aren't always necessary, are they?"

Indeed they weren't, as Juliet was clearly discovering. Marc's hand moved through her silken hair; his fingertips brushing over her scalp were evoking shivers of awareness, and the passionate message his eyes were conveying was unmistakably recognizable. Suddenly the caution she had been carrying like a shield for the past several days seemed to be disintegrating rapidly; she wondered for a frantic instant if she could muster the willpower to refrain from succumbing to his touch's mesmerizing assault on her senses. *Of course, I can,* she chided herself. It was only sensible not to resume an intimate relationship with him. Yet that was much easier said than done; an intensifying need to be close to him warred with her very real fears about what gossip could do to her career. She looked at Marc, unaware that her inner conflict was betrayed by the expression overlaying her even features. She unknowingly nibbled her lower lip. "Marc, I—"

"Julie," he whispered. "Spend the night with me."

"I shouldn't and you know why. Nothing's different."

"Everything's different. We're not in Boone now; we're

in New York. We can be together without your having to worry about gossip." He moved closer while drawing her inexorably toward him, his warm smile coaxing. "And if I recall correctly, you said we couldn't be together at the lodge because the crew stays there too. Well, this isn't the lodge, and the crew isn't here."

Juliet couldn't help returning his smile. "I guess I did say that, didn't I?"

"Yes, you did, and I certainly hope you meant it because . . . Julie, I want you," he muttered huskily, kissing the gentle arches of her brows, her eyelids and temples, then the smooth line of her jaw and the tip of her chin. "And I think you want me too."

Juliet tried to fight temptation but failed in the attempt. As Marc's lips sought her own her hands floated up, almost of their own volition, to drift across his chest and the warmth of his kiss and the feel of his virile hard body aroused a sensuous excitement in her that she couldn't resist. Juliet felt keenly alive now, with all of her senses heightened. Marc's deepening kisses, his every caress, his whispered endearments, were electric; a fever seemed to burn outward in her from the very core of her being. She began to tremble with loving desire, and soon her slender curved body was brushing against the potently masculine line of his until her flesh felt ablaze with fires. She lifted her arms to his broad shoulders, tangling her fingers in his thick hair. Her mouth opened invitingly beneath his and when the tip of her tongue teased the curve of his lips, he groaned softly and wrapped her in his arms, hard against him as their kisses became more impassioned and lengthened.

"My sweet delight," he whispered roughly, and then Juliet was lost. Hot rushes of desire rose to a crescendo in her; her hands moved inside his shirt, eager to touch bare male skin. She feathered her fingertips over the corded muscles of his back, probing the structure of flesh and bone, and a woman's smile curved her lips as her evocative caresses increased the tenor of his breathing.

Not one to rush the preliminaries, Marc lowered Juliet and himself onto the sofa, his long lean body half covering her. His lips played over the tender shape of her between possessive kisses while searching hands explored the shapely curves of her body as she explored him. His touch was white-hot even through the silk of her ice-blue dress. When he undid the tiny buttons down the front of her bodice, then sought the rising swell of her breasts and the scented hollow between with his hard yet gentle mouth, she felt she might erupt in flames at any minute. Her breathing was shallow and quick; her senses swirled dizzily, causing her to cling to him in ardent abandon, unable to get close enough to him. And when his lips took hers again, his tongue tasting the sweetness of her mouth, she ached for the more intimate and more satisfying union between them.

"Marc," she sighed, giving him back kiss for passionate kiss. Her skirt had twisted up around her, exposing bare thighs, and with seductive intent, she sinuously entangled her legs with his.

"Come to bed, Julie," he commanded softly, his deep voice rough-edged, his tone appealingly urgent. Rising from the sofa, he pulled her up with him, his arm around her shoulders holding her close to his side, smiling as hers went round his waist. He led her out of the study down a long hallway to his room, where he switched on a lamp then stood simply gazing at her for several long poignant moments before saying at last, "You're so lovely."

Juliet waited in silence as he removed his shoes, and when he finished and moved toward her, her heart drummed with her building anticipation. A tremor ran over her as he stroked her shining hair then drew his hands slowly along the slender column of her neck across her shoulders and down her arms to catch her fingers in his. Powerful thrills coursed through her when he lifted each of her palms in turn to his lips, and strong even teeth nibbled tenderly at her skin. Her fingertips feathered over the taut planes of his cheeks. The faint smile she gave him was mystically bewitching, and sheer happiness surged up in her when he smiled back.

Marc released Juliet's hands to begin unbuttoning his shirt, but Juliet quickly reached up and brushed his hands aside. "I think I'll do that," she said. "It's much more fun this way."

"I think so too," he murmured, beginning to unfasten the remaining buttons of her dress. She pushed aside his shirt. Moving closer, she lightly massaged his lean sides and trailed playful kisses over his chest and flat midriff, pleased when he whispered her name unevenly in response. They paused frequently in the mutual undressing to come together in a lingering kiss but when all barriers of clothing were removed, their eyes met in a silent agreement to prolong the pleasures they were finding in each other.

"You have the softest skin I've ever touched," Marc said, cupping her ivory, rose-tipped breasts in gentle darkly tanned hands. The edges of his thumbs played over the swiftly firming peaks and his warm blue eyes captured and held hers when she responded to his caress with a quick intake of breath followed by a hushed sigh of delight. Lowering his head, he grazed his lips over the curves of resilient feminine flesh. A moment later his hands spanned her bare waist and he held her from him, allowing his narrowed gaze to roam freely over her as her fingertips traced the subtly muscled contours of his long arms. His hold on her tightened. "It's nice to be able to see and touch you again."

Juliet's answering smile was sweetly provocative. "And I love touching you. But I think you know that."

"I hope you do. I'd planned for us to make up for the past few nights. . . . I've missed you, Julie."

"I've missed you. It's been very lonely in my bed, and it's been hard to fall asleep."

Burning desire flared brightly in Marc's eyes. "Well, you won't be alone tonight, but I don't intend to let you get very much sleep."

"Promise?" she breathed, cupping his face in her hands, love for him banishing all inhibitions.

"I promise, Julie, love," he whispered hoarsely, swiftly bringing her into his encircling arms and fast against him as his mouth came down to possess hers. He drew away only to lead her to his bed, where he flung back the covers and urged her down upon the wide expanse of cool smooth sheets. He moved above her, his upper body covering hers as his elbows supported him, and he explored the exquisite features of her face with light wandering fingertips. His compelling eyes seemed to draw her very soul from the depths of her body. Juliet gazed up at him, adoring him for the wealth of tenderness that always tempered his passion and that, for her, made making love with him totally irresistible. Her hands clasped his lean flanks, her fingertips moving in slow circular motions over his lower back. She tilted her head back slightly on the pillow when he leaned down to scatter kisses along the length of her neck, some of which lingered tantalizingly on the rapidly thudding pulse in her throat.

"I could keep touching you forever," he murmured, his low gruff voice muffled. "You feel so good, Julie, like warm fine silk."

"And you taste delicious," she said breathlessly, taking the lobe of his ear between small white teeth and feeling the responsive tremor that ran over him. He raised his head to look down at her; his gaze hot, magnetic, and fiercely possessive. His control over her was complete, but that was all right with Juliet, because she was controlling him too and knew.it. Seductive, smooth, winsomely pliant, she brushed a finger across his carved lips, smiling dreamily when he caught the tip in a tender bite. Her hand curved along his strong jaw and slipping her fingers through his vibrantly clean sandy hair, she drew him nearer and kissed him, set adrift in a wondrous realm as their lips met and parted languidly then met again and again. Turning toward Marc when he moved onto his side, she rested a shapely bare arm on his as he clasped her waist. His hand swept upward to sensitized breasts, squeezing and stroking their cushioned fullness and toying with surging tight nipples. Sensations plunged through her; an aching emptiness clamored to be filled and she arched acquiescently against him with a softly gasped *"Marc."*

With a deep-throated rumble of sound, Marc pressed her down into the mattress, his weight evocatively heavy, his mouth plundering the moist sweetness of hers before he groaned. "Temptress. I don't think I'll ever get enough of you. You drive me crazy."

"Ummm, I want you to tell me how to please you," she coaxed, eager to give and to find the purest ecstasy in the giving. "Tell me everything you like."

"I promise to. But first . . ." he whispered, parting her satiny thighs with an upstroking hand.

Soon time lost all meaning. Nothing existed except Juliet and Marc and the bed beneath them. Bathed in soft lamplight, they explored each other fully, sharing exquisitely pleasurable experiences that Juliet knew instinctively she would never ever want to share with any man other than Marc. With him nothing seemed beyond limits, and love freed her to drift upward with him in that ever-increasing spiral of erotic tension. Her entire body began to throb with the keen sensations awakened by the caresses and kisses he bestowed on every inch on her. And she glorified in her ability to arouse him, joy steadily growing with his obvious delight in the ways she tried to please him. Unhurriedly they made the night a deliciously sensuous adventure and evoked needs in each other stronger than either of them had ever experienced before.

Much, much later, when mutual desire had peaked again to a feverish pitch and neither of them could wait another moment for the ultimate intimacy, Marc moved Juliet above him, his hands encircling her narrow waist as he guided her down toward him. He watched her, saw the soft glow that came into her emerald eyes, and heard the low, satisfied sound she made as they merged perfectly together, their bodies seeming to become one and to move in slow erotic synchronization. And she saw the fiery passion conveyed by his darkening gaze accompany the intent tightening of his jaw when her flesh yielded completely to receive the vital strength of his.

Swept with emotion, happiness misting her eyes, Juliet brushed her parted lips over his, beckoning, inviting, tempting.

"You're so warm, Julie," he murmured, his breath filling her throat. Curving a hand round the back of her neck, he looked up at her, his gaze unwavering yet endearingly gently. "And so giving."

She did give . . . everything both physically and spiritually if not in words. Aroused and in love, guided by feminine instinct, she reveled in her womanhood and in the ecstasy she found with this special man. Without conscious intent she was able to compensate him and also herself for the nights she had chosen to be absent from his bed, savoring fully and gladly in each long slow stroke of their lovemaking. Her breathing was as ragged as Marc's when the pinnacle of piercing sensations was nearly reached; as he swept her demandingly beneath him sweet fulfillment claimed them both, exploding in her like a sunburst of warmth in crashing waves of rapture.

Marc crooned her name. She held him hard against her. Some minutes later they lay together spent and contented in a tangle of limbs, their glistening bodies touching closely. She brushed a hand across his chest, smiling lazily at him when he caught up her fingers to kiss each tip.

"Julie," he whispered, his tone somehow both teasing and serious. "You've become a very hot-blooded woman, much to my delight."

"I can't imagine why you'd say that about me," she protested, her voice lazy, her accent thick. Still smiling, she floated into a deep sleep.

Juliet awoke to partial darkness. After she had fallen asleep, Marc had switched off the lamp, and as she turned to look at him he was a silhouetted form against the very pale window light behind him, his features barely distinguishable. Even so, she continued to watch him and relax in a wonderful feeling of physical well-being. A tiny smile still graced her lips, and after stretching with fluid grace, she moved silently from the bed. She opened the drawer of a tall dresser, then another, until she found one of Marc's pajama tops and slipped it on, shunning the buttons to wrap it simply around her. Padding barefoot to the window, she looked out at the gray dawn blanketing Gramercy Park and slowly lightening the dark shapes of the trees. For a dreamy moment she wondered how it would be to awaken every morning here—with Marc— then she turned to look at him again and walked back across the brightening room to his side.

In his repose Marc's lean face seemed arranged in relaxed lines; the firm outline of his lips was more softly sensuous, and the thick sweep of his dark brown lashes lay against tanned skin. His jaw was lightly shadowed with a night's growth of beard. As Juliet stood watching him sleep, her love for him knew no bounds. Needing to touch him, she sat down on the edge of the bed to run her fingertips over his tousled sandy hair. She bent down, brushed a kiss against his cheek and when she lifted her head again, he was opening his eyes.

Marc gave her a sleepy smile. "Is it very late, Julie?"

"As a matter of fact, it's very very early," she told him, her voice near whispery. "But since you woke me up at dawn one morning, I thought I'd return the favor."

The last shadows of sleepiness vanished from his clear blue eyes as his smile altered to more a mischievous grin. "Is it possible you're waking me up for the same reason I woke you?"

"The idea did cross my mind," she admitted, drawing the edge of one finger across his lips.

"Wanton hussy," he teased, his hands coming out to clasp her arms. But his expression abruptly sobered. "Tell me something, Julie. After our meeting with Pete today, you'll fly back to Boone and I'll follow day after tomorrow. When we're back there together, you're not going to go cold on me again, are you? Simply because the crew will be around?"

Juliet hesitated. "I . . . don't know. I—"

"Wait. Let me tell you something you obviously don't realize: Every member of that crew has respect for you, lady," he interrupted quietly, intently. "You're a fine field producer, and they all know that. Even if they guess what kind of relationship we have, they'll probably gossip; but their talk won't be malicious. They won't assume you're trying to sleep your way up the ladder of success because they know you don't have to do that. They'll simply be co-workers interested in any romantic intrigue they can talk about. Can you look at the situation that way, Julie?"

196

She understood the logic of what he was saying. Yet . . . "I understand what you mean," she answered at last, "but I guess I just need more time to convince myself you're right."

"All I ask is that you think about it," he said, then allowed his darkening gaze to wander down over her slight curvaceous body swallowed up in his pajama top with its sleeves reaching down to practically cover her hands. He pushed the sides back, his own hands gliding in to move over her bare creamy smooth midriff. His fingers grazed the uprising curves of her breasts. "You look quite fetching in my pajamas, Miss York, but I know for a fact that you look even more fetching with nothing on at all."

Alive with sensations evoked by his touch, she smiled back at him. "Well, then?" she murmured provocatively.

"Take it off for me, Julie," he commanded softly. "I need to see you."

Rising to her feet, Juliet slowly dropped the thigh-length top from her shoulders and let it slip off completely and drift down to the floor at her feet. The passion she saw flare up in the depths of Marc's eyes made her catch her breath, but when he turned back a corner of the sheet covering him, she unhesitantly went into his bed and into his arms, seeking the warm strength of his hard aroused body. Willingly pursuing her newfound role as seductress, she initiated a long deepening kiss, her tender parted lips playing with his. And before rational thought was swept away, she thought fleetingly of the woman she had been before meeting Marc. Strictly professional, immersed in her career, she hadn't really had much of a personal life. Now she was different. She was finding sheer joy in her own womanhood. Because she loved Marc, she had allowed him to change her to the vitally alive woman she was now, and she was glad.

CHAPTER TWELVE

Almost immediately after Juliet returned to North Carolina, the harassment resumed. A new car had been dispatched to trail her—this time a gray station wagon—but from a distance the two men in it appeared to be the same ones who had occupied the dark sedan. Also, much to her disgust, intimidating calls in the daytime increased in frequency; by Thursday morning, her nerves were frazzled, and her patience nearly nonexistent. When yet another call came just before noon and she heard the first few threatening words spoken by a deliberately gravelly voice, she slammed the receiver down with such violence that the bell in the phone gave a merry little jingle, a sound certainly not indicative of her mood.

"Damn those people," she muttered half aloud just as Paul walked into room. A tiny muscle worked in her clenched jaw, and her eyes glittered with angry impatience when she looked up at him. "Surely it must be dawning on them that we're not going to go away and leave this assignment unfinished, so why don't they just stop these ridiculous threats?"

"Too scared. They obviously have a lot to hide," said Paul, approaching Juliet's desk with a concerned frown. "What did he say to you this time?"

"I never listen past the first two or three words. Why bother? What can they be planning to say? That the next time they'll try harder to drive me off the side of the mountain?"

"I guess so," replied Paul glumly, shuffling his feet, hunching his shoulders, and digging his fists into his trouser pockets. His troubled gaze rested on her for several long moments before he added with something akin to reluctant hesitation, "You are being very careful, aren't you, Juliet? Especially at night?"

"I'm being as careful as possible without staying in my room in solitary confinement," she told him.

Paul glanced away, his eyes flitting around at various objects in the room. "Good. I wouldn't want you to let down your guard, even a little, because then if something unexpected happened, you'd be even more terrified."

"Yes. Marc told me the same thing."

"It's good advice. As for these phone calls, maybe you should have Tom thoroughly screen—"

"I have to take calls, Paul, you know that. It might be someone with important information for us, someone who wouldn't trust my assistant's assurances of confidentiality," she said, smiling her appreciation for his concern. "Anyway my heavy breather is more annoying than frightening. I can put up with him." She dismissed the entire unpleasant subject with a flick of her wrist and steered the conversation elsewhere. "I suppose the crew's prepared for the interview with the sheriff this afternoon?"

"All ready to start setting up in his office at two. I've told everybody we need to make this taping go as smoothly as possible. It's taken weeks to get the sheriff to grant an interview, and we can't botch it now. Let's just hope Marc's flight connections aren't delayed and he gets here in time to conduct it."

"Oh, Lord. Don't even mention the possibility of Marc getting here too late," Juliet softly exclaimed, pressing her palms against her temples with a comical grimace. "The mere thought of that happening might cause me to go into cardiac arrest."

"He'll be here; he'll be here. I'm sure of it," Paul responded with a laugh, much to her exaggerated dismay. "After all, you've already performed a miracle, so the entire interview is destined to be an unqualified success. And by the way, just how did you persuade Sheriff Thomas to agree to talk to Marc on-camera?"

"How else? I dazzled with my great beauty, charm, and wit," Juliet quipped then spread her hands expressively. "Actually I simply told him the truth: that if he wouldn't talk to us, we would tell the audience he refused during the aired segment and that, of course, would make him seem guilty even if he happened to be innocent."

"At least he was wise enough to believe you. But, changing the subject, have you heard from the D.A.?"

Juliet smiled. "About a half hour ago. He had a chance to look over the mayor's out-of-town bank statement last night and he's very optimistic about getting an indictment against him. He said it was just the additional evidence he needed."

"Now this story's going somewhere again," said Paul, his expression conveying an understandable hint of professional pride. His mood now seemed more upbeat than it had a few minutes ago, and there was a nearly jaunty spring in his step as he started toward the door. "Well, back to work. See you. . . ." The sudden shrill jangle of the phone ringing interrupted him and made Juliet jump just as he was glancing back over his shoulder, allowing him to witness her response. He halted, his expression hardening. "Want me to get that for you?"

"No, thanks. I'll . . ." Juliet began, but abruptly hesitated. She managed to muster a fairly convincing grin. "Then again, maybe you should. I chipped a nail awhile ago when I slammed the receiver down, and that lout on the other end certainly isn't worth that. *If* this happens to be him again—"

"We'll soon find out. I'll take it," Paul muttered, returning to the desk to snatch up the receiver and growl a greeting. Avoiding Juliet's curious and somewhat wary gaze, he listened silently for several long moments before he, too, replaced the receiver in the cradle with more force than was necessary. Immediately he stared at the floor, as if he were concentrating on the pattern of hardwood grain.

Juliet sighed. "Okay, what did he have to say this time?"

Paul turned in the direction of the door again. "Oh, nothing much. Same old line," he mumbled. "I hung up before he finished."

Watching him walk away, Juliet suddenly suspected there was something he had left unsaid. A vague uneasiness uncurled in the pit of her stomach but, attributing it to an overactive imagination, she tried to dismiss the feeling and instead smile at Paul, who paused in the doorway.

"If you see Marc before I do, would you tell him I'd like to see him?" the director requested, adding on his way out of the room, "I just hope he gets back here early enough to talk to me before the interview."

Juliet hoped Marc would return early too; the earlier the better. Although she hadn't admitted the fact to anyone, the harassing phone calls had begun to nag at her, and she knew that somehow she felt safer with Marc than she did with anyone else. Besides, since she had left him in New York Tuesday, she had missed him terribly. The hours had dragged by at a snail's pace, and she had felt oddly incomplete, as if a very vital part of herself was missing.

"Being in love must be making you a little crazy," she said to herself, smiling wryly as she tidied the material on her desk and wondered if Marc had missed her too. She

201

also couldn't help wondering what his reaction would be when she told him she had thought frequently about continuing their relationship here in Boone and had finally decided he was probably right about the crew. Undoubtedly the members would gossip if it were realized she and Marc were lovers, but the gossip might not be derogatory if the crew did indeed respect her. And there was no reason why they shouldn't—every day she was proving herself a more-than-capable producer.

With her decision made, Juliet felt freer than she had ever felt in her life. This time she was going to be doing what she wanted to do rather than worrying about other people. And accompanying her newfound sense of freedom was a rising excitement: she would be seeing Marc soon, within the next couple of hours. She longed to be close to him again, to see the slow, lazy smile that often touched his lips. After breathing a sigh, she sat up straighter in her chair and shook her head as if to reassemble her thoughts There was only one way to make time pass faster and she picked up her pen and immediately began to jot down a tentative schedule for the rest of the week

About four thirty that afternoon, after the interview with the sheriff was over, Juliet conferred with Marc and Paul in the temporary office at the lodge. Sitting on the edge of her desk, she glanced over the notes she had taken during the interview, then looked at Marc who was in the chair beside her.

"That's done at last, and I think it was a fine interview," she said with a somewhat relieved smile. "You were just hard enough on Sheriff Thomas to get him to talk."

Meeting her gaze directly, Marc spread his hands. "No harder than he should have expected. He wasn't very cooperative, was he?"

"No, and in a way that's a shame, because there was something about the way he defended himself that was rather compelling. Did either of you get the impression that he might be telling the truth?" she asked both Paul and Marc, received two noncommittal answers, and continued. "What I mean is that he did hold his own despite the tough questions, although he's certainly not a smooth talker like Mayor Haynes. But maybe it was his slow, deliberate answers and his earnest expression that made him so convincing."

"Convincing, Julie?" Marc inquired laconically, watching her face. "Are you telling us you believe Sheriff Thomas was *not* involved in any way in the bid-rigging or the bribes?

"Of course, there was always the possibility that ne wasn't," she said, casting a sideways glance at Paul "What do you think?"

The director grinned. "I'm taking the easy way out and reserving judgment for a while."

"That's the only reasonable thing to do for the time being, Julie," Marc put in. "We can't simply decide Thomas is innocent and stop investigating his possible involvement. There've been too many serious accusations made against him."

"Accusations don't necessarily make a case. In fact, sometimes they're deliberately misleading." Juliet persisted good-naturedly. "It could be that the sheriff's name was drawn into this whole scandal just to divert some attention away from the mayor, the judge, and the senator. Did you notice Sheriff Thomas didn't act as if he had much respect for any of them, especially the senator? Just the mention of his name seemed to make him bristle."

"Can't say I blame him," Paul commented dryly. "Benson Velvy isn't the most likable man in the world."

"He certainly isn't," Juliet agreed wholeheartedly. "I

was working on an interview with him last year, and he impressed me as being an outrageously insensitive and inflexible person."

"That's because he is. But my opinion of him isn't important. Neither is Paul's or yours, Julie," Marc reminded her flatly. "The fact that the sheriff seemed to dislike Velvy and complained about having to provide a motorcade every time he visited the county doesn't necessarily prove he couldn't have been involved with the senator in some of the shady dealings."

"No, it doesn't prove that. But still, it's not nearly as likely Sheriff Thomas would be involved in illegal activities with someone he despises," Juliet stated emphatically. "I don't—"

"Come now, children," Paul interceded, chuckling. "Let's not argue."

Juliet laughed. "We're not arguing," she said but hesitated briefly while meeting Marc's gaze. Suddenly realizing he hadn't quite been himself since his return from New York, she wondered if something might be wrong. But what could it be? Uncertainty and concern were mirrored fleetingly in her eyes, then vanished as she considered he could simply be weary after two days of rushing to polish his previous assignment followed by the flight here. That was probably all there was to it, she decided, and her smile brightened again. "At least I'm not arguing. Are you, Marc?"

"Not that I know of," was his easy answer as he stretched out his long legs and situated himself more comfortably in his chair. "I was just having a discussion."

"Good. Now the point I was trying to make is that we have to be careful not to treat Sheriff Thomas unfairly," Juliet went on. "We're not on assignment to persecute innocent people; none of us want to ruin the reputation of anyone who has done nothing wrong."

"There's a simple way to avoid that. We have to dig up as many facts as we possibly can, then make a decision," said Marc. "If we decide the sheriff has probably been unjustly implicated and if the D.A. doesn't intend to press charges against him, we simply don't include today's interview in the segment that's to be aired. But before we can decide anything we have to have more facts."

"That's why I plan to have the researchers do a thorough check of all the sources who implicated Thomas." Reaching behind her for a yellow legal pad and a pencil, Juliet began a short listing of names. "We might discover some or all these people don't exactly have shining reputations themselves."

Marc smiled. "Or we might not."

"Or we might not. We'll have to wait and see what T.J.'s people come up with," she agreed as she handed the finished list to Paul. "I sent Tom on an errand so would you find T.J. and give him this Tell him to have a couple of the researchers find out everything they can about these people. Okay?"

Clucking his tongue against the back of his teeth, Paul shook his head but couldn't suppress a smile. "Turning me into an errand boy," he pretended to complain as he was leaving. "Wait till my union hears about this."

Marc's low laugh drew Juliet's attention again and her smile lingered as she simply looked at him. The moment he had returned from New York earlier this afternoon, Paul had waylaid him and she had had no opportunity since then to speak to him in private. Now they were alone together and it didn't surprise her much to notice her heartbeat seemed to have quickened a bit. Ignoring that physiological reminder of her vulnerability where Marc was concerned, she leaned back on her hands.

"How did it go?" she asked softly. "Did you get your follow-up on the child abuse story all wrapped up?"

With a brief nod, Marc stood, reached for her, and pulled her to him. "It's finished. Miss me?" he asked, his breath tickling her when he bent down to kiss the hollow just beneath her left ear. "I missed you, Julie."

"Ummm, I missed you too . . . when I had time."

"And did you have much time?"

Leaning back in the circle of his arms, she smiled up at him. "Let's just say these past two days seemed to last about two weeks."

Some oddly unfathomable emotion darkened Marc's blue eyes, but he said nothing more before seeking her lips with his. Juliet moved closer, slipping her arms around his neck and, although the kisses they exchanged were warm and exciting, she sensed a certain restraint in him, a certain tension in his embrace. He must be very tired, Juliet thought. With that, she felt an overpowering tenderness for him and an abiding need to soothe away his weariness. Her slim fingers massaged the taut tendons near the nape of his neck while her other hand rubbed over his back.

"Julie, come here," Marc said softly after a moment, drawing away only to take her former place on the edge of the desk and draw her toward him between his long legs. Reaching out, he played with the flaxen tendril of wayward hair on her temple, gently winding it around one tanned finger. "I want to talk to you."

"And I want to talk to you," she answered, feeling now was as good a time as any to tell him her decision. "I've been thinking about what you said about the crew gossiping. . . ."

"I've been thinking about that, too, and you're probably right," he broke in softly. "We really can't afford to be free spirits, not while we're here anyway, with crew members all around us. If they know we're . . . personally involved with each other, of course, they're going to talk a great deal, and it would be wise of us to avoid gossip like that."

For a long moment Juliet was too stunned to speak, although she tried valiantly to mask the inner turmoil she felt. Aware of the dull, heavy thudding of her heart, she simply stared at Marc, hoping neither her eyes nor her expression reflected the sudden abysmal emptiness spreading within her. What he had just said had been the last thing in the world she had expected to hear, and confusion gnawed at her relentlessly. At last she recovered use of her voice and asked, "What . . . made you change your mind about this?"

Marc's broad shoulders rose and fell with a slight shrug. "We have to think of our careers. That's more important than anything else, and it's possible gossip could damage us both irreparably."

How very cold and unemotional the words sounded, Juliet thought. Although she had used that same argument with him previously, everything was different now. Marc had become more important than anything else in her life, so important that she had been willing to risk another scandal simply to be with him. But apparently she was just not that important to him, and there was nothing she could do but accept his decision with as much dignity —or bravado—as she could muster.

"I'm glad you finally understand what I've been trying to tell you all along," she lied, her voice low-pitched as she forced herself to look directly into his eyes. She hated uttering the lie, but pride made her do it. "That's what I was just about to say: I did think about what you said the other night, but I've decided it would be a foolish risk."

"It is best this way," he agreed, releasing her hair and allowing his hand to drop away from her face. The half-smile that moved his hard mouth didn't look particularly sincere. "But maybe after this assignment's ended, we—"

"We'll just have to wait and see how we both feel then, won't we?" Juliet murmured, stepping backward, needing desperately to put some distance between them as a dreadful suspicion flowered in her. *He had no reason to worry about their relationship hurting his career.* Incredibly popular with television viewers, he was influential enough at Union Broadcasting to maintain his position, no matter how risqué his personal life might be. And suddenly Juliet realized he had to be aware of how much power he had. He was free to do as he pleased, so perhaps he merely engineered this little scene as his way of letting her down easy and extricating himself from an involvement that was beginning to bore him. Well, if that was his intention, she certainly wasn't going to make it difficult for him to escape. Inhaling deeply, she turned her hands in a seemingly careless gesture and aimed a smile at him. "Who knows? Could be that after this story's finished, we won't be the least bit interested in resuming our . . . relationship."

"Could be," he agreed, rising from the desk and brushing back the sides of his coat to slide his hands into his trouser pockets. "As you said, we'll just have to wait and see how we feel then."

"That's that, then," said Juliet as lightly as possible, hoping he didn't detect the note of finality she herself noticed in her voice. Eager to escape him and be alone in total privacy to nurse the wounds he had inflicted, she glanced at her watch. "Marc, would you excuse me? I've been looking forward to a long hot bath before dinner all day."

"One more thing before you go, Julie," he said, moving swiftly to block her path round the desk. "Paul told me a different car's been following you since you came back, and that the intimidating phone calls are coming much more often now. He thinks you may be beginning to get a little upset."

"Upset?" With a toss of her head, she pretended to dismiss the very idea. "I'm not upset. Aggravated, yes, but

208

Paul doesn't have to worry about me. I can handle the phone calls just fine."

"But you don't have to handle them by yourself, Julie," Marc persisted, hands still in his pockets. "We're all in this together, and if the calls begin to get to you, I want you to tell me. I'll do what I can to help whenever you need me."

Was this another pitch? His roundabout way of suggesting they be friends as well as colleagues? Two days ago they had been lovers, involved in a passionate affair, and if he thought they could become the greatest of chums now . . . Juliet lifted her chin; she was filled with hurt and resentment. Maybe she should be sophisticated enough to be buddy-buddy with an ex-lover, but at the moment she didn't much feel like being blasé about the end of the affair. She simply wanted to get away from Marc, and she didn't want him sending her off with obligatory promises of being supportive and there if she needed him. She didn't need him that way and said so diplomatically. "Thanks for the offer, Marc. I'll keep it in mind. But I'm sure I'll be able to handle the calls. Would you lock up when you leave? See you during dinner."

Giving Marc no chance to detain her again, she quickly walked out of the office down the inside corridor to the room that had been his but which she now occupied. After pushing the door shut behind her, she locked it and went to drop down across her bed. Turning over, she buried her face in her folded arms and heaved a long tremulous sigh. She couldn't recall ever having felt this lonely and assailed by a sense of loss.

"That's what you get for falling in love with him, fool," she muttered almost inaudibly. From the beginning she had feared he would tire of her eventually—she simply hadn't expected it to happen this soon. But it had, and the irony of his timing was almost darkly humorous. A bleak smile twisted her lips. How long had Marc been trying to convince her that getting involved with him wouldn't hurt her reputation or career? And just when she had decided he might be right and was willing to chance it even if he wasn't, he called the whole thing off. Why?

Juliet had no idea. In his apartment Monday night he had seemed closer to her than he'd ever been; he had been so tender and loving that she had actually begun to harbor the hope that he might be falling in love with her. Now it was quite obvious she had been completely wrong. Yet it seemed unlikely to her that a man could tire of a woman so quickly, in two days time. Then again, what did she know about men? Very little; she had deliberately avoided any serious involvements until meeting Marc. Now it looked as if she were going to have to pay dearly for her lack of experience in man-woman relationships.

Uncaring that her navy linen skirt twisted into a mass of wrinkles around her thighs, Juliet turned onto her back and stared up the wood-beamed ceiling. A near-strangling constriction gripping her throat made it difficult to swallow, and the pressure of tears that needed to be shed ached behind her eyes, but she refused to cry, afraid she might have trouble stopping once she started.

"I'll be damned if I'll go down to dinner with red puffy eyes," she muttered to herself. Maybe later tonight, when she was in bed and able to bury her face in the pillow, she would cry it all out but not now. She just couldn't go before her crew with a tear-streaked face and splotchy skin. It simply wasn't the thing to do, and Juliet was swiftly coming to the conclusion that she would be wise to revert to her old personal habit of doing exactly what was expected of her. If she had to sacrifice some adventure and joy, so be it. Life certainly seemed safer that way.

Lying on the bed, feeling suddenly exhausted and a little lost, Juliet allowed her mind to wander until she remembered the kisses Marc had given her less than a half hour ago after Paul had left them alone in the office. She touched her fingertips to her lips, which immediately pressed together in a tight grim line. Those kisses had meant nothing to him and his words *I missed you, Julie* rang in her memory. Heat flooded her cheeks. She was embarrassed he had thought it necessary to let her down that easy and even to pretend they might resume their relationship in the future. He had needed to go that far; yet try as she did to be angry at him, she couldn't be. It really wasn't his fault she had been reckless enough to become too involved with him.

An unbidden thought reared up in Juliet's mind and she moaned softly, awash with humiliation. *I am too attached to him.* Had he sensed that? Was that the real reason why he had decided to end everything between them? Perhaps he had thought she might become far too possessive if their relationship continued and might even press him to make a permanent commitment. Mortified by the possibility that that could have been his motive, she turned her face into the quilted coverlet again. He should have known she would never have considered trying to pressure him into a commitment; after all, he had practically said outright that his career came first and far beyond any personal relationship. And she had believed him. She wouldn't have pushed then, and she wouldn't push now. She wondered if he perhaps was uneasy because he thought she might still try to salvage their relationship. Gnawing her bottom lip, she wished there was some way to let him know that as far as she was concerned, it was over. He had ended it. And, as the saying went, you can't go home again.

There was only one true way to reassure him. Until they had wrapped up and left Boone behind, she would avoid Marc as much as possible; when she couldn't avoid him, she would relate to him as a colleague. Never anything more than that. She had to be friendly, of course, but she would convey a strictly professional friendliness that couldn't embarrass him and would, in a minor way, assuage her battered pride. It wouldn't be easy but she would survive. She had been happy and content before Marc came into her life. She would be happy and content in the future. It might take awhile to get over loving him, but the day would come when all she had shared with him was no more than a bittersweet memory. But even as Juliet hammered all those truths into her mind, she couldn't help wondering how long and lonely the days and nights would be until that happy, content time did come again.

CHAPTER THIRTEEN

Monday, a week and a half later, Juliet tried once more to persuade the dispatcher in the sheriff's department to tell whatever she might know about Senator Velvy. Once more she failed and retreated, but with every intention to try again another day. The woman was hiding something; Juliet sensed it and didn't believe the dispatcher was keeping quiet because she feared losing her job. If the sheriff himself was innocent of any wrongdoing—and indications were pointing strongly that way—he certainly wouldn't fire an employee for talking about the senator. There had to be some other reason the woman had recently begun refusing to answer any questions at all and Juliet wanted very much to discover what that reason was.

Deep in thought, she left the sheriff's offices housed in a fairly new brick building in the outskirts of Trenton. The hot midafternoon sun bore down on her unprotected head as she crossed the graveled parking lot and went to her car, parked in the shade of a sprawling oak bough. Cooler air greeted her, but just as she started to open the driver's door, her eyes began adjusting to the dimmer light and suddenly noticed the tires. The front and rear were both totally flat, and when Juliet dashed around to the other side, she discovered she had a complete set of flats. She could hardly believe her eyes, particularly when, on closer inspection, she found deep slash marks in the rubber.

213

"Hell and damnation," she swore softly, running a hand over her hair. "These people are going too far."

"Trouble, ma'am? Something I can do to help?" a man's voice asked behind her.

Juliet spun around, startled and more than a little wary until she took in the appearance of the man stepping around the huge thick trunk of the oak. Thirtyish but boyishly slim and wearing a friendly smile, he was clad in expensive sport shirt and slacks and looked no more like a thug than she did, despite the fact he had on dark glasses. Relaxing somewhat, Juliet swept a hand toward the ruined tires.

"You might be able to help if you happen to have four spares I can borrow," she answered with a rueful smile. "Which I'm sure you don't."

"No, ma'am," he said, coming closer. "But I can give you some advice. If you know what's good for you, you'll pack up your television crew and get the hell out of North Carolina. There are plenty of people that don't like all your meddling around. You understand that?"

Juliet stared at him, her jaw nearly going slack she was so surprised. Her heart racing, she took an involuntary backward step, coming up against the handle of the passenger door, which dug into the small of her back. And abruptly the physical discomfort fueled her resentment and her shoulders squared as she glared frostily at him. He merely smiled smugly and unpleasantly in response.

"You can threaten all you like, but you're wasting your time," she uttered bluntly, her eyes snapping. "Go back and tell whoever hired you that *Perspective* is here to stay until this story's finished. And even if you did manage to scare me away, another producer would just be given this assignment, so your threats aren't worth much, are they?"

"Don't smart-mouth me, lady," the intimidator snarled, reaching out for her throat with the swiftness of

214

a striking snake and amazingly pressing the back of her neck hard against the top of the doorframe. Bending over Juliet, his hot breath searing her face, he lowered his voice to a vicious whisper. "You're sticking your nose in what's none of your business, and I'm telling you to stop. *Now.* You might be real sorry if you don't."

Juliet's wide eyes darted in every direction, seeking the crew member who was riding shotgun with her today, until she realized he must be parked out of her view from this side of the car. And if she couldn't see him, he couldn't see her either! Oh, why had she parked where she couldn't be easily seen? She had made it easier for this degenerate to accost her, and now she had to handle him by herself. Fear seemed to trickle down her spine and squeeze her stomach, but she was determined not to show it.

"Take your hands off me," she demanded raspingly. "This instant."

"Sure, lady." Releasing her abruptly and moving back, he smirked and jabbed one pointed index finger toward her in the air. "Just you remember what I said: You might be real sorry if you don't take your people and get away from here."

Before Juliet could react, he circumvented the tree, loped to the edge of the narrow secondary road beyond, and leaped into rumbling silver sports car that screeched to a halt beside him. The driver floored it; tires squealed as the car spun away and disappeared around a curve in a matter of seconds. Lifting herself away from her car, her entire body violently shaking, Juliet pressed her fingers hard against the frantically throbbing pulse in her temples as she tried to take several deep steadying breaths. Her legs felt rubbery; as if they might buckle beneath her weight. The man had succeeded in frightening her—there was no doubt about that. Although Marc had told her to

215

be prepared for the unexpected, she hadn't anticipated being threatened face-to-face. Still feeling the imprint of the man's fingers around her neck, she rubbed her skin and managed to compose herself before stepping from behind the tree to search for the van the crew used. Yet when she spotted it, her composure slipped again, and it took a great deal of self-control to restrain herself from running wildly to it and to its driver.

Two hours later Juliet's rental car had four brand-new tires and she had a splitting headache. In her room at the lodge she sat curled up in the easy chair beside her bed, resting her forehead against the wing, waiting for the aspirin she had taken to alleviate the tension-induced pain. Her nerves were calmer now, though her hands were still a bit unsteady, and full-fledged resentment and anger were slowly but surely replacing the fright she had felt. A slightly stubborn streak she had always possessed flared to life with a vengeance; she knew she wouldn't rest until this corruption story was as complete as she could make it and ready to be aired, all the loose ends tied up to her satisfaction. Except for scaring her half out of her skin, today's episode had backfired and merely reinforced her determination.

Lifting her head, Juliet rested it back against the cushion and closed her eyes against the glare of late afternoon light. She reached for the glass of lemonade on the table beside her but before she could take a refreshing ice-cold sip, there was a knock on her door. Deciding the chair was too comfortable to surrender, she simply called out for her unknown visitor to enter. And when Marc opened the door, came in, and moved across the room toward her, his strides long and purposeful, his expression grim, she sat immobile, the rim of her glass poised close to her lips. She looked up when Marc stopped directly in front of her and hooked his hands in the back pockets of his khaki pants.

216

"I was about to go for a walk when Joe told me what happened at the sheriff's department this afternoon," he began at once, his voice stern. "Why didn't *you* come and tell me about it?"

Shrugging, Juliet took a slow sip of lemonade, then set it aside. "There wasn't much to tell actually. The whole episode boiled down to an outrageous charge for four steel-belted radials on my expense account."

"Who cares about the damn tires?" Marc ground out, tiny lines appearing around his mouth as he bent over her, a hand on each arm of her chair. "I know they were slashed—that doesn't surprise me. But Joe said you were grabbed by some man. Are you all right?"

"I have a little tension headache, but other than that I'm fine," she assured him calmly, drawing back almost imperceptibly, too aware of the disturbingly familiar spicy male scent of him. The throb in her temples sharpened, but she smiled anyhow. "Really, I am. The man didn't hurt me."

"Then how the devil did you get those bruises on your neck?" Marc growled, leaning closer, his eyes narrowing nearly to slits as she compulsively brought her hands up to her throat. "If he didn't hurt you, where did those come from?"

"I guess he did squeeze a little hard," she admitted, unwittingly wincing as her fingers probed a particularly tender area of skin. "But he wasn't as rough as it looks like. I just bruise easily."

"For God's sake, you almost sound like you're defending the bastard," Marc uttered, his voice becoming deceptively soft. Pushing her hands away, her ran his own incredibly gentle fingertips over the darkening splotches on her creamy smooth neck. "He assaulted you, Julie. Did you report him to Sheriff Thomas?"

"Sure. I thought he'd want to know what had happened right in his own parking lot."

"You signed a complaint against that hoodlum?"

"Yes, for whatever that was worth. The sheriff agreed with me that he was probably long gone but he did radio his deputies to be on the lookout for him."

"Then you were able to give a description of the car he got away in?"

Juliet nodded. "A silver sports car. An MG, I think."

"Could you make an educated guess about the year and the model?"

"Heavens, no. MGs aren't my thing," she quipped recklessly. "I like Jaguars."

Marc's eyes iced to a glacier-blue and seemed to impale hers with piercing hardness as he continued to lean over her, too close for comfort. "I suppose you did get the license number?" he asked, the words clipped. And when she shook her head, he exhaled audibly through clenched teeth. "When will you learn, Julie? Haven't I told you often enough to always be aware of license numbers?"

"The car was too far away for me to see the plate," she fabricated slightly. The car *had* been too far away, but even if hadn't, it had never crossed her mind to try to see the number when her attacker was escaping. At the time she had been too overwrought, too amazed for common sense thought but she wasn't about to admit that to Marc. Right now, he wasn't acting particularly understanding. After scooting farther back on the cushion, she shrugged again. "Besides, Thomas didn't hold out much hope of stopping the car. By the time I finished telling him everything, he figured those men were probably already in another county, maybe even across the state line, in Tennessee. The license number wouldn't have helped."

"But they might be back, so you would remember the man if you saw him again?"

"Without a doubt. That face is etched indelibly in my mind."

"Give me a description."

"Dark brown hair. He was wearing sunglasses, so I couldn't tell the color of his eyes. A thin face, light complexion," Juliet rattled off the list of physical characteristics. "He had very white, very straight teeth and a nice pleasant smile, but that didn't last long. And he spoke with a northern accent."

"Height?"

"Ummm, tall but not as tall as you are."

"Be more specific."

"Oh, five ten or eleven, maybe. A couple inches shorter than you."

"Weight?"

"He was slim, almost skinny."

"Be more specific, Julie."

The hint of impatience Juliet heard in Marc's voice made her sit up straighter in her chair and unknowingly lift her chin. "Why all the questions about what he looked like?" she asked heatedly, her headache and her unconquerable feelings for him making her more than a little irritable. "Are you planning to form a posse and go after him?"

"Don't be flip."

"Why shouldn't I be?" she countered tersely. "After all, you're interrogating me, treating me like I'm some kind of criminal you're interviewing. And for no good reason."

"Don't exaggerate; I'm not treating you like a criminal, and I do have a good reason for asking questions. I'd like to know what the man looks like so I can keep an eye out for him."

"I doubt we'll see him again. He's done what he was paid to do and he wouldn't want to risk me identifying him." Juliet wrinkled her nose disdainfully. "I imagine

Senator Velvy has an inexhaustible supply of thugs at his disposal."

Marc's brows lifted questioningly and at last, he moved away from her to sit on the edge of her bed. "What makes you so sure Velvy's behind the harassment? Were you able to get something out of the dispatcher? Did she—"

"She wouldn't say a word. I'd almost bet she's never going to, but nothing changes the fact that she nearly flinches whenever I even mention the senator," Juliet explained. "And isn't he the one with the most to lose in this situation? He's a U.S. senator and already in trouble with the voters—who've started viewing him as mean-hearted, which he is."

A smile tugged at the corner of Marc's mouth. "He is in your opinion."

"An opinion shared by many, including you, I suspect," she parried. "Anyway with an election coming up soon, Velvy can't afford even a hint of scandal. If he did bribe the judge to hand down light sentences to the councilman and the deputy, he'd probably go pretty far in trying to stop our investigation."

Marc nodded thoughtfully. "I'm sure it would be nearly impossible to prove he's behind the harassment though. As you said, he's a powerful man with many connections. One of his aides might have contacted someone, who hired someone else, who sent your attacker here. There probably isn't anything that would tie him directly to the senator. And unfortunately it might turn out to be almost as difficult to tie Velvy to the judge, if he *is* guilty of bribing him."

"I know," Juliet agreed with a weary-sounding sigh while running a hand over the side of her neck and around to massage the tightness gathering in her nape. Her face was wistful. "It certainly would be a hot story if we could find strong evidence of his involvement and a public service too. If he's crooked, he should be thrown out of office."

Closely watching her rub the back of her neck, Marc frowned slightly. "Are you sure you're all right? He didn't hurt you worse than you're admitting, did he, Julie?"

Juliet shook her head. "He wasn't trying to hurt me, just scare me. I'm fine."

He got up and came to her, putting a hand out to touch her hair. "Maybe it wouldn't be a bad idea to have a doctor check you."

"Marc, I'm all right. I don't need a doctor," she insisted softly, tensing beneath his light touch and trying to halt the shivers of sensual awareness that ran over her. She didn't want him making her feel that way again. For nearly two weeks, they had kept each other at a distance, their only interaction professional, never personal. They were friendly, of course—they had to work together—but the closeness they had once shared was gone. Now his warmth and concern for her was merely serving as a reminder of what had been and she didn't want to remember. That hurt too much. Drawing back, she escaped his ministering hand and made herself smile up at him. "I'm really okay. I've put what happened this afternoon right out of my mind."

Darkening perceptive eyes studied her carefully. "If that's true, Julie," he said after a moment, "why are you still trembling?"

"I'm not," she lied, hastily dropping her hands into her lap and clasping them tightly to still their shaking.

"You are," he differed flatly, shaking his head. "Come on, Julie, why this 'tough' act?"

"I'm not trying to *act* tough. I get the impression you think I'm just on the verge of lapsing into hysteria. Sorry to disappoint you, but that just isn't true. So I got manhandled a little this afternoon. I wasn't really hurt, so no big deal."

"Big enough to justify being upset. Why are you trying to hide how you feel from me?"

"But I'm not," she stated quietly, looking deeply into his eyes while holding a firm grip on her emotions. She was determined not to let him talk her into revealing exactly how shaken, how vulnerable she was feeling. She smiled wanly. "Look, Marc, I appreciate your concern, but it isn't necessary. The episode in the parking lot may cause me to have a few bad dreams, but that's all the harm it did. You don't need to hover over me. I don't need coddling."

Marc's pleasantly rough fingertips grazed her cheek, slipped beneath her jaw, and tilted up her chin. "A little coddling now and then never hurt anybody."

"Maybe not," she replied wryly. "But you have to admit you wouldn't think about coddling me if I were a male producer who had been knocked around a—"

"Whoa, spare me the feminist speech," Marc interrupted, raising a silencing hand and nearly grinning. "I'm all for the cause, but the rhetoric's beginning to wear on me."

"Even so, if I were a man—"

"But you're not. And if it's coddling you to help you get rid of your tension headache, so be it," he said, wasting no time reaching down to nimbly undo the second and third buttons of her pristine white blouse. Ignoring her exclamation of surprise and protesting gestures, he pushed the garment back on her shoulders then walked behind her chair. "A gentle neck massage will work wonders, and I'll be careful not to touch the bruises."

Juliet's entire body tensed when Marc's large warm hands came down softly on her shoulders and glided inward over the bare sensitive skin toward her neck. Feelings too intense and too disruptive rushed through her, and she closed her eyes for a fraction of a second. She

222

didn't need this. His touch was too much a pleasure and too much a torment. She twisted around on the cushion to look back at him.

"You don't have to do this," she protested. "I already took aspirin."

"Turn around. Relax," he coaxed though in a firm enough tone to indicate he didn't intend to be swayed from his objective. "Feeling how bunched up and tight your muscles are, I'm not surprised you have a headache. Loosen up, Julie. Lean your head forward a little."

Juliet obeyed but couldn't actually relax. She didn't dare. She had to steel herself against the effect of the moving kneading hands slipping beneath her hair. With every fleeting brush of a fingertip against her scalp, her breath seemed to catch down deep in her chest, and she was disturbed by her silly heart's thudding reaction to his nearness. She wished she could learn to be much less responsive to him, both emotionally and physically. But that was easier said than done. She longed to feel at ease around him, but thus far hadn't had any luck at it. It was a little absurd. She was an adult woman. And Marc was just a man. . . . *No, he wasn't.* He was the one man she loved very much and that made all the difference. His touch was special, and for her, almost irresistible.

"You're still tense, Julie," he murmured, his lean strong fingers applying light pressure in circular motions along the length of her neck. "If you were to lie down, I could do this more effectively."

Juliet's eyes were drawn up toward her bed, and she knew it would be absolute insanity to let him continue the massage there. Lying down, knowing he was beside her, feeling his masterly arousing hands on her, she might— Oh, no. She knew only too well the depths of her feelings, knew how badly she wanted and needed him and at that

223

moment, her bed seemed the most dangerous place in the world. She shook her head.

"Oh, I don't want to move now; this feels too good to be interrupted," she exaggerated. "I think my head's already beginning to hurt less."

"It might stop hurting altogether if you could relax more," he told her quietly, shaping the contracted muscles below her nape with his thumbs. "You still feel like you're in knots. Can't you loosen up your shoulders?"

Juliet tried, and slowly, under the patient expert hands, began to succumb. Her muscles started to tingle and gradually unbunch as more and more tension was being slowly, very slowly, melted away in a building physical warmth. Marc knew what he was doing. His powerful fingers swept over her neck and upper shoulders in rippling pressuring strokes and soon Juliet was slowly turning her head from side to side in silent encouragement, occasionally grazing her jaw against his hard knuckles. Her eyes had fluttered shut, and she made a soft contented sound.

"That's better," said Marc, raising his resonant low-timbred voice barely above a whisper, as if reluctant to disturb her. "I can tell you're more relaxed now."

"Ummm, this is lovely," she murmured. "Pardon me while I drop off to sleep."

Within moments, however, Juliet's drowsiness vanished. Her body's natural need for rest and her mind's for the forgetfulness found in sleep gave way to another need as powerful and far more intriguing. Marc had pulled her blouse farther down her back; his fingers were tracing the straight line of her spine, applying pressure in slow circular motions, roaming lower and lower toward the hook of her bra. And suddenly that contact of flesh on flesh sent a radiating thrill rushing over her and made her ache for him to unfasten that hook, slip his hands around to cup her breasts and tease the sensitive peaks to throbbing hardness. Desire surged so strongly in her that she longed to turn her face in to the curve of his hand and scatter enticing lingering kisses over his palm then move swiftly into his arms, inviting his lovemaking. But she couldn't do any of these things, not even the first of them, knowing she would only betray herself if she did. For days she had controlled her awesome need to be close to Marc; she could not relinquish control simply because his warming soothing massage had weakened mental resolve and physical resistance. Now she realized she was too relaxed and too vulnerable—and much too tempted—to lose herself in an ardent response. She had to call a halt to what he was doing to her before she passed the point where she couldn't stop at all.

"Thanks, Marc. That's fine," she spoke up, an odd little cadence to her voice. "I feel much better now." But when his hands left her and empty air remained to lie against her heated skin, she really didn't feel better. She felt bereft and lonely and lost. Yet there was no quick remedy for such feelings, and she knew very well that she would simply have to endure them until they passed. Only after drawing her blouse around her again and fastening all except the topmost button did she raise her head to look at Marc. She managed a smile she hoped appeared appreciative as she added, "I think my headache will be completely gone soon."

"A long hot shower before dinner might chase it away for good," he suggested, tucking his hands back into his pockets and rocking back on his heels. For an instant he looked down at her, his eyes inscrutable and darkly thoughtful, then planted his feet firmly on the floor again, moved past her, and away toward the door. "I'll go for my walk and leave you alone so you can at least give it a try."

"Thanks again, Marc," Juliet said quietly when he paused and glanced back at her.

"Anytime," was his answer as he left.

And after he had closed the door behind him on his way out, she sat staring after him for a while, feeling both relief and regret because he was gone.

About dusk Wednesday night Marc's car was parked by the edge of an isolated rural road, and in the front passenger seat Juliet made herself as comfortable as possible. She looked out through the stand of road-bordering maples to the rolling meadowland beyond, growing darker with each moment of ebbing twilight.

"Our mysterious informant sure picked an out-of-the-way place for us to meet him in," she commented to Marc, who was sitting beside her, one long arm draped casually across the steering wheel. Lifting her wrist, she peered at her watch, trying to discern the placement of the hands on the face despite the gathering darkness. "It's about eight, and he said he'd be here as soon as it started getting really dark so we shouldn't have to wait long."

"If he comes at all," Marc said with a shrug. "Would-be informants are notorious for backing out at the last minute."

"Maybe this one won't," replied Juliet hopefully, smoothing her skirt with her hands for lack of anything better to do. Out of the corners of her eyes, she glanced sideways at Marc, wondering what she could say next to break the absolute quiet in the car. She had to say something; these days she felt compelled to keep conversation going while she was with Marc. Before, while their relationship had been intimate, silences between them had been comfortable and companionable. That wasn't the case any longer. Now, any silence between them, no matter how brief, filled her with tension and seemed to enclose

226

her in a choking mist as this one was doing now, making her more and more on edge with each second it continued. Yet she had to search her brain for something—anything —to talk about. In the past two weeks the possible topics of conversation she could have with Marc had dwindled practically to zero and she didn't have much choice except to initiate yet another discussion of their assignment. Better than nothing though, she supposed. Drawing in a silent fortifying breath, she tucked her feet, in canvas espadrilles, up beside her on the seat as she turned toward Marc, able to see him more clearly now in the light of the particularly brilliant quarter moon rising in the sky.

"I talked to the D.A. today," she announced, seizing upon that little bit of information simply because it was the first to come to mind. "He didn't say so outright, but I got the impression that he probably won't try for an indictment against Sheriff Thomas, although he doesn't seem to completely believe in his innocence yet."

"Neither do I. Completely believe, that is," said Marc, strumming his fingers on the steering wheel. "I think he's probably innocent, but I can't be sure of it since there are those who swear he isn't."

"I wouldn't trust any of those people as far as I could throw this car. According to our researchers, all of them have reputations for being dishonest. They're not exactly what you'd call reliable informants."

"I agree but, even though they're not pillars of the community and have been known to lie, you can't necessarily assume they're lying this time," Marc said, draping his right arm across the top of the seat behind her. "Sometimes it's wise to hold on to a few doubts, Julie, especially in this business. And you don't seem to have any about Thomas. Maybe you should."

Juliet smiled. "Maybe so, but you're right: I don't doubt

the sheriff's innocence. For some reason, I have this strong feeling he is. Chalk it up to woman's intuition."

"Intuition, woman's or any other kind, isn't infallible."

"I know, but this time, I'm pretty sure I can trust mine," she said, a hint of quiet determination in her tone, which then lightened as she looked out the window at the narrow two-lane blacktop. "And my intuition also tells me we could stay here till doomsday, and this guy still might not show up."

"We won't wait for him quite that long," Marc assured her, smiling. "Sometimes people who voluntarily offer information need a long while to get up enough nerve to give it. We'll wait an hour or so. Too bad we didn't bring a deck of cards to help us pass the time."

"Too dark anyway. We'd never be able to see them." Lifting a hand to her mouth, Juliet stifled a yawn. "Well, I suppose we could always tell each other ghost stories."

Marc laughed softly. "Overnight camp revisited, but I'm willing if you are. Know any good ones?"

"Oh, I used to know a few guaranteed to make your hair stand on end," she said with some enthusiasm, then wrinkled her nose. "But I guess they'd only effect you that way if you were twelve years old or younger. You wouldn't be interested in hearing them."

"Try me."

Juliet shook her head.

"I'll tell you one then." Marc moved across the seat, closer to her, his voice lowering. "It's not your average ghost story, but the desk clerk at the lodge told Paul and me about it the other night, and he says it's true."

Juliet's interest was piqued. She leaned nearer. "Really? What did he tell you?"

"According to Bob, sometime a few years back, there was a horrendously gruesome murder committed here in the county," Marc began softly, then added, "As a matter of fact, I believe he said it happened somewhere along this road."

"You're kidding?"

"No, I'm not. Bob said it happened in a meadow near a stand of trees close to the road." Marc looked up and out her side window. He raised his eyebrows. "Actually I guess it could have happened right along here. This place certainly fits the description."

Playing along, Juliet pretended to glance compulsively back over her shoulder then look back at him with wide eyes. She cleared her throat nervously. "I . . . don't think I want to hear about—"

"Sure you do. The story's not all that horrid," Marc added quite solemnly. "Anyway, it seems there were these two men, business partners for twenty years or more, and one of them wanted to sell the business but the other refused flatly to do that—"

"Marc, you devil, that's enough," Juliet murmured, and was no longer able to contain the laughter that was bubbling up in her. Pale moonlight danced merrily in her eyes as he automatically caught her wrist in one large hand when she lightly cuffed his arm. She shook her head at him. "I know this is no true story. You're making up every word of it as you go."

"How did you know?" he asked, laughing with her until suddenly, in a tiny fragment of a moment, everything was different. Their soft laughter stopped; smiles faded, and they were simply looking at each other, gazes locked as if neither of them possessed the will to look away. Certainly Juliet didn't, and even when the edge of Marc's thumb began to play slowly over the quickening pulse in her wrist and warning signals clanged in her brain, she scarcely noticed them; she didn't even attempt to pull her hand away. She continued simply to look at him, fascinated, nearly mesmerized by the gently intent expression on his face. A light summer breeze swayed the branches of the nearest tree. Moonlight filtered between the leaves and through the windshield, casting a bronze glow on Marc's skin. And Juliet could clearly distinguish his carved features when he lowered his hand from the back of seat, curved it over her left shoulder, and drew her toward him.

As if in a trance, she moved toward him, enthralled by the warmth emanating from his broad chest, by the hard feel of him as her hands floated up against his shoulders, and by the softly sensuous yet firm curve of his mouth. In that instant all was forgotten except the driving need to be close to him once again. Her fingers spread open across his shirtfront. Her heart raced when he took her chin between thumb and forefinger to uptilt her face. The pale light gilded his sandy hair as he leaned forward to lay a feathery light kiss on her lips. He drew away then but only for a moment before seeking her mouth again, withdrawing, seeking again and again as her response became an invitation he had no desire to refuse.

Juliet's emotions careened out of control; she was powerless against the tide of sensations that brought her fully alive again. Her mouth was opening like a sweet fragile flower to his, her soft lips brushing, caressing, the firmer shape of his. The familiar passion exploded between the couple, white-hot and all-consuming, spreading like a burst of wildfire over both of them.

With a muffled groan Marc pressed Juliet back against the seat, his upper body covering hers, evocatively heavy and masculinely firm against her slender shapely form. When her arms went round his waist, his mouth took swift possession of hers, and as she kissed him back, the tip of her tongue playfully parrying his, a shudder ran through him.

Fingers swept through the silken strands of her hair, tangling in them. Marc tilted her head to one side to rain hot searching kisses over her neck and down into the hollow at the base of her throat. Trembling, she pressed him closer. Then his lips were seeking the sweetness o. hers again and she was kissing him with an urgent hunger that equaled his. Even as she was set adrift in a realm of sensual pleasure and promise, a tiny voice of reason in the far recesses of her mind cried out for control. She ignored it. Emotions and needs much more powerful than mere logic held sway now. It seemed an eternity since she and Marc had been this close. She had been lonely and had longed to be in his arms again. Now she was, and for several heavenly minutes she could not deny herself the odd sense of completion she felt.

It was only when Marc moved his hands beneath her blouse and over the rounded swell of her breasts that she began to come to her senses. When his long lean fingers slipped into her bra, playing over and around the firm peaks, arousing them to budding hardness, she felt almost faint with delight but she also felt the dawning of fear as she started to realize exactly what it was she was doing—inviting more pain for herself. All Marc seemed to want from her was an on-again, off-again relationship, but she didn't think she could endure adjusting to many more of the off periods. She didn't dare let her feelings tonight lure her into repeating the entire process. Both passion and pleasure waned as she considered the heightened pain she would have to face if she didn't put an end to this madness here and now.

"Marc, no. Stop," she breathed, pushing at his hands and dragging herself away from him to the far side of the seat against the car door. Unwilling to look at him, she sat tense, staring straight ahead out the windshield. She tried to take a deep breath. "How . . . crazy," she murmured at last. "We didn't drive out here to park and neck . ."

Marc said nothing and continued to say nothing for the following fifteen minutes. With each second that dragged by, Juliet's nerves became a little bit more frayed. The tension between them and the unspoken words that perhaps should have been said hung over her like a pall in the silence of the car, and she knew that if Marc did not speak soon, she would have to, if only to put an end to the tormenting quiet. Clenching her hands together in her lap, she hazarded a quick glance at Marc and was dismayed by what she saw. There was a hard, implacable set to his chiseled profile that indicated he had no desire to strike up a conversation. If she wanted to end the silence, she would have to do so herself.

With the tip of her tongue Juliet moistened suddenly dry lips. "I don't think our informant's going to show," she began at last, some strain in her voice. "Maybe he never meant to. It could be our friends are tired of trying to scare off this assignment and decided to get rid of us by boring us to death instead. It's a little farfetched, but do you think they may have brought us out here on a wild-goose chase?"

"Or a set-up," Marc muttered, looking at her now, his eyes dark, narrowed. He swore beneath his breath, then leaned forward to turn the key and start the engine. "The possibility never occurred to me, but it should have. I shouldn't have brought you out here with me, and we're leaving right now."

Juliet didn't argue. She wanted to leave. As Marc shifted gears and spun away from the trees onto the roadway, she sank down in the seat, not caring that the informant might arrive late, after they were gone, and they would miss him. And she didn't care if there was a slim possibility she and Marc had been lured out here for some extracurricular harassment. At that moment she didn't even care much about her precious assignment. Her career wasn't everything. Her personal life was important, too, and right now it seemed to be in a shambles. Tears pricked her eyes as they sped back toward the lodge. Surreptitiously, she looked at Marc, and as usual experienced a hot, tight aching in her chest. It was all so insane. She wanted him; he wanted her—it should have been simple. But it certainly wasn't, because she also wanted love, while he obviously didn't; that made for an irreconcilable situation.

CHAPTER FOURTEEN

At times it seemed to Juliet that she had been on this assignment for years instead of weeks. With many sources too intimidated to talk openly, progress was exceedingly slow and occasionally came to a virtual standstill. Yet, fitting together bits and pieces of information, Juliet and the *Perspective* team were beginning to see more and more evidence that indicated Senator Velvy probably had bribed the district judge to hand down light sentences in the corruption trial—his motive being to protect his old crony, Mayor Haynes. Velvy and Haynes were thick as thieves, and had been for years; it was logical to assume the mayor hadn't wanted his bid-rigging cohorts—the councilman and the deputy—to receive such stiff sentences that they might be tempted to try to get them reduced by testifying that he also had been involved. Still, establishing a possible motive for the senator was not enough, and Juliet knew *Perspective* needed something more to implicate him justifiably. Finding that something was the problem.

On a rainy Thursday afternoon she sat staring at the telephone on her desk and heaved a frustrated sigh. It had been one of those days when everything she did quickly led to a dead end, and she was close to throwing up her hands in defeat, at least for a couple of hours. It had been a long unproductive afternoon. Mayor Haynes, who now knew the D.A. had his out-of-town bank records as evidence against him, was trying to stonewall. Marc and Juliet had gone to his office, but he had flatly refused to see them. Later they had visited the district judge in his chamber but he had been so hostile that even Marc had trouble getting him to tell them where he had gone to law school. And to cap it all off, back at the lodge Juliet had tried to reach the senator in Washington to request an on-camera interview but never got past a very snooty and unpleasant secretary, who said quite haughtily that even Velvy's aides were too busy with important matters to talk to her.

Juliet was disgusted. In some of her blacker moods, she wondered if the senator had covered his involvement so well that *Perspective* would never succeed in getting at the truth. Her thoughts were drifting in that direction now, and she lay back in her swivel chair, closed her eyes, and searched her brain for the best way to proceed from there. Perhaps she was trying too hard, because no ideas at all came to her. Finally, she allowed her mind to wander, wishing she would miraculously zero in on the perfect solution. No such luck. Twenty minutes later she opened her eyes and found chief researcher, T. J. Fletcher, entering the room through the open doorway, a huge grin on his angular face.

Juliet straightened in her chair, a spark of hope appearing in her lambent emerald eyes. "I hope that smile means you've found something—anything—to go on?"

"I do believe we have. Haven't I always said I have a fantastic research team?" T.J. said with much satisfaction. He plopped down in the chair across from Juliet and began flipping through the notebook he'd brought with him. "Of course, it will take some time to locate the people and convince them to make statements on camera."

"Everything takes time; we're used to that. But what

people are you talking about?" Juliet asked excitedly. "Come on, T.J. If you have good news, let's have it. I need to hear some about now."

Fletcher's grin widened. "All right. I'd almost wager I know exactly how Velvy bribed Judge Markham, what he promised him. There's a federal judgeship vacancy coming up very soon—someone's retiring—and Markham has a reputation for being highly ambitious, ambitious enough perhaps to do just about anything to be appointed to fill it."

"And?" Juliet questioned expectantly, knowing there must be more. "What else did you find?"

"Believe it or not, Markham's apparently indiscreet as well as ambitious. There are rumors flying that he's bragged to a few people that he has the appointment sewed up."

"You're kidding! You're not kidding. Oh, Lord, this could be just what we've been looking for." Juliet's face brightened, fairly glowed even as she tried to control her euphoria. This new information was important but, as it stood, it was by no means conclusive. Nibbling a fingernail, she looked thoughtfully at T.J. "But all we have right now are the rumors?"

"For the moment, but I think we'll have much more than that soon," T.J. answered confidently, tapping his notebook with a fingertip. "This is the hottest story on the courthouse grapevine these days, and we found a particularly helpful and blessedly talkative court stenographer who supplied names of some of the people Markham bragged to about this. All we have to do now is locate these people, interview them, and try to get them to make on-camera statements. That's why I came to see you. You do want me to follow through on this, don't you?"

"Oh, absolutely, go to it. In fact, I'd like you to try to get addresses and phone numbers for these people this afternoon, if you possibly can. Then I can give them a call tomorrow morning and arrange to meet them. Oh, and T.J.," Juliet added as he immediately rose from his chair, "if we could find some indication that Velvy's already tried to use his influence to get Markham the appointment, we'd really have something."

The researcher nodded. "I've already called Washington and put somebody on that."

"Terrific. Of course, even if the senator has recommended Markham, he's probably going to defend himself by claiming the judge deserves the appointment because of his distinguished law career."

"Then he'll be lying, and it should be relatively easy to prove he is," T.J. assured her. "The truth of the matter is that Markham's professional life has been quite lackluster. He had a mediocre law practice and has a mediocre record on the bench. And Velvy's not even going to be able to claim he wants Markham appointed because they are old close friends. Everything we've found indicates they didn't know each other until about the time of the corruption trial."

"You've done a fantastic job researching this, and I want you to know you've made my day," Juliet said sincerely, her smile enthusiastic. "Of course, we have to thank Markham for being a blabbermouth and Velvy for obviously believing he can do anything he pleases without fear of being caught."

"Well, we're going to prove him wrong, starting right now," T.J. said and, eager to follow up on the leads, left.

Alone again, Juliet found it impossible to sit still. She was too excited. Minutes ago, she had been on the verge of depression, but now all of a sudden she felt there was light at the end of the tunnel once more. T.J.'s discovery might very well break this story wide open.

"This could be it," she sang softly to herself. Surrender-

237

ing to impulse, she executed a carefree, graceful pirouette in the center of the room, then dashed back to the phone on the desk to call Marc and share the good news and map out strategy. There was no answer when she rang his room so she called downstairs and asked the lodge manager to locate him. While she waited for him to join her, she kept herself busy with necessary paperwork, and it wasn't until several minutes later that she glanced up from the desk and saw a strange man hovering in the doorway. He had been about to knock, but she saved him the trouble by beckoning him into the room.

"Yes. Can I help you?"

"Indeed, you can. You are Juliet York, I presume," the young man in the standard unimaginative dark blue suit and narrow tie responded smoothly. When she nodded, he came across the room and offered his hand, which she took. He flashed a brilliant smile. "I can't begin to tell you what a pleasure it is to meet you."

Juliet gently extracted the hand he still held. "How nice of you to say so, Mr.—"

"Yes, why don't you tell us who you are and how you knew to find Miss York here?" Marc spoke up as he entered the room and strode over to the desk. Coatless, he flicked back the sides of his unbuttoned vest, placed his hands on his hips, and looked expectantly at the unknown man.

"Well, well, Marc Tyner. I've often seen you on television, and it's a great pleasure to meet you too," the man said, once again extending his hand and firmly shaking Marc's. "And to answer your question, the clerk downstairs told me where I could find Miss York. I'm Porter Johnston, aide to Senator Benson Velvy."

Juliet and Marc exchanged quick glances then she sat back in her chair, tapping the eraser end of a pencil lightly against her lips. "Why don't you both have a seat," she suggested, and turned a speculative gaze on the aide. "This is quite a coincidence, Mr. Johnston. I just called the senator's office but couldn't get past the secretary, and now here you are, in person no less."

Johnston pursed his lips. "I must apologize for Mrs. White. She must not have realized who you were or she certainly would have connected you to one of our aides. I'll be sure to speak to her about her unfortunate error when I return to Washington."

"That won't be necessary. I'm sure Mrs. White was simply following someone's orders," Juliet said flatly, then tossed the pencil onto the desktop and rested her chin on steepled fingers. She got right down to brass tacks. "What can I do for you, Mr. Johnston?"

His practiced smile appeared again. "I'm here at the senator's request, to see both you and Mr. Tyner, actually." He carefully adjusted the perfect creases in his dark blue trousers as he got to the point of his visit at last. "Senator Velvy would be very pleased to have both of you as houseguests this weekend in his home in Georgetown. Of course, he'll send his plane here to fly you in Friday evening, and you'll also be flown back Sunday afternoon."

Once again Marc and Juliet glanced at each other and, despite the bland expressions on their faces, their eyes exchanged a message. Then Juliet gave the aide a polite smile. "It's very generous of Senator Velvy to offer us the use of his private plane, but *Perspective* teams arrange their own transportation when it's necessary to travel to get an on-camera interview. Company policy, you understand."

"Oh, yes, indeed I do. I understand perfectly," Johnston effused and shook his head. "But I obviously didn't make the senator's invitation clear. He isn't granting an interview. He simply wants you to come as his guests to

239

a small houseparty he and Mrs. Velvy are giving this weekend. A purely social occasion, I assure you."

"Oh?" Juliet's gently arched brows lifted. "Then I'm afraid it's impossible for Mr. Tyner and me to accept. As I'm sure the senator realizes, we're working on a story that involves an investigation of his activities, and if we were to spend a weekend as guests in his home, we might place ourselves in a position where we could be accused of a conflict of interests."

"She's right, Mr. Johnston," Marc interceded pleasantly. "Journalists have to be almost as careful as politicians to avoid damaging their credibility."

"Careful, yes, but not overcautious surely," the aide countered with a suspiciously rehearsed chuckle. "I can see nothing inappropriate in the two of you accepting this invitation. After all, many politicians have close friends in the news media. And because Senator Velvy greatly admires the work you both do, he naturally wants to meet you and become acquainted on a personal level."

Juliet doubted that. A snake just doesn't slither over and introduce himself to a mongoose. And she had the distinct feeling those two creatures might have more in common than the senator and Marc and she would. Velvy was well aware of that fact too; she was certain of it. He was simply hoping to do something to convince them to drop their investigation. Maybe he planned to try to bribe them too. She studied Porter Johnston for a few short moments, then shook her head.

"Mr. Tyner and I cannot accept the invitation," she reiterated. "We won't change our minds."

"That is regrettable," Johnston said, his tone cooling slightly. "Senator and Mrs. Velvy will be very disappointed."

Juliet inclined her head. "Please give them our regrets."

"And also tell him we're very interested in getting an

interview with him," Marc added, leaning forward in his chair to rest his elbows on his knees, as if wanting to observe more closely the aide's reaction. "At his convenience of course."

"The senator's an extremely busy man; he rarely grants interviews," Johnston pronounced. "But naturally I'll mention your request to him."

"We appreciate that," Juliet said, expecting Johnston to leave, since he had failed to convince them to accept the invitation. Surprised and rather disgruntled when he repositioned himself in his chair, as if he meant to stay awhile longer, she tilted her head to one side inquiringly. "Is there something else you want to discuss with us?"

Johnston cleared his throat. "As a matter of fact, there is. It's about your investigation of Senator Velvy. Of course, the senator understands you must check him out simply because he's an acquaintance of Mayor Haynes's."

"An acquaintance?" Marc quietly challenged. "It's common knowledge that they've been close friends for a number of years. Isn't that so?"

"I wouldn't know exactly how close they once were," the aide responded glibly. "All I know is that Senator Velvy was very disappointed and saddened by the rumors he's heard, rumors that indicate Haynes was indeed involved in illegal activities. I assure you he's just shocked by the entire distasteful situation."

"Oh, I imagine so," Juliet said, managing to suppress the sarcasm that threatened to edge her voice. Velvy was shocked all right, shocked that his abuse of power was about to catch up with him. The man was a disgrace, the kind of elected official who gave all politicians a bad name, and Juliet had no desire even to deal with one of his lackeys. "But why do you feel it's necessary to tell us this?"

"I wanted to make the senator's position clear. And

also—now, this may sound odd but there is another reason why I came here today—I want to help you, Miss York. I want to put this as delicately as possible." Porter Johnston winced, as if pained by what it was he was about to say. He cleared his throat once more and tried to appear apologetic as he continued, "We on the senator's staff know why you left Lancaster Broadcasting—the, uh, gossip about you and Henry Alexander, and we'd hate for you to have to go through another similar episode. We certainly wouldn't want that to happen. Your career could really suffer."

Juliet saw Marc's jaw suddenly tighten and saw the glint of anger that flared in his eyes, but it was no more intense than the glitter in her own. She glowered at Johnston. "Get to the point," she demanded icily. "If there is one."

"This is embarrassing for me, and it certainly was for Senator Velvy. He was appalled when he heard what Haynes had done and was planning to do." The aide made a show of sadly shaking his head. "That's why I felt I had to warn you that Haynes may attempt to blackmail you, Miss York, if you don't drop this story about him. It, uh, seems he has in his possession some proof that you and . . . Mr. Tyner are, uh, lovers."

Juliet's heart seemed to stop for a long moment and she could only stare at Johnston, speechless. Fortunately Marc intervened.

"Be more specific," he commanded with admirable calm although disdain was written in the grim lines of his face as he surveyed the aide. "Exactly what kind of proof does the mayor have?"

"Photographs, supposedly."

"Photographs. Describe them."

"Well, of course, none of us on the senator's staff has ever seen any photographs. We've only heard they exist,"

Johnston blustered, unnecessarily straightening his narrow tie. "We're told they show you and Miss York embracing and in various stages of, uh, undress."

"Nude, you mean?"

"Some of them. Yes. At least that's what we've heard."

"Photographs. Of Marc and me?" Juliet said softly, her heart sinking while her stomach tied itself in tight knots. She was stunned and felt very much like crawling beneath her desk to hide from the whole world. But she wasn't about to do anything remotely like that in front of this despicable man, and she managed to force a lazy smile to her lips. "Someone actually has photographs of Marc and me together? Why, how exciting! Mr. Johnston, would you please tell the senator that I'd love to have copies of all of them. I can paste them in my scrapbook. And how about you, Marc? Would you like a set of prints?"

Marc laughed aloud and shot her a glance that was congratulatory.

"This is no laughing matter, Mr. Tyner. And, Miss York, you apparently misunderstood me—Senator Velvy has nothing to do with these photographs," Johnston insisted, shifting in his chair. "If such pictures exist, it's the mayor who has them and is threatening to use them. That's why I came to warn—"

"I didn't misunderstand you. And don't insult my intelligence, Mr. Johnston," Juliet interrupted tersely, her smile fading, her voice hard. "I'm not stupid. What good would it do Mayor Haynes to try to blackmail me now? The D.A. already has enough evidence to indict him and he knows that. So no, it isn't Haynes who's threatening to use the pictures. It's Velvy, through you, his ever-faithful errand boy. But it isn't going to work, I promise you."

"You're getting this all wrong. It's Haynes who has the pictures," the aide insisted. "And we hear he plans to send them to your executive producer."

243

"Mr. Johnston, if such pictures actually do exist, *you* may send them wherever you please."

"Does Velvy know you're here?" Marc inquired, getting up to stand towering over the aide's chair. "I know he's not an overly intelligent man, but somehow I don't think he'd be stupid enough to send you to make such asinine threats. Even Velvy's not that blatant, and besides, he'd realize such tactics would only make us more determined to get this story—all of it. If coming here was your own brilliant idea, Johnston, your boss probably isn't going to be very pleased."

"I can see I'm wasting my time," Johnston proclaimed, trying to mask with a superior smirk the nervous little tic that suddenly appeared to pull at one corner of his mouth. He looked from Juliet up at Marc then back at her again. "I'm sorry this had to happen, Miss York, but you must understand that Haynes is a desperate man, and I doubt the senator or anyone else can persuade him not to use the pictures . . . if he does have them. I just hope you won't live to regret refusing to take his threat seriously."

"Time to go, Johnston," Marc ground out, a dangerous flare-up of light in his eyes. He stared down at the other man, who hastily stood and took one step back, then recklessly hesitated as if he meant to say something else. Marc moved toward him, his lithe, subtly muscled body conveying ominous power. "Now."

The aide held his ground for a second, thought better of it, and started for the door.

"Tell Senator Velvy we'll certainly be in touch with him soon," Juliet made herself say calmly. But when Johnston stepped from the room into the hallway and Marc had closed the door after him, she released her breath in a long shaky sigh and covered her face with her hands.

Marc came to her, moved a hand over her hair. "Julie," he murmured above her. "Try not to worry."

Dropping her hands limply into her lap, she looked up at him, seeking reassurances. "Do you think they really have pictures of us together?"

"It's a possibility, I suppose" was his honest answer. Sitting on the edge of the desk directly in front of her, he reached down to take her hands in his. "If the drapes across the French windows weren't completely closed one of those nights in my room, I guess someone could have taken pictures from the balcony. I tend to doubt that though."

"But if they don't have photographs, how could they even know that we—"

"People like this have ways of knowing things. They might even have had someone following us when we were in New York and because you did spent the night at my place with me, they knew we'd realize there *could* be pictures. It all may be a big bluff."

"And if it isn't? Oh, God, I never imagined even these creeps could sink this low," Juliet exclaimed softly, a slight wobble to her chin, her eyes dark with unhappiness. Her small hands tightly grasped his, giving some indication of the hurt and anger she was feeling. "*Damn them.* If Johnston wasn't lying . . . Oh, I can't stand to think they turned something so private and personal into a peep show."

"No, it isn't a pleasant thought, but try to remember that they couldn't have gotten much from the balcony. At least the bed isn't visible from there."

There was some solace in what Marc said. Not much, but a little, and although she managed a wan smile, it quickly faded. "But I guess just pictures of us undressing each other would more than shock some people," she murmured, searching his face. "If they exist and someone sends them to Pete . . . what do you think he might do?"

"Destroy them," Marc answered without hesitation,

lifting a hand to gently smooth back the wayward tendril of her hair. "I don't think you have to worry about Pete's reaction, Julie."

"I think maybe I better."

"If someone has pictures, Julie, you're not in them alone. I'm in them too."

"I know, but our situations are very different," Juliet softly reminded him. "Pete's worked with you for years; he respects you. But I've been with Union Broadcasting such a short time that he doesn't know much about me or the quality of my work."

"But he'll have to know that you must be doing a hell of a job on this assignment if the senator's people would go to such lengths to try to stop you."

"And he also knows what happened at Lancaster . . . all that gossip about Henry and me. I don't need anything else making me look like a—"

"Our personal lives are none of Pete's business."

"Maybe not, but with pictures in front of him, he might not be as objective as you think. He could still fire me."

"Julie," Marc whispered, lifting her chin with one finger. "Do you really think I'd let that happen?"

She gazed up at him, loving him all the more for his promise to defend her. Yet she had no desire to keep her position at Union through his influence. She wanted to keep it because Pete thought she was too valuable a producer to be fired. She would hardly feel like a success if Marc had to save her job for her. But maybe it wouldn't come to that. She could only hope and channel her thoughts in some other direction. Unfortunately the path they took was even more emotionally draining. "You know," she mused, "what bothers me most is that someone may have dared to intrude on what was just ours to share."

Marc's eyes looked deeply into hers. "It's still just as

special, Julie. Even if there was a voyeur or two on the balcony watching the preliminaries, that doesn't change what being together meant to us. At least it doesn't change it for me."

In a way he was right. She loved him. Nothing in the world could change that, and their nights together had been, especially to her, unforgettably special. But still . . .

"Try not to think about it," Marc suggested, apparently seeing her uncertainty. "Tell me why you sent for me. What did you want to talk about?"

T.J.'s news lifted her spirits slightly as she shared it with Marc but her enthusiasm never reached the level where it had been before Johnston's nasty visit. Yet she kept her mind on the business at hand while they discussed how he would approach the new sources once T.J. had located them. It was only after they had discussed the practical details that her thoughts drifted back to Johnston's threats.

"You're thinking about it again," Marc said perceptively. "If you can't stop yourself, at least try to remember that you handled Johnston very well. You acted like you didn't much care if he uses the pictures, if he has any, and that might make him give up the whole idea." A slow, somewhat mischievous smile moved his mouth as he watched her. He raised one eyebrow and leaned closer to ask, "Would you really like to have a copy of each photo to put in your scrapbook?"

Juliet had to smile a little bit at that, but when Marc bent down and brushed his warm lips against hers in a featherlike kiss, she felt like bursting into tears and wanted to fling herself into his arms for comfort. Naturally the old compulsive self-discipline allowed her to do neither. She simply sighed and then said, "Maybe I should just be alone for a little while so I can put all this in perspective."

Nodding understandingly, Marc stood, gave her shoulder a reassuring squeeze, and left. After he had gone, she sat staring at the floor, her expression growing more morose with each passing second. It seemed her life was rapidly becoming a shambles. Sure, Marc was being supportive in this situation but she needed more from him than that. She loved him and needed his love in return. And, as if that weren't enough to cope with, she was constantly being harassed. Now someone was even attempting blackmail, and the career she had worked so hard for might be in jeopardy. Everything seemed such a hopeless mess and she was tired. Unable to keep a stiff upper lip any longer, Juliet buried her face in her folded arms on her desk and cried at last.

CHAPTER FIFTEEN

Juliet's day went from bad to worse after that. She tried not to think about the senator or his amoral staff or of the possible photographs, but it took all the effort she could muster to think about anything else. She began to look forward to the interview she had granted Chloe Spencer, editor of the university newspaper. At least while she was answering the young girl's questions, she wouldn't have much opportunity to think about the unpleasant event of the day.

Chloe interviewed Marc first then came to Juliet's room. As the interview progressed, most of the questions concerned Marc rather than Juliet but she found that rather amusing and wasn't the least bit offended. She understood Marc's appeal and the public's insatiable interest in him. He was, after all, the star, while she worked behind the scenes and didn't seem nearly as intriguing. She answered the questions about him as best she could until the interview had ended and Chloe was starting to leave.

"I know Mr. Tyner isn't married," the girl blurted out, hand poised on the doorknob as she looked back at Juliet. "But well, do you know if he belongs to anybody?"

Only to himself, Juliet wanted to answer but didn't. Understanding Chloe's infatuation, she simply smiled and shook her head. "I think maybe you better ask him about that."

"You know, I think I will," Chloe replied chipperly, and waved good-bye.

Smiling to herself, Juliet wandered out onto the balcony to the railing. She appreciatively inhaled the sweet clean mountain air and gazed out on the rolling countryside washed pale gold in the early evening sunshine. Hearing the French doors of Marc's room being opened, she turned to greet him, then looked back at the lush green hills while he walked over to join her.

"How did your interview go?" he asked, leaning against the railing and looking at her rather than the scenic view. "Did our Miss Spencer get you to indulge any of your innermost secrets?"

Smiling, Juliet shook her head. "You know I wouldn't do that. I'm too secretive."

"What a disappointment for Chloe. I think she expected both of us to regale her with scorching stories about working in television, and we let her down."

"I'm sure she'll print the interviews anyhow," Juliet said, her tone taking on a teasing note. "It's not every day she gets to question a celebrity like you."

"Yes. That is true," Marc answered, trying to keep a straight face but not quite succeeding. He leaned back on both elbows. "Chloe seems like a nice girl. Very intelligent."

"Uh-huh, and very pretty."

"That too," he said, then changed the subject. "What time did you plan to have dinner?"

"I'm not sure yet. Maybe a little earlier than I usually do so I can go for a swim after," Juliet said, turning to look at him, then yielding to sudden impulse and a very real need to be with him. "Why don't you go with me, Marc?"

He wore a puzzled expression. "I thought you'd be going over to the campus with me to speak to Chloe's newspaper staff."

"Oh? Well, I thought I'd skip that," she said rather tongue-in-cheek, not bothering to tell she hadn't been asked and wondering what exactly Chloe was planning for the evening. Maybe not a staff gathering at all but a little rendezvous where she would have Marc all to herself? The thought should have been, at the very least, mildly amusing, but somehow Juliet wasn't amused at all and mentally chastised herself. If Chloe was setting him up for what she hoped would become a romantic interlude, he could handle the situation . . . if he chose to. Maybe he wouldn't mind the idea. . . . Juliet slammed the brakes on such thoughts then and there—temporarily anyhow. Smiling faintly at Marc, she moved her hands in a resigned gesture. "Maybe we can have our swim some other time then. Now, if you'll excuse me, I want to shower before dinner."

Nonchalantly she strolled away from him and into her room where she drew the draperies closed across the French doors. Grumbling to herself, she went and sat on the edge of her bed, propped an elbow on crossed thighs, and plopped her chin into the cup of her hand.

She felt miserable, ashamed of herself, and resentful of Marc. It certainly was a wretched state of affairs when she actually felt jealous of a twenty-one-year-old coed, even if that particular coed did look and act more like she was thirty.

By ten o'clock that night Juliet felt as if the walls of her room were swooping in on her, smothering her, and making her yearn for escape. Catching a glimpse of herself in the floor-length mirror, she realized she was actually beginning to pace back and forth between dresser and bed. She shook her head in disgust and slapped back the rebellious wisp of her hair. She stared at the book she had left closed in the easy chair and knew it was useless to pick it up again. Much as she had tried to divert her thoughts by immersing herself in reading or by doing anything at all, she had been unable to stop thinking about the alleged photographs and what damage they might do her career if they existed and Velvy's people used them against her. The only times in the past three hours she had managed to rechannel her thoughts, they had flown directly to Marc and those hadn't made her feel very good either.

Now she was weary to the bone and wished she could go to bed with some chance of going to sleep but that wasn't likely. It was hot; her brain was awhirl with fever-ish activity, and she was plagued by nervous energy. She sighed and glanced wistfully at the closed French doors. Despite all Marc's warnings against her going out in the night alone, she felt if she didn't get outside where she could walk awhile in the fresh air that she might very well still be pacing these floors come morning.

Finding that very thought unbearable, she hesitated only a brief moment then slipped her feet into the canvas espadrilles by the bureau. When she realized she was tiptoeing toward the door, she immediately stopped and resumed a normal walk. She didn't have to sneak out of her own room. She had every right to go outside whenever she pleased, day or night. She simply had to be careful; that was all. If some of Velvy's thugs did watch the lodge at night, they probably sat in a car in the parking lot where it would be easier for them to follow her if she drove somewhere or went with anyone else. Therefore, if she confined her walk to the area back of the lodge, they wouldn't be able to see her from the parking lot and would never know she had left her room.

Noiselessly Juliet opened the doors and slipped out onto the balcony, where the cool night air felt like heaven against her bare legs and arms. She went past Marc's room. It was dark. He wasn't back yet, but she wouldn't allow herself to think about where he might be or with whom. She went on toward the stairs located at the west end of the lodge, but as soon as she turned the corner she ran directly into something hard and barely yielding, a dark form that suddenly loomed up at the top of the steps. She stumbled. Her arms were caught in a viselike grip and she made a soft alarmed sound.

"Julie, what the—" Marc exclaimed, pulling her back around into the soft pool of light that filtered out through the drapes in the last room of the building. He looked down at her upturned face, apparently saw fear still in it, and a deep frown furrowed his brow. "What's happened? Why are you out here? Is something wrong?"

Catching her breath at last, she shook her head. "Nothing's wrong now that I know it's you. At first I thought you could be one of—"

"But what are you doing out here?"

Juliet flexed her arms, then stepped back when Marc released them. She wanted to answer his question with a lie but couldn't and murmured almost inaudibly, "I had to come out and get some air, Marc. I couldn't stand it cooped up in that room any longer."

He didn't speak. He didn't need to. In the pale light, the sudden grim hardness that tightened his features was visible and although Juliet couldn't really see anger flash into his eyes, she could guess it had. He uttered an explicit curse, grabbed her by the arm, and headed her in the direction she had come along the balcony.

Halfway to their rooms Juliet tried to shake her arm free. "You don't have to drag me," she protested vehemently but softly so none of the crew would overhear as they passed along the line of rooms. "I can walk."

"Don't press your luck, Julie," he warned beside her, his deep voice rough and ominous. "Right now, I think I could drag you to your room by your hair and enjoy doing it."

253

A retort sprang to her lips but was silenced when Marc brought her to an abrupt halt at her door and unceremoniously reached into her skirt pocket to extract her key and open her door. Even after herding her inside, he didn't release her and they stood toe-to-toe in a face-off, the anger between them almost tangible.

"Are you completely out of your mind?" he at last asked harshly, raking his free hand through his sandy hair. "What the hell does it take to convince you that those thugs out there mean business? You've almost been run off the side of the mountain, accosted in a parking lot, and you still traipse out alone in the dark! Is it so very much to expect you to stay in your room?"

"Yes," she snapped, her emerald eyes flashing defiantly. "It's easy for you to think I should stay locked up in here every night—you're able to come and go as you please. But I'm beginning to feel like a prisoner in my own room and I'm tired of it, tired of letting those idiots control my life. They'd never really do anything to me anyhow. All they want to do is badger me with phone calls and throw out the same old vague threats that never change one iota from one time to the next."

"What they say to you may never change, but the threats they make against you to Paul and me have changed quite a bit in the past few weeks," Marc informed her brusquely, a muscle working in his clenched jaw. "I think it's just as well you don't have to hear what we've been hearing."

Juliet dismissed his words with a toss of one hand. "Why do you even pay any attention to them? They're just trying to get you and Paul to stop pushing so hard to get this story, simply to protect me. They're trying to intimidate you two by using the fact that I'm a woman."

"And doing a damn fine job of it. Paul's intimidated and so am I. If something happened to you . . ."

"But nothing's going to. These people are all talk, and I'm not going to let myself be that afraid of them."

"I don't think you have much choice," Marc nearly growled, jerking her closer. "You certainly can't go around taking foolish chances because Paul and I are hearing threats that aren't at all vague anymore. They're very specific."

"How specific?"

"Very. Just take my word for it."

"But I'd rather not. I think you'd better tell me exactly what kind of threats they're making."

Marc's thunderous expression altered slightly to show something akin to concern as well as the obvious impatience. "All right," he muttered stiffly. "You're a lovely woman, Julie, and Paul and I are often told that it would be a shame if someone decided to scar up that pretty little face of yours."

Juliet almost flinched, then shook her head. "They're bluffing."

"Do you want to stroll out to the parking lot and see whether they are or not? Maybe they *won't* toss you in their car and drive you to some isolated spot someplace," Marc countered bluntly, though his hold on her gentled when she ceased her futile attempts to twist free of his grip. He laid his hands on her shoulders. "Do you want to go find out what they'll do, Julie?"

"No. Of course not," she answered quietly, and just as quietly added, "But dammit, Marc, why haven't you told me what they're threatening before now?"

"I thought I could make you understand you had to be careful without going into all the unpleasant details. Besides, this isn't something you want to have to tell a—"

"Woman?" she challenged rather coolly. "Marc, you don't have to protect me. I've told you I don't want to be coddled. I can take care of myself."

"And what's so wrong with Paul and me wanting to do a little taking care of you too?" Marc asked softly, his hands beginning to move in massaging sweeps over the tight muscles of her shoulders. "You can't be totally independent every second of your life. Nobody can. You have to stop trying to be so tough, Julie. It's making you very tense."

"That's not what's making me tense," she objected weakly, feeling the effect of his hands on her and far too aware of his nearness and the spicy clean male scent of him. Fixing her gaze to the strong tanned column of his neck rising up from his opened collar, she suddenly was overcome by the desire to reach up and trail her fingers over his smooth warm skin, but she clenched her hands at her sides and resisted. Her eyes drifted over him. Endearingly handsome in casual navy blazer and gray pants, he seemed to exude raw sex appeal and with the turn her thoughts were taking, she tried to move away from him. He wouldn't let her. She acted as if it didn't matter and finished what she had started to say. "I'm tense because I'm going stir-crazy. I don't know how much longer I can stand to be stuck in this room night after night. Sometimes I feel like breaking the walls down. I've never felt like this. I'm so restless."

"But not because you have to stay in your room," Marc said softly, drawing her nearer, the light in his blue eyes changing to something more dangerous than anger. "Any time you want, you could ask one of the crew to go out with you. Or Paul. Or me. So you're not trapped in this room. You're restless for a different reason and I know what you need, what I need. It's been too long, Julie."

"No! *Marc*," she gasped as he quickly lowered his head, but it was much too late. The soft sound of his name was caught up then silenced by his gently searching kiss. The touch of the firm lips possessing the softer shape of hers was electric, and though she stood stiff and unyielding she could feel resistance melting, melting in the successive waves of warmth spreading like wildfires over her. She made a muffled imploring sound and tried to pull away but Marc simply caught both her wrists in one large hand behind her back and arching her against his lithe long body, swiftly unbuttoned her blouse halfway down.

"Marc, don't," she breathed when he brushed his lips across the swell of her breasts and flicked the tip of his tongue into the enticing shadowed valley between. *"Don't,"* she repeated again and again, but each time with less emphasis as she became keenly alive to exquisite sensations that at last brought the complete downfall of any hope of resisting. Juliet tugged at her hands, trying to free them from his, and when he released them, she wrapped her arms around him as her parted lips sought his. She swayed against him and whispered her delight when, with a low tortured groan, he brought her in hard muscular arms even closer to him.

He was right. It had been too long, much too long since they had shared pleasure like this and now both of them were trembling in an onrushing tide of desires that could no longer be denied. Marc molded her slender curved body to his and she entwined her fingers in his hair. His hands roamed over her bare shapely arms then down her back to cup the firm curving flesh of her hips. Pressed tight against his hardening thighs, Juliet moved lazily, felt his surging response, and longing quickened deep within her.

"I've wanted to come to you every night," Marc uttered huskily, scattering nibbling little kisses along the graceful curve of her neck and the delicate slope of her shoulders as he pushed back her blouse. Raising his head, his piercing eyes capturing her and conveying all his passionate intent, he clasped the back of her neck in one hand, drawing the edge of his thumb over and around and inside her ear. "I've wanted you so much, Julie. It's been making me crazy knowing you were lying alone in your bed and I was alone in mine when we could have been together, making love."

"I think maybe I've been getting a little crazy too," she confessed, smiling and tracing her fingertips over the fascinating indentations carved in his lean cheeks. Turning her head slightly, she nuzzled the hair-roughened hand on her neck. "I guess I was just crazier than usual tonight."

Marc's answering smile was slow, lazy, and provocative. "There's only one cure for both of us, you know."

"Yes, I know," she whispered, throwing all caution aside, unwilling to deny herself or him the delight that, together, she knew they would find. She feathered her fingers across his firm lips, then stretched up on tiptoe to kiss him, her mouth opening sweetly to his, a shiver dancing over her as his tongue probed the tender-veined inner flesh of her lower lip. She moved her hands inside his blazer, slipped it from his shoulders, then tugged it off completely as he undid the remaining buttons of her blouse. When he pulled it free from beneath her waistband, she hesitated an instant and turned her eyes toward the French doors and the draperies that covered them.

Understanding her instantly, Marc smiled. "You see, they're completely closed. Not even a slim possibility of voyeurs tonight."

Satisfied, Juliet removed his shirt and her blouse then allowed him to finish undressing her, and just as her undergarments floated with a whisper of lace to join the other clothing on the floor, a leaf-rustling wind kicked up outside and a low rumble of thunder rolled in from a distance.

"A perfect night for making love," Marc whispered. He brought her hands to his his belt and, cradling her face in his, kissed her as she unbuckled it. Moments later, he enfolded her in his arms and his long bare legs were hard and pleasantly hair-roughened against the satiny smooth skin of hers. Then with his arm still around her waist, he led her to the bed and tossed the covers back.

Half expecting to be swept up and deposited on the sheets, Juliet couldn't conceal her surprise when he let her go instead and promptly dropped down onto his stomach in the center of the mattress.

Smiling, Marc closed his eyes and crooked a beckoning finger. "Come on, Julie. I massaged your neck the other night. Now it's your turn. A very vigorous back rub, please."

"Yes, master," she murmured, fighting a grin when he opened one eye to look up at her. Joining him on the bed, she knelt astride him and leaned forward slightly on her hands as she moved them slowly up and down alongside his spine. As the wind grew strong enough to occasionally rattle the French doors and bright flashes of sheet lightning pierced the darkness beyond, she pummeled his broad back with soft quick blows then guided her fingers and palms along contouring muscles, kneading and stroking. For a long while, as the rumbles of thunder became crashes which followed jagged cracks of light that split the roiling black sky, she administered a massage that was both expert and impersonal but with the slow passage of time, her touch began to change. A coppery sheen lay over his taut skin in the lampglow and her fingers became more caressing upon it. The fine strong structure of flesh and bone and the powerful rippling of his muscles increasingly intrigued her and her hands moved around and along his taut sides. She leaned down and blew her breath gently up the length of his straight spine, smiling secretively to herself when he shivered as her hair fell forward to graze over him.

"I have you at my mercy," she breathed close to his ear,

nibbling the lobe, then trailing a strand of tasting kisses over his shoulders' broad expanse. She felt the tremor that ran over him and continued, delighting in the feel of him beneath her and in her own ability to arouse him. The role of seductress was coming to her naturally, and she enjoyed promising much with her every caress. She ran her fingers through the vibrant sandy hair that grew down to just brush his nape, tugged gently at the ends, and caught her nails in it. A low rumble rose from deep in Marc's throat, as exciting as the sound of the rolling thunder and loving him, in love with touching him, Juliet moved her fingertips up and down his back then followed the same paths with parted lips. Aroused and arousing, she eased her hands beneath him, moving them sinuously over his flat hard abdomen as the tip of her tongue drew small tantalizing circles on his sunbrowned skin.

Her heart leaped when his entire body suddenly tensed and went taut with the potential power of a tightly coiled spring.

"Temptress," he growled, easily reaching back to grasp one slender arm and flip her down onto the bed beside him and over onto her stomach. "Two can play this game."

"Oh, I hope so. I was counting on that," she murmured, slanting her eyes up at him and laughing softly as she burrowed her cheek into the soft cool pillow beneath her head. Out of the corner of her eyes, she watched as Marc moved above her, his nakedness compelling and fantastically exciting, his sensuous answering smile warming. She shifted lazily between his knees and caught his wandering gaze. "Are you going to give me a back rub too?"

"Not exactly," he said, a hint of playful teasing in his low-timbred voice. His hands spanned her narrow waist, his thumbs following the enticing sweep of the small of her back down along the subtle sloping of her hips. Bending, he kissed her there and lower, his lips thrilling her with featherstrokes on the backs of her thighs and the calves of her legs and the soles of her small slender feet. His white even teeth nibbled at the tips of her toes and as pleasurable sensations plunged through Juliet, he turned her over onto her back. He slipped his hands beneath her, arched her up toward him as he kissed first her mouth, then the tender roseate peaks of her lush full breasts and the small shallow dip of her navel. Juliet drew in a swift breath and cradled his head in her own trembling hands as his lips began a wandering quest over the satiny smooth skin of her abdomen.

Fat plopping drops of rain sounded out on the balcony then began to pepper down on the wooden planking with a mesmerizing rhythm as the storm approached the lodge with more vivid lightning streaks and quicker louder refrains of pealing thunder. In the cozy privacy of Juliet's room, she and Marc lost themselves in a leisurely frolic that was both fun and infinitely rousing: touching each other, kissing each other, teasing each other with caressing hands and lips.

"What a sexy little wench you've become," Marc whispered after a while, gazing down at her as her fingers traced the high hard bones of his cheeks. His teeth caught the tips in little nibbles as they feathered across his mouth. "And irresistibly playful."

"No more playful than you are," she whispered back, her eyes happy, laughing, aglow with a woman's loving passion. "I wonder what would happen to your reputation as a tough, hard-hitting journalist if the world knew what I know."

"I promise to keep all your secrets if you'll keep mine," he murmured, dropping a hand down to curve it around a shapely thigh and squeeze gently. "Deal?"

Shaking with sudden laughter, Juliet tried to push away his hand. "Don't do that. It tickles like mad."

"I know," he answered wickedly. "That's why I do it. I like to hear you giggle."

She raised her eyebrows in mock surprise and shook her head. "I never ever giggle."

"Oh, don't you? Let's find out."

Even the slight pressure exerted by his fingers along her thigh brought a frenzy of excitement to the surface nerves of sensitized skin and Juliet, twisting and writhing, couldn't prevent herself from laughing aloud. "Stop, you fool," she gasped. "Somebody's going to hear us."

"At the moment I don't give a damn if someone does," was his swift easy answer. And he grinned as his hand sought her other thigh.

Juliet was indeed giggling—almost helplessly—and had to retaliate in the only way she knew how. She wasn't the only one who was ticklish. Marc had his own susceptible areas and she had to fight fire with fire. She drew the edges of her nails lightly over his lean sides and felt the flutter of muscles beneath her fingers. Marc's low laughter mingled with hers and they struggled briefly, tumbling together on the mattress in a tangle of limbs. They settled into stillness in the center of the bed, on their sides in each other's arms, each deeply searching the other's eyes. The laughter faded into silence and they exchanged lazy sensuous smiles as Marc gently brushed her tousled hair back from her face. Juliet moved her head and caught the fuller curve of his lower lip between hers, inflaming his senses and her own with successive teasing kisses as her hands roved languidly over his smooth straight back and his swept over her slight curvaceous body in a possessive knowledgeable exploration.

An inner heat from both of them seemed to radiate outward and cocoon them together in warmth. Mutual desire heightened, became an irresistible force as the sensations they created in each other became more and more exquisite, more and more piercing, more and more demanding.

"Julie," Marc murmured huskily, slowly lowering her onto her back and leaning on one elbow above her. "Let me look at you for a while, just look at you the way I did that day up on the hill. Remember?"

"I remember," she whispered, experiencing the same erotic thrill she had then as his eyes seemed to devour her, sweeping hungrily over skin so smooth that it shimmered opalescently in the lamplight's lambent glow. Though seemingly intrigued for several long seconds with the rapid rise and fall of her perfect breasts, Marc raised his eyes to hers then sought her tender parted lips with his mouth. A gentle knee parted her legs. Marc moved between them and whispering her name, entered her welcoming warmth.

The storm gathered in all its force directly above them. Wind lashed at the trees and drove the rain in splattering sheets against the panes of glass in the French doors. Lightning increasingly consumed the darkness; booming thunder filled the night and in the bed Juliet and Marc joined together in an upspiraling celebration of the senses, taking each other higher, ever higher in a magically alive pulsating world of their own. Wrapping herself closer to him, giving everything for love, she was borne up with him to the crest of ecstasy and over. And as tumultuous cascading waves of sensation carried her away in a soft warm sea of delight, she opened her eyes, saw his dark form silhouetted in a brilliant flash of light that pierced the clouds and shattered toward the ground.

Later they lay together in the tangle of sheets without speaking, in silent contentment. The storm was over. The rain had slowed to a drizzle. The moonless sky was shrouded in total darkness again. In the circle of Marc's arms Juliet snuggled closer, resting her head in the hollow of his shoulder. She was able to tell from the slow even tenor of his breathing that he was asleep and sighed softly as a growing heaviness settled in her chest. She did not regret what had happened, yet she was sad because she knew that for her own peace of mind she couldn't allow this to happen ever again. She couldn't go on like this. These occasional nights of passion weren't enough for her; they only made her want more. She doubted even a semi-permanent live-in arrangement with Marc could have satisfied the deep longings she felt. Perhaps she was more old-fashioned than she had ever realized, because way down inside she needed the security and the promise that only a total commitment between two people can achieve. She wanted all of Marc's love, wanted more than he could give. She simply wanted too much and was unwilling to settle for less. Realizing that, she knew this had to be her last night with him.

CHAPTER SIXTEEN

The story came to another screeching halt. None of the three people T.J. located would admit Judge Markham had ever said that he was certain he had the federal appointment tied up. It was obvious all three were afraid to speak up, even the seemingly self-assured law clerk, Brian Jacobs, who worked closely with the judge. When Juliet and Marc went to see him at the county courthouse, he flatly refused to say a word.

"It's going to take some work to get his cooperation," Juliet said to Marc as they walked down the courthouse steps Friday afternoon. "You know, I've always suspected he knew a great deal he wasn't telling."

"He'll talk eventually. He tries to hide how nervous he is but it shows. I think we might have better luck going to visit him in his home," Marc suggested. "If he wants to tell the truth and I think he does, he'll probably let his guard down a little away from the courthouse."

Juliet nodded. "I'll see if T.J. has his home address as soon as I get back to the lodge. I'm on my way back there anyhow—to catch a four o'clock call from New York. I thought I could make the meeting with the police chief but you'll have to see him without me."

"Fine. But wait a minute before you go, Julie," Marc said quietly, cupping her elbow and guiding her into the shade of one of the ancient oak trees. Looking down at her, he pulled once or twice at the knot of his tobacco-brown tie as he continued, "You were up and gone before I woke up this morning and I wanted to talk to you. I still do"

"All right," she murmured, last night's difficult decision knifing through her consciousness, opening up a hollow emptiness inside her. What did he want to say to her? What could she possibly say to him? She didn't know, and at the moment couldn't bear to find out. Forcing a hopefully regretful smile, she looked at her watch. "But I'm afraid we'll have to postpone our talk. It's past three-twenty-five, and the Chief expects you at three thirty."

Marc nodded, his expression darkly solemn. "Tonight then."

"Yes, tonight. See you back at the lodge," she said in way of parting and turning away, left him.

Walking along the sidewalk toward the corner drug-store where she had parked her car, she was lost in thought, quite unaware anyone was behind her until her heel was suddenly trod upon. No apology was forthcoming and with a disgruntled but silent sigh, she resumed a normal gait and walked on only to have her heel stepped on again a few seconds later. Irritated immensely, she started to turn around and give someone a nasty glare, but the instant she turned her head, she caught sight of her reflection in a store's plate-glass window. And mirrored in the glass very close behind her was a burly man in a dark Windbreaker, a man who looked very much like one of the two who followed her everywhere.

Juliet's heart jumped up into her throat, plummeted back down, and began to pound. Although there were other people all around, she quickened her pace and looked for the van with the crew member in it. When she spotted it parked not far from her own car, relief surged through her but she didn't slow down, imagining she

266

could feel the burly man's breath on the back of her neck. Long before she reached her car, she rummaged about in her purse for the keys, and after finding them, squeezed them so tightly in her clenched fist that the sharp edges dug painfully into her palm.

At long last she reached the car and safety—or so she thought for a few brief seconds. No longer caring if she appeared to be running away, she dashed around to the driver's door but as she started to thrust the key into the lock, her arm was caught, enclosed in a crushing grip that made her gasp. A broad face loomed down close to hers.

"Too bad you don't listen, pretty lady," the burly man hissed. "Looks to us like we're going to have to do more than talk to get you to start minding your own business."

Juliet jerked her head around, ready to beckon her protector in the van, but before she could even open her mouth to call out, her tormentor released her arm and moved away swiftly, very swiftly for such a big man. Juliet's shoulders sagged; the breath she had held rushed out with a softly rushed sound and she lifted a violently shaking hand to her forehead as the other fumbled with the key and finally thrust it home into the lock. As she unlocked the door, she watched wide-eyed as the man hurried back the way they had come and she realized he would be long gone before she had any chance of summoning a policeman.

Once the door was open, she sank down in the driver's seat, slammed the door, and locked it again. Sheer habit enabled her to fasten her seatbelt, but after that was done she didn't have energy left to slip the key into the ignition. She simply sat there, almost wishing she had never stopped smoking. A cigarette might have been comforting just now and, at the very least, would have provided her with something to do with her hands, which were still trembling. After a minute or so, she composed herself enough to start the car and back out of the parking space. Driving slowly down the block, she looked up in the rearview mirror and, as predictably as night follows day, the gray station wagon was coming along behind her. As she drove out of town, she caught a glimpse of the van following the wagon and breathed easier.

The road began its circuitous climb, the pavement still wet from the rain that had continued into the morning and suddenly uneasiness crept over Juliet, a feeling of déjà vu as everything about the day struck her as unpleasantly familiar, almost a replay of a past event. Those men had tried to run her off this very road on another overcast day like this. And abruptly the mere thought became accurate premonition when the station wagon bumped her violently from behind. Whipped forward in her seat, Juliet cried out faintly, held on tight to the steering wheel, and slammed down the accelerator. The economy car's four-cylinder engine was no match for the wagon's V-8, however, and her pursuers rammed her again and again as the road dipped down into a sharp curve, then unfurled before her in that long straight stretch. She was going too fast but was afraid to slow down and stepped harder on the gas pedal when the wagon moved up alongside her and veered in. This time her tormentors meant business, meant to terrorize her—perhaps meant to do more than that—and the steering wheel was nearly wrenched from her hands when the wagon slammed against her with a horrific screaming shriek of metal against metal. The vehicles bounced apart then back together again with a shower of sparks shooting up between the front fenders.

Juliet fought to keep her car on the pavement, gripped in a nightmare she couldn't escape. She knew her protector in the van couldn't come to her rescue in this situation; he could only watch and hope she could maintain control of the car, which was her fervent hope too. Her heart was

268

drumming in her ears but she forced her brain to work anyway, thinking of the overlook up ahead, wishing she could stop there yet knowing she didn't dare. If she did, these maniacs would have her trapped and it would be the two of them against the crew member in the van. They could easily overpower him and take her. . . . She bit down hard on her lower lip, remembering the specific threat Marc had said they had made repeatedly and the thoughts that exploded in her mind made her practically sick with fear.

She sped past the overlook. The road began to curve once more and the wagon dropped back again but only to ride her bumper while the driver ceaselessly leaned on his horn, making her want to scream as the blaring reverberated in her ears. Still, she raced on, determined to reach the lodge and safety and, after several minutes that lasted an eternity, she saw the building rising up ahead. She was going to make it.

Coming up fast on the drive, Juliet jerked the steering wheel to the left—but too sharply, and she was suddenly excruciatingly aware of utter helplessness. She was no longer in control of the car; the right wheels plunged off the drive. The car tilted and rolled. Seat and shoulder belts dug painfully into Juliet's flesh as she was thrown to the right and forward. She saw the steering wheel as it seemed to rush up at her. Her head hit it. Then there was only darkness.

Despite the throbbing in her head, Juliet struggled upward from the depths of nothingness, unable to open her eyes as yet but beginning to hear, as if in the far far distance, faint voices and muffled footsteps. She felt disoriented and groggy; it seemed to take every ounce of energy she possessed to force her eyelids even half open. She squinted as she gazed up at a daylight-washed white ceiling that was geometrically scarred with ugly metal tracks. Confused by the unfamiliar sight, she frowned and turned her head to the left, wincing as the movement intensified the throbbing near her right temple, but the pain was momentarily forgotten when she found herself looking between metal bars. Bed rails, she realized, then noticed a slight movement near her feet and Tom moved into her line of vision, his young face a study of concern mingling with some relief.

"Juliet, you're finally awake," he whispered, coming to the side of the bed. "Welcome back."

" 'Lo, Tom," she murmured, her throat parched, her voice cracking. "Could I have some water, please?" After he had poured some from a plasticware pitcher into a glass, then guided a straw to her lips, she sipped and the icy cold water felt and tasted tremendous as it washed away some of her grogginess. She glanced around the room, then tried to give Tom a smile. "What hospital am I in?"

"County. You remember the accident?"

"Vaguely. I remember enough to know the car was probably totaled. Was it?"

Tom grimaced. "Well, it's not in very good shape right now."

"Terrific," Juliet moaned. "The accounting department will have fits when I send that expense voucher in."

"To hell with accounting. It's better the car got the worst of it instead of you. As it is, you got a pretty nasty cut and a concussion. No fracture, thank God, although you weren't very clearheaded when you regained consciousness last night."

"Last night? You mean this is Saturday and not still Friday. I thought—"

"It's Saturday morning, Juliet."

Then where was Marc? If she had been unconscious for

270

hours and in the hospital all night, why hadn't he been here waiting for her to wake up this morning? To Juliet, the answer to the question she asked herself was painfully obvious. Marc simply didn't care enough about her to be here and she couldn't believe how much that realization hurt. Turning her head on the pillow, she closed her eyes, on the verge of tears as she compulsively mumbled, "Where is . . . everybody?"

"Oh, well, that's the good news," Tom answered cheerily. "Marc somehow persuaded that law clerk, Jacobs, to talk on camera and he and Paul and the crew are at Jacobs's house now, taping his statement."

"Oh, damn and I'm missing it," Juliet muttered and to her dismay and Tom's shock tears spilled from her opening eyes to run in rivulets over her cheeks and back toward her hair. "It's probably the interview that breaks this story wide open and I don't even get to be there while they tape it. That's not fair."

"Please don't cry," Tom begged, staring down at her, his hands moving indecisively for a moment before finally reaching for one of hers, which he began to pat. "My God, if I'd known how upset it was going to make you, I wouldn't have told you about the taping. I'm really sorry."

"But it's not your fault. I just have this horrible headache," Juliet said, sniffling, unwilling to let him feel guilty for what was actually a moment of weakness on her part. She took the tissue he pressed into her hand, dried her tears and gave him a wan smile. "And besides, hospitals depress me. When can I get out of here?"

Tom brightened. "Maybe right after lunch, after the doctor checks you. Now why don't you try to go back to sleep for a while. Best thing you can do for that headache."

"Maybe you're right," she said softly, allowing him to

271

keep her hand and continue to pat it as her eyelids began to feel heavier and heavier. She rubbed her cheek against the cool, smooth pillow and tried to think of nothing or no one except good old Tom. She could count on him to stand by her when she could count on nobody else, not even Marc.

Juliet awoke again two hours later.

"Hello there," Marc whispered, his warm smile the first thing she saw when her eyes slowly opened. Bending down, he very gently brushed his lips over hers and touched featherlight fingertips to the stark white bandage nestled in her hair and extending a little way onto her temple. "How are you feeling?"

"Better," she said, and it was true now that he was with her. "My head doesn't hurt as badly as it did when I woke up before. I felt pretty lousy then."

"So Tom told me. He said you were upset that Paul and I went ahead and taped Jacobs's statement. I'm sorry, Julie," Marc said quietly, raking his fingers through his hair. "I thought you'd want us to get it before he could back out. And I also thought it might be a nice surprise for you to wake up and find out it was all wrapped up."

"It is, Marc. I'm glad you went ahead and got it. When Tom was here I wasn't really upset about that anyway." She spread expressive hands, palms up, and smiled a little sheepishly. "That awful headache just made me overreact but now I'm okay. So, how did the taping go? Did Jacobs tell you what we hoped he would?"

"Uh-uh, and I think Senator Benson Velvy's in for some tough questions. We can't prove beyond a shadow of doubt that he bribed Markham—that's not our job anyway. But I'm sure Pete will agree we have enough against Velvy to hand what we have over to the Justice Department and the Senate Ethics Committee."

272

"We've done it then and we're actually going to be able to wrap up this story soon," Juliet said, excitement lighting her eyes and features. Pushing herself up, she sat back against the pillows and noticed for the first time that she was wearing her own ivory silk Charmeuse gown. She touched the softly shirred bodice and gave Mark a questioning look. "How did I happen to end up in this?"

"I asked Tom to bring it over for you." Marc grinned mischievously. "I know how much you enjoy your sexy little nightgowns."

"Well you must admit my gowns beat those hospital things that let your derriere hang out in back," she retorted wryly, smiling as Marc chuckled, then turned her eyes toward the door as a doctor entered and strode over to the bed.

"Guess you don't remember me from last night when you regained consciousness—you were very groggy and went to sleep right away. I'm Frank McCrea." The doctor introduced himself, then greeted Marc. He lowered the side railing on the bed and leaned over Juliet. "How's the head today?"

"Better," she murmured, wincing a bit when Dr. McCrea gently peeled back the bandage to examine underneath it. "It hurts some but not like it did earlier."

"Uh-huh, uh-huh," the doctor said. He pressed the gauze pad back into place and straightened. "Well, it's going to hurt for a time. Pretty deep cut, but the sutures are perfect—if I do say so myself. You may have a little scar there but it won't be bad."

The edge of Juliet's teeth sank into her bottom lip as she nodded then asked wistfully, "How long will I have to stay in here, Doctor McCrea?"

"As long as it takes you to dress and me to walk to the desk to sign your release," he answered with an understanding smile as he moved briskly toward the doorway, where he paused briefly. "I'll want to remove those sutures a week from today. Call my office for an appointment. And, Mr. Tyner, take care of her for the next few days. No work. Plenty of rest and relaxation."

"It won't be easy to convince her but I'll manage somehow," Marc said, catching and holding Juliet's eyes, almost as if conveying a message she couldn't quite comprehend.

Two hours later, Juliet settled in the easy chair in her room at the lodge and laid her head back. "Ah, peace and quiet," she murmured, watching as Marc seated himself on the edge of her bed. She smiled. "The crew really gave me a royal welcome back downstairs. It was very nice."

"I told you they respect you," Marc reminded her, then grinned. "And at least you were able to eat lunch here instead of having to sample the hospital fare."

"Thank goodness. If hospital food is as bad as people say, I might have had a relapse."

"But the little impromptu party the crew cooked up was a little too much for you, I think. You looked as if your head was hurting worse again. Is it?"

"It was a little. But it's better now, since we came up here."

"You feel well enough to have that talk I mentioned yesterday?" Marc asked, his gaze intent upon her when she looked directly at him. "If you don't—"

"Well, actually, I . . ." Juliet hesitated and gathered up all her courage. Might as well get it over with. She nodded. "Sure, I feel fine. What did you want to talk about?"

"Us, Julie," he said rather huskily. "We can't go on this way."

"I know," she answered softly, clenching her hands together in her lap. It was coming—he was going to end it between them again but this time the ending must be permanent. She took a deep breath. "I know we can't, but what is it you think we should do?"

"My contract with Union comes up for renewal in three months, but I won't be renewing it," he told her without mincing words. "I'll take an offer from one of the other networks."

Juliet swallowed hard. He really must be eager to get away from her. And she had to make herself continue to meet his eyes as she nodded. "I see. Has someone offered you more money?"

"Money has nothing to do with it," he insisted, leaning toward his elbows on his knees. "It's just that if I leave Union and you stay with them, then we can be together between assignments without anyone saying you're only involved with me to advance your career."

"Together?" Juliet breathed, staring at him as hope tried to bubble up in her and she tried to suppress it. "What exactly do you mean?"

"I mean together whenever we can be, like we want to be," he said urgently, moving from the bed to come down on his heels before her chair and take her hands in his. His piercing blue eyes impaled hers. "Julie, it's been insanity the past few weeks, trying to stay away from each other."

"But that's how you wanted it," she reminded him, remembering every word he had said. "When you came back from New York, you said we should think of our careers first and—"

"When I came back from New York, my ears were ringing with all the snide remarks I'd overheard about us, about you sleeping your way to the top," he interrupted quietly. "Obviously some of the crew here had mentioned our relationship to someone up there and . . . God, do you think I wanted to stop being with you? I didn't but I couldn't let your career suffer just because of me."

"Oh, Marc," Juliet whispered throatily, easing her

275

hands from his to cradle his face in them. "I did think
. . . Why didn't you tell me the truth?"

"And have you worry yourself sick about your professional reputation?" Marc ruefully countered, shaking his head. "I couldn't do that to you. But now I know it was crazy to try to stay away from you and I can't do it any longer. That's why I'll leave Union. You can move into my place or I'll move into yours and at least we'll be able to be together between assignments."

Live together. Oh, she wanted to but knew she couldn't and took a shuddering breath. "I . . . don't know what to say, Marc."

"Say yes," he commanded softly. "You have to because I love you, Julie."

"Oh, Marc, I love you too. *So much,*" she answered, lost in his gaze. Her lips trembled; bittersweet tears welled in her eyes and she was tempted, sorely tempted, to do as he bid and say yes to him. Some happiness, no matter how brief, was better than nothing. Or was it? What would happen to her when it was over? Would she constantly long for the happy times? She didn't want that, couldn't bear the thought of going through life yearning for the past. She wanted a present and future, even if both did prove to be mundane. She just couldn't have the burden of a tragic love affair heavy on her heart for the rest of her days. Living with Marc temporarily just wouldn't be enough for her. But, oh, she did love him and her hands moved adoringly along his jaw even as she shook her head. "In a way I want to say yes but . . . I can't."

"Why not, Julie?" he questioned roughly, his facial muscles tensing beneath her fingers. "If you love me . . . I don't understand."

"I *do* love you but . . . do you want to know the truth?"

"Of course."

Juliet smiled sadly. "You won't like it."

276

"Find out," he challenged, reaching out to span her waist in demanding hands. "Try me."

"All right. Marc," she began, hesitated, then blurted it all out. "I've done something you'll think is very foolish. I've fallen so much in love with you that I couldn't just live with you now. I want—no, *need*—a total commitment and I'm sure you know what I mean by that. It's not that I think 'making it legal' makes relationships last forever—it's just that two people should at least believe it will last, believe it enough to go through all the formalities."

"And that's what you need then?" Marc asked, his deep voice somber, his gaze searching. "Marriage? Are you proposing to me, Julie?"

A fat tear rolled from her eye and caught in a crystalline droplet in the fringe of her lashes as she shook her head. "No. I'm not proposing. I know how you feel about binding relationships."

"Do you really? How *do* I feel?"

"You said yourself that you're not made for marriage."

"Correction. My ex-wife said I wasn't because she wasn't willing to understand how I could love a career that took me away on assignment, that would never become a nine-to-five job," Marc explained, brushing the back of one hand tenderly across Juliet's cheek. "You and I wouldn't have that problem, Julie. Our work would just be something else we could share. And, despite what you think, I would like very much to be married . . . to you."

"Then why didn't you propose instead of just asking me to live with you?" she asked logically, genuinely confused and at the same time battling the renewed hope surging forth in her. "I don't understand that, Marc."

He smiled indulgently. "Julie, I wasn't even planning to ask you to live with me yet. I know how cautious you are and I thought I'd better take things slowly, wait until I had left Union to suggest we live together. But yesterday when I saw you lying unconscious in that hospital bed ..." His words trailed off; he shook his head and there was something wonderfully vulnerable in his expression as he surveyed her face. "Hell, I was scared, Julie. If something were to happen to you ... Anyway, when Dr. McCrea assured me you'd be all right, I knew I wasn't willing to wait any longer for us to be together, no matter how cautious you are."

"You really mean that, don't you?" she murmured thickly, and a different kind of tears, tears of happiness, sparkled in her lashes as she could actually recognize his love for her in his eyes. With an adoring touch, she slipped her fingers through the shock of sandy hair that brushed to the side across his forehead and gave him a rather apologetic smile. "And to think I was upset this morning when I woke up and only Tom was with me. I thought you didn't care enough to ..."

"I stayed with you all last night, Julie," he chided, but teasingly, then grinned. "Who do you think got you into that sexy nightgown? You didn't imagine I asked Tom to put it on you, did you?"

Juliet laughed softly and shook her head. "No, I didn't imagine that. I just assumed one of the nurses took care of it."

"I wanted to take care of you myself. I still do. Do you mind?"

"Mind?" she asked, bending down to kiss his lips lightly. "People in love should want to take care of each other. I certainly want to take care of you, so why should I mind you feeling the same way?"

His broad shoulders rose and fell in a small shrug as he stood, swept her up in his arms, then sat down in her place with her on his lap. Cradling her close to him, he smiled down at her. "I thought maybe you'd see my wanting to take care of you as a threat to your independence. Actually that's another reason I was waiting to mention our getting married. Some young career women seem very afraid of marriage because they're afraid their husbands might start controlling their lives."

"I know you better than that, Marc. You've always respected me as a person and you've respected my work—you'd never try to take total control of my life," she told him, her hand curved across his shoulder, slowly stroking. Then, with a winsome smile, she turned his previous question back on him. "All this talk of marriage . . . Are you proposing to me, Marc?"

"If I am, are you accepting?"

"Let's name a date. Some time next week all right?" was her response, for which she was rewarded with a long rousing kiss that left them both a bit shaken but content.

"I think we have to get married anyhow," he said softly in her ear as they held each other. "After all, someone out there may have some very compromising photographs of us together. It'd be useless to make them public if we're respectably married."

"So *that's* why you're finally proposing," she teased, laughing up at him. "You're just trying to save your reputation."

"Speaking of reputations," he said, his expression growing more somber. "You do realize, don't you, that some people might still gossip about you and say you only married me to help your career?"

She nodded. "I know that some people *will* say exactly that."

"And will you care?"

"Not very much," she replied honestly. "As long as we know the truth and other people respect me for my abilities, I'm not going to worry about what a few vicious gossipmongers say."

"Good, then there's no reason for me to leave Union

Broadcasting. I'm even going to use some of that clout you're always saying I have, to fix it so you and I are given the same assignments."

"I certainly hope you will. What good does it do to have clout if you don't use it once in a while?"

"Especially for such a good cause," Marc murmured, touching his fingertips near the bandage at her temple. "How's your head now?"

"Spinning. It always spins when I'm with you," Juliet said provocatively, her hand drifting down to curl trustingly against his neck. Many moments of sweet silence passed before she took in a deep breath and asked curiously, "After I turned the car over, what happened to the gray station wagon?"

"Those bastards tried to get away through Talbot County but one of Haynes's deputies stopped them and tossed them in jail. The D.A. managed to get a very high bail set for them but that didn't do much good," Marc said, his voice taking on a steel edge. "Someone posted bail anyway and they took off, of course. Haynes doesn't expect to see either one of them again."

"Someone paid a lot of money to get them out," Juliet mused. "Velvy? Or one of his people?"

"Undoubtedly but very difficult to prove, not that we need to prove anything else. As I said, we've got enough against Benson Velvy to make his life very uncomfortable for some time to come." Marc stroked her hair. "You're the producer of what will probably be one of the hottest stories of the year, and when I talked to Pete today he was already singing your praises."

"Was he really? That's so good to hear," she murmured, a light of enthusiasm in her eyes but a light that was dim compared to the love for him that shone there. "But you know, Marc, important as this assignment was to me, success wouldn't have meant much to me if I couldn't share it with you."

"You're going to have to share everything with me, even the next couple of hours while I sit here and watch you nap." Rising easily with her in his arms, he carried her to her bed and gently put her down. "Dr. McCrea said you should rest and I think you could use some sleep now."

When he started to move away from the side of the bed, Juliet caught his large brown hands in hers. "I don't sleep very well anymore without you," she whispered, beckoning him with bewitching emerald eyes. "Lie down with me."

"Julie," he muttered unevenly. "Your head—"

"It doesn't hurt. And the doctor only said I shouldn't work. He recommended plenty of relaxation and what better way to relax . . ." As Marc hesitated, she inexorably drew him down beside her, turning into his arms and touching her lips to his. "Unless you'd rather not make love to a woman who's going to have a scarred face?"

"Battle scars, love. Journalists tend to collect a few and I love you, scar and all. And if you want to hide it from everyone else, all you have to do is let that naughty little lock of hair of yours do its own thing—the scar won't show. No one will know it's there, except those who know you intimately."

"And 'those' is you—only you," she promised, snuggling against him, the heels of her hands sweeping over his chest in lazy seductive circles. "I love you, Marc."

"*Julie.* I love you," he whispered roughly, helpless to refuse the invitation she so lovingly issued. Bringing her to him, he held her tenderly, caressing her as she unbuttoned his shirt. They kissed many times, her lips sweetly honeyed and parted, his tasting of mint and exerting a gently twisting pressure that opened her mouth beneath his. And when kisses and caresses were no longer enough

281

and their bodies were bare and alive to every touch, he lowered himself down over her. They kissed as he slipped a hand beneath her hips and she arched upward to receive him. And wonderful as it had always been between them, this union became at once supremely different; became an incomparable merging of body, mind, and spirit. The words of love they exchanged made the difference. Free of doubt, they were free to fully take and give, both emotionally and physically. Juliet allowed him to know just how much she adored him; he adored her. It was a precious time out of time and when fulfillment came, it was enough for both of them—it was everything. They found in each other the essence of completion and the fire of love and loving passion that would make all of their life together warmed by that fire.

COMING
IN
AUGUST—

Beginning this August, you can read a romance series unlike all the others — CANDLELIGHT ECSTASY SUPREMES! Ecstasy Supremes are the stories you've been waiting for—longer, and more exciting, filled with more passion, adventure and intrigue. Breathtaking and unforgettable. Love, the way you always imagined it could be. Look for CANDLELIGHT ECSTASY SUPREMES, four new titles every other month.

NEW DELL

TEMPESTUOUS EDEN,
by Heather Graham.
$2.50

Blair Morgan—daughter of a powerful man, widow of a famous senator—sacrifices a world of wealth to work among the needy in the Central American jungle and meets Craig Taylor, a man she can deny nothing.

EMERALD FIRE,
by Barbara Andrews
$2.50

She was stranded on a deserted island with a handsome millionaire—what more could Kelly want? Love.

NEW DELL

LOVERS AND PRETENDERS,
by Prudence Martin
$2.50

Christine and Paul—looking for new lives on a cross-country jaunt, were bound by lies and a passion that grew more dangerously honest ·with each passing day. Would the truth destroy their love?

WARMED BY THE FIRE,
by Donna Kimel Vitek
$2.50

When malicious gossip forces Juliet to switch jobs from one television network to another, she swears an office romance will never threaten her career again— until she meets superstar anchorman Marc Tyner.

Desert Hostage

Diane Dunaway

Behind her is England and her first innocent encounter with love. Before her is a mysterious land of forbidding majesty. Kidnapped, swept across the deserts of Araby, Juliette Barclay sees her past vanish in the endless, shifting sands. Desperate and defiant, she seeks escape only to find harrowing danger, to discover her one hope in the arms of her captor, the Shiek of El Abadan. Fearless and proud, he alone can tame her. She alone can possess his soul. Between them lies the secret that will bind her to him forever, a woman possessed, a slave of love.

A DELL BOOK 11963-4 $3.95